Gomez :   ıinst a
tree and going completely still. Flanagan nodded to Cruz, who stepped out into the fields and started toward the farmhouse.

Flanagan let him get a few yards away before following. He took one step out of the trees and froze.

Six Green Shirts, talking and bitching in Spanish, one of them trying to shake leaves out of his collar, had just stepped out of the woods on the far side of the field.

Cruz was already halfway to the house—the fields weren't all that big, at least not on this side of the farm. He froze for a second, then tried to dash for the house.

Unfortunately, the sudden movement drew one of the Green Shirts' eye. He shouted, lifting his AK-47 and opening fire.

BRANNIGAN'S BLACKHEARTS

WAR TO THE KNIFE

PETER NEALEN

Printed in the United States of America
http://americanpraetorians.com

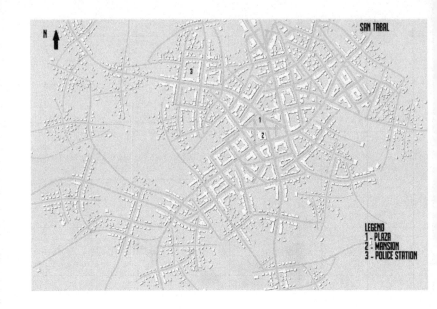

CHAPTER 1

There was no warning.

Miguel Jurado was a heavy sleeper, especially after he'd eaten well and had downed about half a bottle of *aguardiente*. So, he didn't hear the door open, despite the noise outside. He was dead to the world until he found himself shaken roughly. "Mayor Jurado! Mayor Jurado! You need to wake up, *Señor!*"

He cracked one eye, his head already starting to pound. He couldn't handle the *aguardiente* as easily anymore. It took a moment to register that it was Sebastian Casas, his chief of security, who was shaking him.

That can't be good.

He sat up in bed with a groan, squinting against the light that spilled through the open door. He wasn't really fat, not yet, but his body was going soft as he got older and balder, and for some reason, that meant that he always hurt when he got up, despite the alcohol.

Maria, his third wife, twenty years his junior, didn't have that problem. She was sitting up in bed, covering herself with the sheet, staring at Casas with large, dark, frightened eyes.

"What is it?" Jurado peered blearily at the clock beside the massive bed. "What time is it?"

"It is just after one in the morning, *Señor*." Casas' voice was taut. "Please, you have to come with me. We have to get you and the *señora* to safety."

1

That got his attention. Casas was not a man easily frightened. "What has happened?" He was already pulling the sheets aside, casting about the darkened room for his trousers.

"There was a bombing at the rancho, *Señor*."

That made Jurado's blood run cold. Juan Fernando had been throwing a party there. His eldest son and easily a hundred of his friends, many of the scions of the wealthy farmers and businessmen of San Tabal, would have been there. "My son?"

Casas shook his head. "We don't know yet, *Señor*. All we know is that there was an explosion next to the house, and that there are casualties. Please, we need to get you to a safe haven."

The Mayor's mansion, overlooking the Grand Plaza in the center of San Tabal, was not exactly the most secure building in the city. Left over from the Spanish colonial days, its aging construction meant that another car bomb could very well level half of it, and it had never been built with defense in mind in the first place.

Jurado had always found that odd, given the history of the place.

He dressed quickly, urging Maria to do the same. She was frightened and pale, her hands shaking as she struggled into her clothes. Jurado couldn't help but pity her a little, past his flash of irritation.

He was no stranger to the threat of violence. While Colombia was much more peaceful than it had been during the days of *La Violencia* and the cartel wars around Medellin and Cali which had followed, the ever-present *narcos* and revolutionaries such as the FARC and the various other groups—many of them influenced or supported by neighboring Venezuela—meant that the threat never really went away. Maria, however, hadn't lived through the periods he'd seen. He'd been a child during the very end of *La Violencia*, and had come of age during Pablo Escobar's reign of terror. She'd grown up since the peace arrangements with Medellin and Cali, and while Colombia could not have been called *peaceful* since then, with the FARC and ELN waging their perpetual narco-revolutions, it had been nothing like the old days.

2

Pulling on his shoes, he shooed Maria toward the men in suits standing just outside their door. "We have to go." He looked up at Casas. "I need to know what happened, and that my son is all right. Get me Manzano." Carlos Manzano was the San Tabal chief inspector. If he wasn't already aware, he would need to act quickly.

Jurado didn't know why someone might have tried to kill him or his son. That could wait.

"Manzano is already heading that way." Casas ushered the mayor and his young wife toward the stairs and the doors below. "All the police are on alert. They are locking down the city as we speak."

"Then where are we going?" Maria still sounded like she was on the edge of panic.

Jurado put his arm around her as they descended the richly carpeted stairs toward the grand entryway. "The police can only do so much if the terrorists are truly committed. There is a safer place for us, up in the mountains." That had been the old Jurado *villa*, which hadn't been built for defense, either, but after the last threat to his family—when one of the smaller cartels had wanted to seize several of the farms that were San Tabal's lifeblood for coca production—Casas had had a bunker put into the mountainside behind the house.

Casas and the other bodyguards hustled them across the vast hall and toward the massive wooden front doors. Two more security men flanked the doors, Uzi submachineguns in their hands. It was only then that Jurado really registered that Casas had drawn his sidearm, and held it in his right hand, pointed up at the ceiling.

As the mayor and his wife neared the door, one of the men with submachineguns put a hand to his ear and spoke, listening for a moment before he nodded, and the two of them opened the doors and moved out onto the driveway in the mansion's courtyard, where a pair of Mercedes G-Wagens waited for them, their engines already running. Two more security men stood nearby,

3

also carrying Uzis, watching the streets beyond the gate. Casas was taking the threat seriously.

That was why Jurado had always trusted Casas. He wouldn't have kept him on as chief of security otherwise.

Maria was whimpering a little as Jurado rushed her into the back seat of the rear G-Wagen. He wondered briefly if he should have married her, or just kept her as a mistress. She was stunning, and her physical charms were unmatched, but she wasn't exactly the most blinding of intellects. He did care for her, but sometimes he wished she was more like Consuela. *She* had been nearly as tough as Casas.

She'd been a harridan, and he hadn't been able to avoid a faint pang of relief when she'd died, but she'd been tough. He wouldn't have needed to practically drag *her* to safety.

Or maybe he would have. She would have been leading the charge, berating the guards while she tried to grab a gun from one of them.

Jurado climbed into the vehicle and Casas shut the door before hurrying around to the front seat and getting in. The lead G-Wagen was already pulling out the gate and turning left, heading for the mountains.

Jurado patted Maria's hand, and she seized his and hung on as if it were her only lifeline. But she calmed down. Then he reached into his pocket and cursed.

"I forgot my phone. Casas, give me yours." He needed to start getting control of this situation. He needed information.

Casas had just handed the phone back to him when the lead vehicle slowed. At first, Jurado couldn't see what was happening. He just saw the brake lights suddenly blaze red ahead of them as they neared the slums on the edge of the city.

"What…" He never got a chance to finish the question.

He didn't see the RPG round in flight—the ambush was far too close for that. He just saw the armored Mercedes ahead suddenly disappear for a moment in a bright fireball. Their vehicle rocked from the concussion. When Jurado opened his eyes a moment later, the vehicle was burning fiercely.

"Get us out of here!" Casas was looking back over his shoulder as he yelled at the driver. Maria was screaming, and Jurado could only stare at the burning wreck, his mind momentarily frozen. He'd thought himself prepared for anything, given his country's history, but this was far more immediate and personal than anything he'd really been ready for.

Casas got all the way around and finally got a good look out the back window, as Maria shrieked and clutched at her ears. He blanched and yelled at the driver to stop.

Jurado twisted around to look. It took him a moment to realize what had prompted his security chief to stop them.

Another man was standing in the middle of the street behind them, an RPG leveled at the vehicle. Half a dozen more came out of the tumbledown houses on either side. Most of them carried wicked-looking rifles. One held a much longer and heavier machinegun.

"Who are they?" Maria had stopped screaming, but was now staring at the men with guns, her eyes wide with terror.

"I don't know." Jurado was suddenly calm. In fact, he could see in the dim light that all of them were dressed the same. He had his suspicions, now that he had a better look at them. There had been rumors floating around the farms in the vicinity of San Tabal for months now. "Just stay calm. I think they want us alive. Otherwise, they would have blown this car up, too."

He glanced at Casas, who was clearly struggling to maintain his own calm. Even with two Uzis in the front seat, they were no match for the gunmen outside. As soon as anyone pointed a weapon, that man with the rocket launcher would kill them all.

Casas kept staring at the gunmen as more of them came out of the shacks to their right. Jurado wondered that there weren't any on the left. But after a moment, he realized that even if they tried to run for it, the gunmen would probably shoot them down before they even got all the way out of the car.

Finally, Casas met Jurado's eyes. His expression was lost, helpless. They were trapped, and he knew it. He'd failed.

Jurado couldn't accept that, though. There had to be a way out. He didn't want to die. He desperately wanted to live. He could feel the panic bubbling up in his chest as the gunmen closed in on the vehicles. "Do something!"

But Casas just shook his head as he unloaded his Uzi and laid it on the floorboards. "Don't resist. Like you said, if they wanted to kill you, they already would have. If you're alive and in captivity, something can be done."

Jurado wasn't sure about that. But if Casas wasn't going to fight, what could he do?

"Lock the doors." He wasn't just going to go out there and let these people take him prisoner. He surely didn't want to let them have Maria. She might not be the brightest young woman, and she might occasionally be tiresome outside of the bedroom, but he still cared for her. He didn't want to see what might happen to her if she fell into these men's hands.

But Casas shook his head and started to open his own door. "Then they will kill us all." He swung the door open and called out, "We surrender!"

Jurado lunged across the seat and tried to grab him, cursing, but it was too late. Casas stepped out of the vehicle with his hands raised.

A burst of gunfire cut him down, slamming him into the open door. He left a bright smear of red on the inside of the armored glass as he slid lifelessly to the ground.

Maria screamed again, and the driver, a wiry little man named Escudero, cursed and grabbed for his Uzi. But he was too slow. A dark figure appeared in the open door, standing over Casas' corpse, and shot him through the head. Blood and brains spattered off the window and the ruin of Escudero's skull bounced off the steering wheel before resting between the dash and the door, dripping gore onto the floor.

Jurado froze, staring at the rifle muzzle pointed at his face from a mere three feet away. Maria was shrieking in sheer panic, made worse when an arm reached in around the other gunman and unlocked her door. She was suddenly and roughly dragged out, still screaming until a hard blow knocked her to the ground, where she huddled, whimpering in pain and fear.

Another man lunged into the back of the vehicle and grabbed Jurado. The mayor of San Tabal tried to struggle, but he'd never been much of a fighter, not even in his younger days. A hard punch to the jaw drained all the fight out of him.

The gunmen dragged him out onto the ground and one of them shone a light in his eyes. He squinted against the glare and tried to lift a hand to shield his eyes. A boot slammed down on his arm, pinning it to the roadway.

"It's him. Bring him." The voice was cold and emotionless.

"What about the girl?" Jurado thought he could hear a leer in the other voice, but right then he couldn't do anything about it.

"Bring her, too. Maybe he'll be more cooperative if the alternative is watching us gut his whore in front of him."

Rough hands grabbed him under the armpits and dragged him to his feet. A savage blow to his solar plexus finished off any vague idea he might have had to fight back. Then he was dragged toward an old five-ton truck.

Just before they threw him in the back, they pulled a sack over his head. The last thing he saw before darkness descended was one of the gunmen, grinning from ear to ear, dragging Maria by one arm toward the truck.

***

Dawn had only been a few hours away when they'd been ambushed, but it felt like time had stopped while Jurado waited, his hands tied with zip-ties, the bag still over his head and leaving him in complete darkness. As near as he could tell, he'd been imprisoned in a room by himself. There was no other sound after the door slammed. He waited in darkness and silence, as his imagination started to run away with him, painting increasingly gruesome and vivid pictures in his mind of what these savages might have in store for him and his wife.

7

Finally, the door slammed open, and he heard boots on the concrete floor. Hands grabbed him under the arms and yanked him to his feet.

"What is happening? Who are you people? Where are you taking me?" Another punch to the stomach shut him up. He wheezed in pain as they dragged him out of the room.

He was in too much pain to keep track of direction and distance as they hauled him through several turns. He was fairly sure he was still inside, but he couldn't tell much beyond that.

They dragged him up a couple of flights of steps, and he stumbled repeatedly, since he couldn't see the steps. The next stretch was on carpet, and then doors opened ahead, they went through, and he was forced to his knees. The bag was yanked off his head, and he squinted against the light, though the room was not particularly brightly-lit.

He was in the entertainment room, which opened onto the balcony that faced the Grand Plaza. And he was not alone.

Three men stood by the balcony, watching him. The small one in the center he recognized at once.

Ramon Clemente had been a general in the *Ejército Nacional de Colombia*, the Colombian National Army, before he'd been forced to resign in disgrace two years before. Increasingly credible accusations of corruption and drug trafficking had finally become too loud for the government to ignore, and he'd been offered the option of resignation or prison. He'd resigned, but not gracefully. The last anyone had seen of the small, unassuming, mustachioed man standing in front of him now, he'd been cursing every member of the government and vowing bloody revenge.

Now he was standing in Jurado's house, dressed in camouflage trousers and a dark green shirt, a pistol belted around his middle. And the stare he leveled at Jurado was as cold and dead as a shark's.

Jurado looked at the two men who flanked Clemente, but he found no comfort there. One of them he knew. Julio Ballesteros had been a local rancher who had always had just a bit too much

8

money to throw around—and he'd used it to buy influence for himself wherever possible. No one had ever produced *proof* that the fat, sleepy-looking man had worked with the *narcos* or the FARC, but it had been common knowledge, nevertheless.

Somehow, Jurado did not find it surprising that Ballesteros was here.

The other he didn't know. Whip-lean and rangy, he had sunken cheeks, sharp *indio* cheekbones, and burning eyes. A single glance at those hard, feverish eyes was enough. Jurado looked away hastily.

Clemente and Ballesteros might be thugs, but this man was a predator, of a class far beyond them. This man was to be feared.

"Get him on his feet." Clemente had a slight speech impediment; his voice was thick and faintly slurred.

The men to either side of him seized him and hauled him up until he was standing unsteadily in front of Clemente. He towered over the little man, but right then, the difference in size really didn't matter.

His guards were dressed in simple trousers and dark green shirts. In fact, everyone was wearing some variation on the same green shirt. It appeared to be these terrorists' uniform.

"Come to the balcony, *Señor* Jurado." Clemente's tone was vaguely polite, but he couldn't quite manage to completely conceal the vicious, underlying malice to the words. Jurado's knees shook and he wanted to vomit. If he'd had anything in his stomach or his bladder, he probably would have voided them some time ago.

The Green Shirts dragged him toward the balcony. The doors were already open. He staggered out as they shoved him through, and he stumbled against the railing and looked down.

The sun was coming up over the Grand Plaza. Ordinarily, there was some little traffic around the Plaza in the morning, mostly the early risers, those business owners who opened their doors for breakfast. The fountain at the center was usually in the shadow of the forested mountain above until nearly ten in the morning.

Now it was bathed in white light from the headlights of a dozen trucks. And a dozen familiar people knelt in front of that fountain, pinned by those glaring headlights. Some of them wept. Some cowered. Some stared into the light defiantly.

The dark shadows of twenty men stretched out from those headlights toward the kneeling figures. Each man carried a rifle.

More gunmen, backed up by pickup trucks mounting machineguns in their beds or atop their cabs, herded hundreds of the people of San Tabal toward the square. Clearly, Clemente wanted a lot of people to see this.

With a sudden, sickening shock, Jurado realized what was about to happen. But he couldn't even summon up his voice to protest. He could barely hold himself up against the railing.

Clemente stood next to him. "I want you to see this." Malevolence dripped from every syllable. Jurado didn't know why. He'd never met Clemente before this moment. Then Clemente lifted a bullhorn to his lips.

"For too long, these rich farmers and puppets of the American imperialists have oppressed the people of San Tabal! Now, the hour of justice has come! San Tabal is an independent city state as of this moment! And all those who have sucked the blood of the poor who scrape out their living from the cleared jungle, giving their best to these parasites, who live in expensive mansions while they live in tumbledown shacks in the slums, will pay the price!" He turned to the wolfish man who stood on Jurado's right hand and nodded.

"Firing squad! Do your duty! For the revolution and for Ramon Clemente!" The man's voice was as raw and harsh as his eyes.

The twenty men lifted their rifles. With a ragged crash of gunfire that echoed off the mountains, they emptied their magazines into the twelve men and women kneeling by the fountain. Crimson spattered on the stone, while bullets chipped away at the two-hundred-year-old sculpture.

10

When the gunfire fell silent, a dozen twisted bodies lay leaking their lifeblood out onto the stones of the square. The old fountain was pocked with bullet holes, and one of the spigots had been shot off, dribbling water down into the pool below. Those residents who had been dragged out to witness the atrocity could only stare in shock and fear.

Clemente turned to the wolfish looking man again. "Take him away and finish it."

The man with the burning eyes stared at Jurado without a word, and jerked a hand at his guards. Rough hands grabbed him by the arms and dragged him away from the railing. He went without resistance, still staring down at the bodies below. Some had been friends. Some had been enemies. Some had been competitors before he'd become the mayor.

Wordless and shaking, Jurado let himself be led away.

***

When the sun finally topped the peak to the east, spilling its rays down onto the bloodied plaza, it illuminated the body of Miguel Jurado, formerly mayor of San Tabal, as it swung gently beneath a lamppost at the edge of the Grand Plaza. Above, a red, black, and yellow flag drifted in the morning breeze, declaring a new order in the city of San Tabal.

CHAPTER 2

The Rocking K Diner was quiet, but it was the middle of the afternoon on a weekday. Most people in that neck of the woods had to work. John Brannigan had plenty of chores to do around his cabin up the mountain, but his situation was a little different.

And the message he'd gotten from Mark Van Zandt had been more than a little intriguing.

Brannigan threaded his way between the tables toward the back, trading a friendly wave with Ginger, Mama Taft's granddaughter and permanent waitress, who would probably inherit the diner whenever Mama passed away. Granted, Mama Taft was hard as nails, and probably wouldn't die until Death himself came and dragged her away, cussing and punching him in the face. It would be a long time before Ginger inherited, but the cheerful, bouncy young redhead was fine with that.

Van Zandt was sitting in the corner booth, all the way in the back, nursing a cup of coffee. He'd dressed down a bit since the first time he'd come to the Rocking K, wearing jeans and a flannel shirt. The first time, he'd been in slacks and a corporate polo shirt.

Brannigan and Van Zandt had a history. Not a particularly pleasant one at all points, either. It had been Brigadier General Van Zandt who had supervised the unwilling retirement of Colonel John Brannigan from the Marine Corps, because

Brannigan had ignored politics while deployed in East Africa, and had done what he'd thought was right. He'd rescued the people he'd set out to rescue, but killing local soldiers to do it had stepped on some toes, and so he'd been sacrificed. And Van Zandt had been the one to wield the knife.

But that was all behind them. Because they were both in the private sector now. And that was why they were meeting in a diner in the middle of nowhere.

Brannigan slid into the booth across from Van Zandt. "Hello, Mark."

"John." Van Zandt nodded to him as he glanced toward the door. He seemed almost nervous, which was odd for him. He'd always been a bit of a stuffed shirt, but he'd been a Marine. Flighty wasn't in his nature.

He held his peace as Ginger came by and slid another cup of coffee in front of Brannigan. "Anything else I can get you?"

"No, thanks, Ginger." Brannigan cradled the cup in his hands. "It's still too early in the day."

She dimpled and patted him on the shoulder. The Tafts had developed a sort of familial attachment to him, since he'd started coming down the mountain to eat, especially since he often brought some venison with him during hunting season. "You have a good meeting, then."

Van Zandt raised an eyebrow. "She knows this is a meeting?"

Brannigan gave him a long-suffering stare. "You're not from around here, and Hector's come to meet me here before you became a part of this operation, Mark. Of course she knows it's a meeting."

Van Zandt sighed and looked down at the table. "I guess you're right."

Brannigan took a sip. The coffee was good, and scalding hot. "You're not usually this jumpy. What's up?"

"I've got another job for you." Van Zandt still wasn't looking him in the eye. Brannigan's frown deepened. Something was off. "But it's… not exactly standard."

14

"We're mercenaries specializing in deniable operations, Mark. Everything we do is 'non-standard.'"

But Van Zandt was still frowning. "Not like this. This is… weird."

Brannigan leaned back in his seat and crossed his arms. "Okay, lay it out for me."

"Have you ever heard of a city called San Tabal?" Van Zandt brought a thin folder out and put it on the table.

Brannigan's eyes narrowed as he saw just how thin that folder was. Their target packages were usually much more substantial. "Can't say as I have."

"It's a small city in northeastern Colombia, awfully close to the Venezuelan border. Most of its economy is entirely dependent on farming and ranching in the mountains nearby." Van Zandt pulled a map out of the folder. It didn't look like there was much else in there. He slid it across to Brannigan, who studied it.

Awfully close to the Venezuelan border is right. It looked like the city was less than ten miles from the line. And there wasn't much more than mountains and jungle covering that ten miles.

"Two weeks ago, a disgraced Colombian general named Ramon Clemente seized control of the city with a small army. They don't have a name, but they are generally referred to as the Green Shirts, because that's the closest they've got to a uniform." Van Zandt ran a hand over his face. "There's close to zero information on these people aside from a handful of pictures that have gotten out. Pictures of a mass execution in the town square and the mayor getting lynched shortly thereafter."

"That's pretty close to FARC territory." Brannigan looked up at Van Zandt, who was still looking down at the map, his hands folded in front of his face. "Are they FARC? ELN? Or somebody new?"

Van Zandt shrugged. "We don't know for sure. The one statement that's made it out sounds *really* Communist, but like I said, there's not much information readily available."

Brannigan turned his eyes back down to the map. It wasn't much more than a topographic map of the Colombia-Venezuela border region. San Tabal, nestled between two taller mountain ranges, had been circled, but that was about it. The map was about as informative as the rest of Van Zandt's brief so far.

"So, what's the mission? I'd suspect something like Khadarkh, where we had to go in and rescue some hostages, but you make it sound like it's something different." His expression turned thunderous. "If it's some half-baked takeover attempt, count us out. I want no part of any Silvercorp nonsense."

Van Zandt's mouth thinned. "Yeah." He pulled a single sheet of paper out of the folder and slid it across the table. "Someone with all the right clearances wants Clemente dead. And he's already got everything planned out."

Brannigan didn't even look at the sheet of paper. "No way in hell."

Van Zandt sighed. "I know. That's why I said it's non-standard. It's sketchy as hell." He ran both hands over his face and dropped them to the tabletop, looking around helplessly. "Unfortunately, we're in a crack."

"How so?" Brannigan was starting to get that distinct sinking feeling in his gut. His voice took on a dangerous edge. "What have you gotten us into, Mark?"

"It wasn't my doing." The protestation of innocence might have sounded petulant under different circumstances, but right then Van Zandt just sounded tired. "Unfortunately, the fact that most of what your little crew has done has been for Uncle Sam means that this little operation can't be entirely airtight. It was probably inevitable that *somebody* was going to try to stick their oar in."

"That doesn't mean we just have to take every Good Idea Fairy mission that comes along." Brannigan's voice was as hard and unforgiving as his stare. "We're contractors, not employees or sworn agents."

"And I'd agree with you, if this particular politico wasn't a very powerful and very unscrupulous asshole." Van Zandt sighed again. "We don't have much of a choice on this one, John."

"Who is it?"

Van Zandt's glance got suddenly sharp, as he detected the threat implicit in Brannigan's tone. "Don't even think about it, John. There's no scaring this one into line. Not now."

"Who. Is. It?" Brannigan was relentless.

Another sigh. "It's a Senator. One with a chair on the Intelligence Committee, who can cause us a *lot* of difficulties if we give him a reason. And it has been made abundantly clear to me that turning this mission down *will* be considered that reason. You might have been in the right—*we* might have been in the right—but that won't stop him from digging us up and finding *something* to nail us all to the wall. And given the generally illegal and under-the-table nature of your missions, that isn't going to be hard." He sighed. "Hell, all he's got to do is get wind of that business down in New Mexico, and you're screwed."

Brannigan's silence was thunderous. His knuckles whitened around his coffee cup. He stared at the map, searching it for a way out.

Because he knew that Van Zandt was right. They'd run that risk as soon as they'd taken on the Khadarkh job. Mercenary operations in foreign countries were not something that American politicians liked to go public. They were embarrassing, despite how many other countries did it without even bothering to shrug. That made them a political weapon, never mind how justified they might have been.

And it made Brannigan's Blackhearts targets.

Van Zandt steepled his fingers and lowered his voice. "Now, before you lose your temper, hear me out. There's more to this than meets the eye. Like I said, it's sketchy as hell, and it has me *very* suspicious. I've dealt with this particular Senator before. Calling him an arrogant jackass is an insult to arrogant jackasses the world over. And I say that as one of them."

Brannigan raised an eyebrow, but otherwise didn't comment. He'd never heard Van Zandt be self-deprecating before.

"I guaran-damn-tee he's got some kind of angle going here. I don't know what it is, yet, but the fact that we got a canned plan—all the way down to the timeline, ambush site, and

17

everything—tells me a lot. He wants Clemente dead, and no questions asked. Well, he apparently thinks that your little hit squad is just that—a no questions asked hit squad. And he's arrogant enough that he figures that we'll just go along with the plan because we don't want to be exposed."

He jabbed a finger at the paper that Brannigan still hadn't read. "We've got three weeks before this is supposed to go down. That's a lot of time, if you get moving now. Plenty of time for reconnaissance." He leaned forward. "Possibly enough time to learn what has the Senator so interested in one man's death."

Brannigan's eyes narrowed, but he held his peace. He could kind of see Van Zandt's point. If the Senator was on the Intelligence Committee, and therefore had some access to whatever shadowy office Van Zandt worked for, he might be able to blackmail both Van Zandt's people and the Blackhearts to do this. For certain, not all of their operations had been sanctioned and aboveboard—and even if they had been, Brannigan had enough experience under his belt to know that politicians really didn't care about such things. If they wanted, they could turn a legit mission into a perceived rogue operation overnight. He'd seen it done before.

Hell, it was why he was retired.

"We might have to take this mission." Van Zandt was in earnest. "But there's nothing saying we've got to be patsies." He jabbed a finger at the map. "Get in there and do what you do best. If nothing else, you should be able to find out what the Senator's interest is, and we can adjust as needed from there." He grinned like a death's head. "If we're really lucky, we'll be able to use that interest against him. He's got to have a reason why he doesn't want you doing anything but flying in, setting charges, blowing up one vehicle, and leaving."

Brannigan thought about it, finally sipping his coffee. It had cooled, though Mama Taft always served it scalding hot to begin with, so it wasn't cold.

As much as he hated to admit it, Van Zandt was right. He'd seen it before. The only reason that this Senator—and he had

18

a pretty good idea who it was—might risk something like this would be because he figured that he had the Blackhearts—and Van Zandt's office—over a barrel. Such people always thought they were untouchable. And if they turned it down, he had no doubt that the FBI would be knocking on their doors within the week.

He wouldn't apologize for anything they'd done. They'd been on the right side, even if the law could technically be brought to bear against them for any of their past operations. He'd made sure of that. They were warriors, not thugs.

But he had a responsibility to the other Blackhearts. He might be an aging widower who could stand to go to prison if that was the price for doing the right thing. But many of the others weren't. Flanagan was due to get married before the end of the year. Santelli had saved his own marriage and was now a father. None of them deserved prison for what they'd done. They'd killed terrorists and rescued innocent people, and possibly prevented countless deaths.

He'd never apologize for that.

So, despite searching his mind for an alternative, the best option he could come up with was Van Zandt's plan. Play along until they could find out what was really going on.

Then cram it down the Senator's throat.

He sighed. "Why haven't the Colombians intervened? This is technically a Colombian problem."

Van Zandt shrugged, even as he visibly relaxed. Brannigan might not have said as much, but the question had already established that he'd taken the job. "Nobody knows for sure. It's possible that Clemente has something to hold over someone important's head in Bogota, or he's got an arrangement with somebody in high places. More likely at the moment, the proximity to Venezuela and the remaining FARC and ELN camps is a deterrent. Apparently, the Venezuelan Army has been running exercises in the mountains on the other side of the line for the last month. Colombia's got all kinds of problems since their peace deal with the FARC didn't result in sunshine and rainbows, and we believe that a potential war with Venezuela is more than they're willing to risk."

"That suggests that this Clemente has connections in Venezuela." Brannigan stroked his graying handlebar mustache.

"It would fit with the Communist rhetoric," Van Zandt agreed.

"What about logistics?" Brannigan finally pulled the plan toward himself and started to skim it.

"We can arrange transport via charter air. I'll get on it as soon as I get back to the office." Van Zandt pointed to the page in Brannigan's hands. "Weapons will have to be procured down there—that's already in the plan. There's even a local contact, but I think that you should consider him compromised."

Brannigan nodded, then folded the page and slid it into his shirt pocket. "I'll need to start making some arrangements. The less that you know, the less that Senator can pry out of you when he comes sniffing around."

Van Zandt nodded in turn. "Agreed. Can't say as I like it, but you're right."

Brannigan downed the last of the coffee and stood up.

"John?" Van Zandt was looking up at him, concern in his eyes. It was an expression that Brannigan wouldn't necessarily have expected to see on the other man's face even a few years before. "Watch your back."

"You too, Mark."

CHAPTER 3

Brannigan was leaning against the corner of the cabin as Flanagan pulled up in his old Ford. The truck was well cared for, but it was pushing fifty years old, and some rattles were just par for the course.

Flanagan parked the truck, shutting off the engine and swinging the door open. Brannigan waited, taking in their surroundings.

He'd never been to Flanagan's place before. It wasn't quite like his own cabin, but Flanagan was a backwoodsman and didn't like cities. Fortunately, Rachel appeared to like his taste in houses just fine.

"John." Flanagan walked around the back and dropped the tailgate. Two five-gallon buckets were sitting back there, next to a fishing rod and a good-sized tackle box. "I'd ask what brings you out here, but from the look on your face, I doubt that it's just to see how the fishing's been. It's been great, by the way." He pulled the two five-gallon buckets down, and Brannigan saw that both of them were pretty full of trout, perch, and a couple of walleyes. Flanagan had limited out for the day.

"I kinda wish that was exactly why I'm here." Brannigan took one of the buckets and joined the shorter, black-bearded man as he walked toward the front door. "That's quite a haul. The melt's still stirring the silt up where I'm at."

"You can still catch plenty during the melt, if you read the water right. They're still there, and they still gotta eat." Flanagan unlocked the door and led the way in. Even up in the hills, miles from his closest neighbors, Joe Flanagan was security-minded enough to lock his doors.

Given what they both did for a living, a little paranoia was probably not unreasonable.

Brannigan helped the younger man, who'd been one of his junior Marines back in the day, get the fish cleaned and stored. They didn't talk about the job, not yet. Brannigan asked after Rachel—he knew that the two of them weren't living together yet; they were saving that for after the wedding—and Flanagan told him that she was away at her parents' house, making some more arrangements for the wedding, which was now just over a month away.

"Not my thing. I'll let her do whatever she wants for it." Flanagan shrugged. "Honestly, she's told me that it's not so much her thing, either, but her mom's going to take it personally if it isn't just right."

Flanagan put the last of the fish he was preserving into the freezer, shut the door, and went to the sink to wash his hands. "Okay, what's the job?"

"Shady and suspicious as hell." Brannigan sank onto one of Flanagan's wooden chairs, his bulk making it creak a little. He was a big man, easily six foot four, broad shouldered and deep chested.

"What else is new?" Flanagan leaned against the counter next to the sink and folded his arms. "But somehow, from the way you say that, this is somehow shadier and more suspicious than usual."

Brannigan filled him in. He watched Flanagan's frown deepen and his scowl get darker as he talked.

"So, we're getting blackmailed into becoming a government hit squad." Flanagan was not happy. "Have I got that about right?"

"On the surface, yeah, that about covers it."

Flanagan's eyes narrowed. "Maybe I'm particularly slow today, but if there's something else going on beneath the surface, I think you're going to have to spell it out for me."

So Brannigan told him what he and Van Zandt suspected. "I think Mark's right. I think this is somebody's political or criminal gamesmanship, and we're supposed to simply be pawns in the game. Well, I don't care to play somebody's pawn, not even if they're a Senator."

Flanagan snorted. "*Especially* not if they're a Senator."

Brannigan inclined his head in agreement. "So, we're going to go down early, do some snooping around, and find out what's really going on. Then we'll decide on what course of action to take from there. Honestly, from what Mark told me, and what little I've been able to confirm, it sounds like this Clemente probably deserves to die, anyway. And if the Colombians are too scared to touch him because the Venezuelans might intervene, well…"

"Somebody's got to do it." Flanagan sighed. "And that's kind of why Brannigan's Blackhearts exist in the first place, right?"

"True enough."

Flanagan scratched his beard. "Who else knows about this?"

But Brannigan shook his head. "Right now? You, me, and Mark." At Flanagan's raised eyebrow, he shrugged. "I used to call Roger first. Now that you're the Number Two man, you get first word."

Flanagan nodded, looking down at the floor. "Big shoes to fill."

"I can't think of a Blackheart better suited to fill them. And I'm not just blowing smoke. You know me better than that. Roger would agree."

Roger Hancock had been the Blackhearts' second in command since their first mission on Khadarkh. He'd been Brannigan's right hand up until a mission in Argentina, where he'd taken a bullet to the head while charging an enemy spider hole.

He'd already been dying, gut shot down in the Humanity Front's underground research facility. He'd gone out like he probably had wanted to: with his boots on, his barrel hot, facing the threat and engaging the enemy.

Every one of them still missed him.

"I'll do what I can. I call half, you call half?"

Brannigan nodded somberly. "That's how we've worked it. Let's meet at the usual spot in… three days? We've got three weeks until time on target."

"We'll be there with bells on."

***

John Wade was an angry man.

Now, most of the men who'd known him over the years—especially his former comrades in the 75th Ranger Regiment—would have agreed with that statement just on principle. He was somewhat infamous for being a hard, unforgiving, and angry taskmaster.

But this had nothing to do with the constant, low-level background roar that was daily life for John Wade. No, this was because of his ex.

He was looking for something to punch when his phone rang. Gritting his teeth, he snatched it out of his pocket, ready to start snarling until he saw who it was.

"What's up, Joe?" He was a little proud of how steady his voice was.

"Got a job. You free?" Flanagan wasn't a man of many words, and even though he probably heard the simmering anger in the back of Wade's voice, he wouldn't comment on it unless it became an issue.

"If it means killing people, you'd better believe it." *Let the NSA chew on that if they're listening in.*

"It might." Flanagan paused for a moment. When he spoke again, he sounded almost grudging. "There something I need to know about?" Flanagan had gotten out as a Sergeant.

24

Wade had retired as a Master Sergeant. It probably felt weird, playing a leadership role to a man with Wade's background.

But Wade didn't care what rank Flanagan had held, any more than he cared much about his own. That had been then. The Blackhearts was now. Brannigan trusted Flanagan to be the 2IC, so Wade trusted him, too. *He* certainly had no particular interest in the job.

"Nah. Just fighting with my ex-wife. She's kicking up a shitstorm about custody of my kid, again." He snorted in renewed fury. "Once she found out how much I've been teaching my daughter to shoot, she decided to go running to CPS, claiming I'm putting her in danger." He gritted his teeth. "Bitch."

"Will it require you to stay Stateside for a while?" Wade realized that Flanagan was thinking a little farther ahead than he was.

"I don't think so. This isn't the first time this has happened, and I've got a good lawyer. I'll be good to go. Just so long as it isn't pure recon or babysitting duty, or something. I need to get my kill on."

"It's... complicated. Odds are there's going to be some action, though, one way or another." Flanagan clearly didn't want to say more over the phone, and Wade didn't blame him.

"Great. Usual spot?" By then, all the Blackhearts knew the campsite they'd turned into their de facto briefing room.

"Usual spot. See you there in three days."

***

Vincent Bianco just started banging his head against the table.

"Come on, Vinnie, it's not *that* bad." Tom Glenn was a long-time friend and a co-conspirator when it came to trying to get *The Legend of Morval* off the ground. Unfortunately, his optimism wasn't particularly helpful right at the moment.

"It *is* that bad." Bianco sat up and gestured to the multiple legal pads strewn across the table. "It won't work."

25

"It just needs some tweaking." Glenn rubbed the back of his head as he looked down at the lines of numbers and stats. "Maybe we're trying to get too complicated."

"No 'maybe' about it." Bianco ran his hands over his face. "We're trying to codify too much. Maybe we need to just stick with the bare-bones basic stats. Nobody wants to spend eight hours rolling up a character."

"I don't think we really need to go *completely* bare-bones." Glenn wasn't just Bianco's gaming buddy. Unlike most of their circle, Glenn was also a combat vet. He'd been in Marjah, back in the day, and had the scars to prove it. He was also a huge nerd, possibly more so than Bianco. "I mean, if our system is the same as a dozen other RPGs, then why should people bother?"

"Because the rest of the rules are different." Bianco stuck his thumbs in his eyes. "Hell, if I'd known this whole game design thing was this complicated, I'd never have started."

"Bull." Glenn snorted. "You love this crap."

Bianco just groaned. When his phone rang a moment later, he grabbed for it almost as if it was a lifeline. Anything but staring at those legal pads and giving himself a headache trying to figure this out.

"Vinnie, it's Joe." Flanagan's voice actually triggered a wave of relief.

Bianco sat up straighter. "We got a job?"

"We've got a job. It's complicated, but we'll explain at the briefing. Usual place, three days."

"I'll be there." Bianco glanced over at Glenn, who was frowning a little, and briefly considered bringing his friend in. They could probably use another shooter.

But no. Glenn's scars went deeper than what the naked eye could see. Unlike a lot of vets who were one hundred percent disabled, according to the VA, Glenn was in no shape to go running around in the weeds with a rifle. Not anymore. He'd sustained some serious wounds in Marjah, and still needed to go to the VA hospital regularly. Bringing him along wouldn't be doing him or the rest of the Blackhearts any favors.

Especially since he'd feel honor-bound to try to hang if Bianco even brought it up. He knew Tom well enough to be sure of that.

"We'll see you in a couple days, then." Flanagan hadn't heard Bianco's brief inner monologue. Bianco shook himself a little.

"Roger that." Flanagan hung up first. Bianco shoved the phone back in his pocket, and then, with a sinking feeling, realized that if the meetup was in three days, he still had time to work on this.

***

"Hank!" Brannigan looked around the cabin as he got out of his truck. It had been a few months since the younger Brannigan had come to live with his dad, helping out around the place. Sure enough, he was splitting firewood in the back. "Come inside for a minute."

He led the way into the small cabin, which he had built for himself and Rebecca before cancer had claimed her. He wasn't exactly looking forward to this conversation.

Hank came in behind him, wiping his boots off and dusting his hands. He'd worked up a good sweat—he must have been at it for a bit. The young man was almost the spitting image of his father, if shorter and slighter of build, his hair still dark and cut short. Brannigan waved him to a seat at the table, then took the other.

"I'm guessing we've got another job." Hank sounded eager. Somewhat more eager than Brannigan might have expected. Or liked.

"We've got another job. At least, the Blackhearts have another job." Brannigan steepled his hands in front of him, leaning on the table. "The question is, are you going to come or not?"

Hank frowned. "I thought I did okay in Azerbaijan."

Brannigan nodded gravely. "You did. That's not the issue." He sighed. "Son, I need you to be damned good and sure this is what you want to do. Because this mission's not just combat dangerous. If it goes sideways, the US government might just

27

come down on all our heads." Better to get all the cards out on the table.

But Hank just spread his hands. "I watched them scapegoat you for East Africa. I saw just how quick the knives come out when I was a Company Commander. That doesn't worry me. It's always been a risk. If it happens, we'll deal with it."

That wasn't exactly the answer Brannigan had wanted to hear. He realized that while he was proud of his son's warrior spirit, a part of him really didn't want him coming out and risking his neck with the rest of them. Hank was all he had left since Rebecca had died. "You're sure? You might have gotten through your first mission, but they don't get any less hairy."

Hank shrugged. "I'm not that used to being the low man on the totem pole anymore, but I can deal." He sighed and squinted up at his father for a moment. "I know why you're asking, Dad. But yeah, I do want to come. I can't think of anything else I'd do."

"That's a poor reason to carry a gun for money." But Brannigan sighed. As much as he didn't know that he wanted the merc life for his son, Hank was a grown man, and a warrior. He could make these decisions for himself. "All right. But we're going to have to watch our backs."

"What else is new?"

CHAPTER 4

Brannigan put the phone down. That had been his second try to get through to Gomez, without an answer.

If it had been anyone but Mario Gomez, he would have just figured that the other man had decided that he'd had enough and was leaving the Blackhearts. Gomez was generally a man of few words, anyway. He was even more taciturn than Flanagan.

But Gomez was also a stone-cold killer, and about as unlikely to just walk away as he was to suddenly join the Peace Corps. Something else was going on.

He'd just turned to call the next man on the list when the phone rang.

Brannigan glared at the phone, tilting his head to see who was calling. He'd never been eager to get a cell phone in the first place, but the fact that the Blackhearts were spread all over the country meant that it was kind of necessary. And if either Van Zandt or Hector Chavez needed to contact him, then it made it easier to keep things low-key.

He still hated the damned thing. Even though the number of people who had this number was extremely small.

He recognized the incoming number. He'd just called it.

"You've been harder to get ahold of than usual, Mario. Everything all right?"

"Everything's fine. We have a job?" Gomez sounded as calm and deadpan as ever.

"We have a job. Can you get up here in three days?" Brannigan was staring at the wall, his eyes slightly narrowed.

"Easy. We had some issues down here, but everything's under control now."

Brannigan's frown deepened. "Anything you need help with? I can get in touch with Drake."

"No. Like I said, it's all under control." He might have heard an echo of Gomez's faint, wolfish smile, about the most expression he'd ever seen on the man's face. "I'll be there."

Brannigan hung up, his eyes still narrowed. *I wonder just how many bodies are currently attracting the buzzards down there in New Mexico?*

***

Erekle "Herc" Javakhishvili scanned the scrub-covered flats around Kitengela as the eastern horizon began to lighten. He wasn't visibly armed, but the AKS-74 in his pack was still within easy reach.

Tom Burgess, his long hair pulled back in a ponytail, his salt-and-pepper beard neatly trimmed, joined him, opening the driver's side door of the ancient Land Rover. "Any sign of them yet?"

"Not yet." Javakhishvili kept his eyes out as he climbed in and Burgess started the truck.

At first glance, especially here in Kenya, the two men might have been mistaken for brothers. Both lean and rangy, both with long hair, and both white men in a decidedly black part of Africa. "Is David coming?"

"He should be along in a couple minutes." Burgess kept the engine running, though he kept the gears in neutral. "Father Metaxas wasn't all that happy about this little expedition."

"Because we're doing it, or because we're bringing David?" With the door shut, Javakhishvili pulled the Kalashnikov out, flipped the stock open, and set it on the floor under his feet. He wanted to have it handy if this went badly.

"Because of David. You know Father Metaxas." The priest in charge of the St Anastasius of Sinai Mission had no particular objection to the two trained soldiers of fortune stepping in to protect his flock. But he was fiercely protective of that same flock, and David Kinyanjui was barely into his teens.

Kenya wasn't the safest place to grow up, though, especially a mere two hundred miles from the Somali border. Al Shabaab and other jihadi groups had made far too many inroads, despite the Kenyans' efforts to curtail them.

And it had been David who'd learned about the impending attack on the mission in the first place.

Running footsteps came up from behind the vehicle, and Javakhishvili glanced in the rear-view mirror. David skidded to a halt next to the rear door, pulled it open, and jumped in.

"Grab that bag in the back seat." Burgess jerked a thumb toward the duffel he'd shoved in there earlier as he put the Land Rover in gear. "But it's only for a last resort situation, you understand? You're still staying with the vehicle."

David reached into the duffel and pulled out the old AKMS. It had clearly seen better days, but while Javakhishvili often called himself the "Shady Slav"—in fact, that was his callsign among the mercenaries who called themselves Brannigan's Blackhearts—there were limits as to just what he could find.

The boy might only be thirteen, but both Javakhishvili and Burgess had taught him well. They'd taught as many of the men and boys of the small Eastern Orthodox parish as had been willing to learn. He checked the chamber, keeping the muzzle pointed down at the floorboards, then rocked in one of the two magazines, racked the bolt, checked the chamber again, and then flipped the selector lever up to "safe."

Burgess had already started them moving. If what David had overheard was true, they didn't have much time.

It was a short drive. David had known one of the young men who were their targets. And he knew where the young man lived.

31

The farm lay about five miles southwest of Kyumvi. Burgess parked the Land Rover in the shade of an acacia tree about half a mile away. They'd gone without headlights for the last couple of miles—there was no cover and no place to hide for miles out there. Leaving David with the vehicle, the two men pulled out their rifles and started across the plain.

They covered the distance relatively quickly. The sun was almost up, and they turned south first, so that they could approach the farm with the sun at their backs. Javakhishvili wondered briefly if they had enough time, but he'd had enough experience with these kinds of jihadis that he doubted that they'd get up early just to go slaughter some Christians nearby.

Apparently, a visiting imam had condemned the presence of the Eastern Orthodox mission, and David had overheard one of the boys at a nearby soccer field bragging about what he and several of his friends were going to do to the "cross worshipers." And that they had powerful friends bringing them the weapons to do it with.

Now, Burgess and Javakhishvili crept up on the low wall around the farm, weapons at the ready. So far, they'd heard and seen nothing to suggest that they'd been detected.

Reaching the wall, Javakhishvili crouched beneath it, rising just high enough that he could peer over the top.

Two Toyota Hiluxes sat in the yard, facing the gate on the other side. Figures were beginning to move around, several of them converging on the trucks. And they were all armed. He counted three AKs, two G3s, four M16s, and a Sterling submachinegun. No RPGs or PKMs, at least not in the open.

He crouched back down, thinking hard. They couldn't just let the attack happen. Even if they were dug in at the church, innocent people were going to get hurt. But two men against ten didn't make for good odds, even with the element of surprise on their side.

Burgess was crouching down again, too. He'd seen—Javakhishvili didn't need to fill him in.

"I say we mag-dump into the trucks," Burgess whispered. "Disable them if we can. In any case, it might scare the hell out of them enough that they call the attack off."

Javakhishvili wasn't sure. He'd seen plenty of jihadis use resistance to their attacks as justification for even more violence. But they were in position, they were loaded for bear, and there was no time like the present.

As one, the two men rose up over the top of the wall, leveling their rifles, the selector levers already down to "Auto."

They opened fire, the Kalashnikovs thundering and rattling, spitting fire as they raked the two trucks with fire. Glass shattered and flecks of paint and metal flew. The nearest jihadis scrambled back, yelling in terror, and the nearest actually dropped his rifle and turned to run, only to trip and sprawl on his face in the dirt.

Javakhishvili's magazine ran dry with a *click*, and he dropped behind cover, ripping a fresh mag out of his go bag, using it to hit the mag release and strip out the empty, then rocked it in and racked the bolt.

When he rose up again, he saw that one of the Hiluxes was smoking, both were sitting slightly askew on flattened tires, and every one of the would-be jihadi warriors was running for the shacks.

Burgess had just reloaded, and Javakhishvili motioned that they should retreat. Hopefully, they'd sent the message. They'd get back to the church and prepare to defend it if the jihadis decided to come after them anyway.

The two of them faded away, staying low as they moved straight northeast toward the truck, keeping the sun off to their flank. They moved fast, not quite a jog, but faster than a mere walk.

A few minutes later, they reached the Land Rover without seeing any sign of pursuit. The murderous little jackals hadn't expected to get hit on their own turf.

As they climbed in, after making sure David didn't mistake them for bad guys, Javakhishvili felt his pack start to vibrate. He peered inside as Burgess pulled the vehicle away from the tree, turning back toward Kitengela.

It was his satellite phone. Pulling it out and extending the antenna, he hit the "receive" button.

"Herc?" Brannigan, like the rest of the Blackhearts, had never found Javakhishvili's full first name all that pronounceable, so they'd adopted the nickname he'd gotten during his time in the Navy. "Where the hell are you?"

"Africa." He had to plug one ear so that he could hear somewhat clearly over the creaks and bangs the Land Rover was making as they bounced over the terrain. "Tom and I came out to do some missionary work. We got a job?"

"Yeah, we've got a job. Can you be here in three days?"

"Easy. We're not that far from Nairobi, and a one-way ticket isn't *that* expensive." Especially given what they'd been paid for the last few missions. As a single man with simple tastes, Javakhishvili wasn't hurting for money.

"We'll see you here, then. And Herc? Watch your back when you get here. This one's... complicated."

"Aren't they all?"

***

Flanagan glowered as he got out of his truck. *We don't have time for this.*

The dingy roach motel just outside of Vegas looked like something out of a true crime documentary. It was hardly The Strip. But under the circumstances, he'd expected that.

Scanning the parking lot, he couldn't see any trouble right at the moment. But that could change quickly. And with Kevin Curtis involved, it probably would.

He found Room 107 and knocked. There was no reaction at first, but he might have seen the curtains move, and the peephole in the door darken for a moment, before the door cracked open.

"Joe! I knew you'd come find me!" Kevin Curtis stood a good head shorter than Flanagan, quite a few shades darker, and almost thirty pounds heavier. And all of it was muscle. For all his excesses and gambling, Curtis rarely missed a session in the gym.

Flanagan shouldered into the room. The inside was as run down and sketchy as the outside. The cheap carpet had some strange stains, the furniture looked extremely cheap, the single lamp on the end table was dim and yellow, and the place smelled slightly of cigarette smoke and piss. Curtis shut the door behind him, still peering through the peephole, and Flanagan confronted him and the girl in the tube top and short skirt who was sitting on the bed.

"For fuck's sake, Kevin. I thought we were getting past this." The girl—who was quite attractive, if in a slightly trashy sort of way, looked at him with wide and slightly frightened eyes. "I've been trying to reach you for the last day."

"It's not my fault!" Curtis turned away from the door. "We were minding our own business!"

"You're always minding your own business right up until the point you're hiding out in a sleazy hotel room from the local mob, Kevin." Flanagan didn't raise his voice, but kept it to a low, dangerous growl. There was a reason he had his .45 in his waistband and a couple of extra mags in his back pocket, aside from the two reloads he usually carried.

"I didn't know she was Vitti's daughter!" Curtis had moved to stand next to the girl, who immediately held his hand. "I sure as hell didn't expect him to get this pissed off that she was with a black guy!"

"He's a mobster with the name 'Vitti.'" Flanagan was not amused, though he found that he was less angry this time. He was more tired than anything else. "What else did you expect?" He sighed. "Come on. We've got a job, anyway. As long as we can get out of the parking lot before the goombas show up, we should be alright."

Curtis didn't move. He stayed there by the bed, holding the girl's hand. "We've got to bring her with us."

Flanagan turned a baleful eye on him, but he was already thinking it through, and even before Curtis spoke again, he knew that the other man was right, tomcat or not.

"You know what Vitti's going to do to her!" Curtis was still holding the girl's hand, as she looked up at him with something like devotion in her eyes. "We can't leave her for him to find her."

Flanagan sighed. "Ah, hell." He looked at the girl. "What's your name?"

"Monica."

"Okay, Monica, we're going to move fast, and I don't just mean to my truck. Kevin and I have some serious work to do in a couple of days, so we've got that long to get you set up in some sort of 'witness protection' arrangement. Fortunately, we know a few people who can make that happen." He moved to the window and peered out past the curtain. "The coast *looks* clear." He turned back and fixed Curtis with a glare. "Are you armed?"

"Of course I'm armed, Joseph. I'm irresponsible, not stupid."

Flanagan rolled his eyes. "I'll go first. Give me ten seconds to get out in the parking lot and confirm that it's clear, then follow. I'm parked just outside." He narrowed his eyes at Curtis again. "You get to call Frank and get things rolling to get her into hiding. This is your mess; you get to do most of the legwork."

Then he was going out the door, clearing visually to his right and left, his hand near the butt of his .45.

The parking lot was still relatively empty and still. His eyes were drawn to movement over by the corner of the building, but it was just a drunk, passed out on the porch, moving in his sleep. Under some circumstances, that might be a bad guy, but he didn't think that the mob was quite that tactically sophisticated, especially not when their target was one gambling, bodybuilding tomcat who'd bedded the boss's daughter.

Satisfied, he climbed into the cab and started the truck. A heartbeat later, Curtis appeared, pulling the girl after him as he rushed to the truck. He helped Monica into the middle, then climbed in and slammed the door. "It's okay, baby. Everything's going to be fine."

Flanagan already had the truck in reverse, and moved out quickly, pulling a Y-turn and roaring out onto the road. He saw headlights in the distance, coming from the city, but he was already turning right, out into the desert.

Half a mile away, he looked in the rearview mirror and saw the headlights turning into the parking lot. It looked like they'd just made it.

"Get on the phone, Kevin. We don't have a lot of time."

***

Carlo Santelli walked out the door and down toward his car with a mixture of satisfaction and sadness. He was about halfway to the vehicle when the phone rang.

"Yessir." He'd been expecting Brannigan to call. After all, today was the day that they finally got Sam Childress installed in a house of his own, with full-time care and state-of-the-art security. After getting shot in the spine in Transnistria, the young mercenary had then been kidnapped out of the hospital by operatives working for the Humanity Front. They'd worked him over pretty good, fractured his skull, and left him with some permanent brain damage. The Blackhearts had found allies who had gotten him to a secret hospital site out in the country, but it had been far from any of the Blackhearts' homes, and it had taken a good deal of resources.

And the man couldn't live the rest of his life in a hospital.

Now, while Childress was a backwoods boy who'd never liked cities, he was just down the block from Santelli's own house in the Boston suburbs. That meant that not only could they get him the care he needed, but Santelli could keep an eye on him. He'd had a fatherly concern for the younger man since their days in the Marine Corps, when Sergeant Major Santelli had needed to discipline the hotheaded Corporal—or Lance Corporal, depending on the month—Childress a few times.

37

"How's our boy?" Brannigan must have been busy, since he hadn't been there to get Childress settled in. Which meant they had a job.

"Getting used to the wheelchair. I don't think he'll ever get used to being fussed over. I might have made a mistake—the permanent nurse we found is awfully pretty. And she's really good at fussing over him, too." Santelli chuckled a little, even as he tensed up a bit.

He knew there was a job in the offing. And he'd been wrestling with the fact that he wasn't sure he was up to it anymore since before Azerbaijan.

It wasn't that he was scared. Not really. At least, he wasn't scared for himself. He'd lived with death since he'd been a teenager, first in the old neighborhood, then in the Marine Corps, and finally with the Blackhearts.

No, he was afraid for his family. He had a retirement, but he could only imagine how that might get screwed up if the VA found out that he'd bought it on an illegal mercenary mission somewhere in a country Americans weren't supposed to be.

Carlo Junior hadn't been born yet when they'd gone to Khadarkh. He hadn't had this concern when they'd started.

"I think he's getting better, Colonel." He tried to continue the conversation as normally as he could. "He's always going to have some short-term memory problems—don't we all—but he's more alert now. More aware of what's going on around him."

"Good." Brannigan sounded a little pensive. "We've got a job."

Santelli stopped in his tracks, angry at just how tense and nervous he felt. But if he'd given anything away by his silence, Brannigan acted as if he hadn't noticed.

"I want you here for the brief, but under the circumstances, with your family and Sam's situation, I want you to stay back and handle logistics and information support." He paused for a moment, and Santelli heard him sigh a little. "I don't want you to take this the wrong way, Carlo. I'm not just doing this because I think you need to take some down time. We've been

38

leaving a lot of our support to offices and people we can't see. I want somebody back here who's one of us, who can be the first point of contact if things go bad. We've been out in the wind without a parachute for eight missions, now. We should have known better. *I* should have known better, and made better arrangements. The fact that you've got a family to worry about and Sam just moved in down the street just puts you in the best position."

Santelli hated himself a little for the wave of relief that passed through him. He knew that he'd hate himself even more after the Blackhearts left. But Brannigan was right. Azerbaijan had been extremely hairy. Building more of a support network was long overdue.

"Roger that, sir. I'll be there."

CHAPTER 5

The fire crackled in the middle of the little campsite. It was the only sound in the aftermath of Brannigan's summation of the situation and the mission.

Wade finally leaned forward, his elbows on his knees. "Well, now. 'Be at this spot at this time, whack this guy, and don't ask questions.' That's not suspicious at all." He shrugged. "Don't get me wrong, I'm fine with murdering a Communist dictator, whatever he's done, but this really sounds like a setup."

"We're almost certain that it is, in fact, a setup." Brannigan took a deep drag on his cigar and blew the cloud toward the treetops. "But as I said, we're also pretty sure that we can't just say, 'No,' without some serious repercussions. Which is why we're meeting almost three weeks before the planned time on target and making contingency plans."

"I've been digging already." Santelli wasn't sitting on one of the log rounds—he'd brought a camp chair so he could lean back while he sat by the fire. "This Clemente character hasn't been on anyone's radar up here before now. Hell, he barely is now. I found one mention of San Tabal or any kind of takeover in the media, and that was some small, alternative online newspaper. It's like nobody cares."

"If this is so minor, and this guy's such a nobody, then why is somebody in DC so keen to see him get whacked?"

Burgess had also brought his own chair, and was sprawled in it, stroking his short beard thoughtfully as he stared at the flames. "It don't add up."

"No, it doesn't." Brannigan looked around at the rest of the Blackhearts. "Which is why Van Zandt gave us some extra warning. We need to get in and run some reconnaissance before the hit's supposed to go down. We're on a relatively short timeline, here—not that that's anything new." A low, humorless chuckle went around the fire. None of the Blackhearts' missions had allowed for anything like a generous amount of preparation time.

"Van Zandt's office is arranging charter flights. Originally, it was going to be all of us in one go, but we've since arranged for two flights. Joe and I will go in first and do our initial reconnaissance. The rest will fly in two days later."

"What about weapons?" Wade was usually their self-appointed weapons guy.

"We'll have to sort that out on the ground, unfortunately." Brannigan had fully expected the grimaces that went around the fire. "Whoever's behind this little game, they don't want official American fingerprints on this, so they've put all of it in our court. Full deniability."

"Getting weapons in Colombia's going to mean dealing with some shady characters." Flanagan kept his voice even, but Brannigan knew he was remembering Dubai. "I doubt that Colombia has regular gun stores, never mind the kind we can find in, say, Texas." The Blackhearts had gotten most of the hardware for the Tourmaline Delta op in an ordinary gun store in south Texas. Santelli, being from Boston, had been mildly shocked at what kind of weaponry they could get over the counter there. Happy, but shocked.

"They don't." Santelli had already been looking into it. "There's no way you're getting weapons outside of the black market there. The Colombian Army has a monopoly on legal gun sales, all weapons have to be registered with them, permits are required, and only Colombian citizens can get a permit." He folded his thick arms over his barrel chest. "We might need to lean on Van Zandt to include some weapons. Charter flights should make it easier, especially since he's got full control over the birds. They should have some smuggling compartments, or something."

Brannigan shook his head. "I've brought it up. The birds still have to get through Customs, and apparently the crews are fine with moving spies and operators around, but don't want to run the risk. They won't fly with weapons aboard."

"Great." Curtis was leaning against a tree. "So, how is Joe going to make a deal with the cartels or the FARC without starting World War Three? I think you need somebody who's a little bit better with people."

"Like who?" Flanagan looked over with a raised eyebrow. "The guy who dates crazy chicks who try to stab him, or the guy who ends up hiding out in a hotel from the local mob?"

"That is below the belt, Joseph. Two incidents do not invalidate all the other times I've glided through all levels of society and charmed the pants off supermodels, millionaires, and all kinds of other people." Curtis huffed.

"'Charmed.' Is that the word?" Flanagan grinned. "Not what I'd use, given some of your history. I at least don't consistently get into trouble. Some people actually trust the quiet guy more than the loudmouth, especially in this sort of a situation."

Curtis sputtered. "'Loudmouth?' Is that what the socially inept one calls the guy who actually engages with people instead of sitting back and just watching and looking mysterious?"

"Are you two done?" Santelli was shaking his head, though there was a little bit of a smile on his face. It turned a little sad after a moment. There had been a time when Roger Hancock would have growled at the two friends to shut up so they could get back to the business at hand. With Roger gone, things just weren't quite the same anymore.

"Seriously, though, as much as I hate to say it, Kevin's right." Wade rubbed his chin. "If we've got to get weapons in-country, the list of possibilities is pretty short, and we really can't trust any of them. Hell, what are the odds that FARC or ELN doesn't have something to do with Clemente's little revolution?"

"Pretty slim." Flanagan had sobered, too.

"I mean, we've kinda been here before—this wouldn't be the first time we dealt with organized crime to get geared up for a mission. Hell, Dmitri just saved our asses in Azerbaijan, as much as I don't trust that oily sonofabitch." Wade grinned. "I kinda like him, but I sure as hell don't trust him. And I'm pretty sure that Dalca chick isn't exactly the most upstanding citizen, either."

"She isn't." Brannigan probably knew more about Erika Dalca's background and activities than the rest. She'd helped them insert onto the Tourmaline Delta, and she had offered the information that had led them to Eugen Codreanu in Transnistria, not to mention the Humanity Front's secret base in the Altiplano. She'd been an active player in a surprisingly—or disturbingly—large number of the Blackhearts' operations.

She had also made a pass at Brannigan himself a time or two. The rest didn't know about that part, and they didn't need to know.

"What about her?" Flanagan looked up. He hadn't been looking at the fire, the way some of the others had. Despite the fact that they were probably in about the safest, most secure spot they could find, miles up in the woods in a wilderness area, Flanagan was too much the woodsman to sacrifice his night eyes by staring into a fire. "She's got to have contacts in Colombia."

"I'm sure she does." Brannigan scowled. "But I'm not bringing her in if we can help it. She's already positioned herself to have a lot more leverage over us than I like. If we're being effectively blackmailed into this, the last thing I want to do is put us into a position where someone like Dalca can hold even more over our heads. She's been helpful so far, but I don't imagine for a second that she did it for any other reason than that it benefited her and her interests. The fact of the matter is, she's still an organized crime kingpin. Hell, for all we know, Clemente's one of her clients. Or vice versa, if he's growing coca to support his little fiefdom."

"She's said that she doesn't deal in drugs." If Curtis was trying to sound hopeful, he managed to sound more like he really didn't believe it, himself.

"And that may or may not be true. My concerns stand, and since I am, ultimately, calling the shots in this outfit, I say that she stays out of this until we don't have any other choice." Brannigan said it around the cigar.

"And while I would tend to agree, it still puts us back at square one." Bianco didn't usually venture an opinion during planning sessions, but this situation seemed to have disturbed him enough to break through his reticence. "How many of us have spent any great amount of time in South America?"

No one answered as the Blackhearts looked around at each other. The only American soldiers who'd really been down in Latin America over the last few years had been Special Forces and a few other SOF units. All eyes turned to Jenkins, who had been quieter than usual. In fact, the former SEAL had been downright subdued ever since Santelli and Gomez had found out he'd been using a self-defense class as a front for his own hookup operation, just before the Azerbaijan mission. He looked a little startled, but then shook his head. "I did some time in Mexico, but never Colombia."

Flanagan's eyes narrowed in thought. "I'd be willing to bet Kirk's spent some time down there. He might know somebody."

There were a few nods, some more enthusiastic than others. Ignatius Kirk had been a Blackheart for two missions, one of them Stateside. He'd taken a sucking chest wound in Argentina, his first overseas job, and had been in and out of surgery since then. He was still a Blackheart, though he had mostly kept to himself since he'd been wounded.

"Will he be willing to help?" Santelli voiced the concern that was on Brannigan's mind. Kirk hadn't exactly been keeping in close contact with the other Blackhearts lately.

"I think so." Burgess knew Kirk better than any of them—the two of them had worked together on contract some time before. "He's grumpy and solitary, but he's only kept his distance because he feels useless while he's still all stove up. If he were on his feet, he'd be here right now."

"I'll go talk to him, then." Flanagan stood and stretched. "I'm not entirely sure what more we can really plan until then. Maybe we can rehearse the ambush tomorrow—*if* we're going to even plan on executing according to the canned plan."

"We're not, but a quick run-through might not be a bad idea. We could probably all use the tactics refresher, just to bust the rust off." Brannigan took one more drag on the cigar before tossing the stub into the fire. "Carlo will run things—I want you to head out and see if you can talk to Kirk in the morning, Joe."

***

Ignatius Kirk was at home, somewhat to Flanagan's surprise. As he knocked on the door, he reflected that he probably shouldn't have been surprised—he didn't know the other man nearly as well as Burgess did, but he'd always struck Flanagan as the kind of man who wouldn't want to stay in the hospital any longer than absolutely necessary.

Kirk's cabin was well back in the woods, invisible from the main road. The track through the trees to get to it was narrow and hard to spot. The cabin itself was built from cargo containers, partially buried. Somehow, Flanagan expected that Kirk probably had trail cams and early warning devices all through the woods around it. He had no doubt that the older man knew he was coming.

He waited, slightly offset from the door. Some of that was habit. Some of it was because he had a healthy respect for Kirk's paranoia. Any man who lived by himself way out here like this was probably not eager for visitors, and while Burgess was pretty sure that Kirk was still a Blackheart, Flanagan didn't know him well enough to be able to say what his reaction might be when one of them showed up on his doorstep.

But when the door opened, Kirk grinned a little. "Hey, Joe. Come on in."

Kirk had been a barrel-chested man with a massive, Grizzly Adams beard the last time Flanagan had seen him. He'd lost a lot of the weight, and it looked like he was still growing the beard back. He was still moving slowly and haltingly as he ushered Flanagan inside.

Flanagan had never been to Kirk's cabin, and he looked around, impressed that it didn't look like the survivalist den that it had appeared to be on the outside. The walls were wood-paneled, the windows let in plenty of light, and those same walls were lined with hunting trophies, photos, and mementos from a long career in Special Forces and the contracting world, after that.

Kirk pointed Flanagan to the couch in front of the fireplace. "Make yourself at home. Want a beer?"

"Sure." Flanagan sank into the couch, adjusting the 1911 on his hip as he did so. "How are you holding up?"

"I'm surviving." Kirk tried to hide a wince as he straightened from the refrigerator, but Flanagan caught it. He definitely wasn't healed up entirely from the latest surgery. "Still not put back together enough to go back out, but I should be soon." He handed Flanagan the beer then settled in his own recliner, obviously stifling a groan. "I hate feeling useless. This isn't the first time I've been shot, but it seems like the recovery didn't take as long, last time."

"We were all younger men once, and was the last time a sucking chest wound?" Flanagan lifted the beer and took a swig. It was in an unlabeled bottle with a flip top, and after a moment, he decided it was some of the best beer he'd ever had. Kirk must brew it himself.

"No, but that doesn't really make it any better." Kirk took a swig of his own. "It sucks getting old, especially when I know you guys have already been out once without me." At Flanagan's raised eyebrow, he shrugged. "Tom told me."

"Well, you might be able to help this time, even if you're stove up." Flanagan took another swig of the beer. The look in Kirk's eyes, the almost pained hope, had been uncomfortable for a moment.

He leaned forward. "We're heading to Colombia. The Colonel and I are going in first, then the rest will follow a couple days later. It's complicated, but we need a contact down there, someone who we can trust, who might also have access to weapons and gear."

"Finding somebody you can trust in Colombia's no easy trick." Kirk took another sip, but his eyes were focused now, and he clearly already had a plan in mind. "That place has been fucked six ways from Sunday since *La Violencia*, and the people still carry the scars. Where are you going? Or can you tell me?"

"Northeast. Near the Venezuelan border."

Kirk swore with feeling. "Right into FARC and ELN territory. Those your targets?"

"Maybe. We're running on short intel." Flanagan filled Kirk in on the situation and the mission, watching the older man's expression darken.

"That's a hell of a fix, man." He stared at the fireplace for a moment. "There's no way you can just tell 'em to fuck off?"

"Brannigan doesn't think so. I'm inclined to agree. The fact that the people pushing this wanted us specifically doesn't bode well."

"No, I suppose it doesn't." Kirk frowned. "Well, I think I can help you. I spent a few years down that way. I've got quite a few friends who are either cops, military, or retired from either. One was even both, but he's probably old enough that he won't want to get involved." He started to get up and winced again. "Let me do some digging. We'll find *somebody* who should be on our side.

"Provided the bad guys haven't gotten to them since I was down there last…"

CHAPTER 6

Brannigan had to admit to himself that he was glad that they'd gotten a taxi at the airport, rather than trying to drive themselves. It had been a while since he'd tried to negotiate Latin American traffic, and it was every bit as bad as Middle Eastern traffic. It was utter chaos. Bogota was generally considered the worst city in the world for traffic, and he could see why. They were motionless, stuck in a jam-packed mass of cars, vans, and trucks, for the fifth time since leaving the airport, despite the multiple attempts the taxi driver had already made to cut lanes and get around.

With the way the man drove, Brannigan was slightly surprised he hadn't already tried to get up on the sidewalk.

Flanagan was watching out the right side of the car, his eyes never still. Bogota might be relatively peaceful, compared to past decades, but nowhere was ever *entirely* safe, and the Blackhearts themselves were not given to complacency. They'd been in too many warzones for that. Even at home, they were always alert.

Well, most of them.

Brannigan was mostly watching ahead and the other side. The streets were as narrow as they were crowded, and while there were a lot of green plants and flowers around, the signs of the uneasy security situation were everywhere. Open warfare with the

FARC and the cartels might not be the rule any longer, but almost every window and door he saw was barred and gated. Crime was clearly still a problem, and a major one.

He'd seen it before. Much of what they'd seen of Argentina had been similar. Latin America had problems—not that the US didn't, but only certain neighborhoods there had bars on all the windows.

It didn't make him feel any better about flying in without weapons.

***

The hotel was a three-story brick building that had clearly seen better days. All of Bogota wasn't run down—they'd seen some very shiny, very modern parts on the way from the airport. But all of them could be expected to have some degree of surveillance on them, either governmental or criminal. Or both. And this was a lot closer to where they were headed.

The rooms weren't great, either. Brannigan didn't *see* any cockroaches, but something about the sketchy carpet and cracking plaster on the walls made him expect that they were there, whether he could see them or not.

Flanagan didn't say much, but just looked around the room appraisingly before going to check that the door leading to the adjacent room was locked. After testing the handle, he grabbed a metal chair and wedged it under the handle. Flanagan was not a trusting man.

He moved to one of the beds, dropped his day pack on it, and sat experimentally. The frame creaked alarmingly under his weight, but it held. He shrugged. He wasn't especially particular about sleeping arrangements while deployed. Neither of them were; they'd both slept in much worse places. Brannigan was still half inclined to just move the covers onto the floor rather than risk the bed collapsing under him in the night.

"Well, that took longer than planned." Brannigan checked his watch. The advantage to working in the Western Hemisphere was that the jet lag wasn't nearly as bad. It almost felt like they were still on a normal schedule, despite the delay involved in getting to the hotel. "Looks like we're going to have to roll right into Phase Two."

"Fine with me." Flanagan wasn't going to get stirred up about it. "I'm kinda hungry, anyway."

Brannigan nodded as he swung his overnight bag onto the bed. "Unfortunately, given our contact instructions, it might end up being a while before we actually get to eat."

Flanagan shrugged. "Wouldn't be the first time a messed-up timeline meant going hungry for a while. Fortunately, I'm not a hedonist, like some people I could mention."

Brannigan snorted. "Joe, compared to Curtis, you're an ascetic."

Before they left the room, both men dug into the lining of their bags, pulling out slim polymer daggers. Slightly longer than a pen, the weapons might not be great for cutting, and were much less versatile than a steel knife or a gun, but they were much harder to detect in a country where civilian weapon carry was illegal. The weapons went into Brannigan's boot and the back of Flanagan's belt. Satisfied that they could handle just about anything short of an armed robbery at gunpoint—or getting rolled up by the Colombian police—they headed out.

The café was just across the street. It was a bit of a hole in the wall, with a full glass front and a corrugated metal sign above that read, "*Casa de Grande Pollo*." Stools faced a small bar against one wall, and regular tables lined the other, with the counter at the back, in front of the kitchen. The place smelled amazing, and Brannigan felt his stomach growl as they entered. He hoped that his own prediction about their dinner turned out to be erroneous—he *was* hungry.

They found a table near the back, where they could sit and watch both doors. The place was getting fairly busy, so it took a moment before the waitress came to their table. She was stunningly beautiful, though probably young enough to be Brannigan's daughter.

"*Buenos dias, señores*." She was looking from one to the other of them curiously—there weren't many gringos in this café.

51

In fact, they were the only ones. "What do you want today?" Her English was halting and hesitant, but clear enough.

"We'd like something that a friend told us about." Brannigan smiled easily. "He said it's not on the menu, so we'd have to special request it. *Chuleta Valluna*." He knew he was probably mangling the name—most of the Spanish he knew was of the Mexican flavor, and some words the Colombians pronounced a little differently.

Her brow furrowed a little. "I... do not think we can..." Then something seemed to click in her head. A memory, perhaps. "Let me ask."

She disappeared into the back. Brannigan and Flanagan traded a glance and went back to watching their surroundings carefully. They were getting some curious looks from the locals against the other wall. Fortunately, it was still a little early, so the café wasn't crowded yet.

A few minutes later, a stocky man, going a little bald, came out of the kitchen, wiping his hands on a towel. He sized the two of them up as he approached the table.

Both men were doing the same thing. *He's no ordinary cook. There's a lot of muscle under that paunch, and he doesn't carry himself like a cake-eating civilian. And he's sizing us up for threats, not just wondering about two gringos who asked for pork in a restaurant that mostly serves chicken.*

"Hello, gentlemen." The thickset man's English was accented, but he was noticeably more fluent than the waitress. "I'm afraid that your friend might have led you wrong. We don't have *Chuleta Valluna* here. I can suggest something else, but we simply don't have the ingredients for *Chuleta Valluna*."

"Well, that's disappointing." Brannigan hadn't been sure what the reaction would have been, but this wasn't quite it. Kirk had told Flanagan that his friend would probably draw them into the back to talk when he heard their order, but this guy wasn't doing that. "What would you recommend, then?"

"I'd suggest the *Arroz con Pollo*," the man said. He was still watching them, but Brannigan noticed that his eyes were never quite still. It wasn't a nervous tic, either. He was watching the front as well.

"We'll have that, then." The man nodded, said a quick word in Spanish to the waitress, and disappeared into the kitchen again.

Brannigan frowned. Flanagan's expression was carefully neutral, but he'd clearly noticed the same thing. "Not what Kirk told me to expect."

"How long has it been since he's been down here?" Brannigan was still keeping an eye on the kitchen door.

"It's been a few years." Flanagan grimaced slightly. "Things may have changed."

"Which means that this could go south in a hurry in the next few minutes." But he wasn't willing to completely abandon the rendezvous until they knew for sure.

The waitress came out a moment later, with two bowls and plates. The rice and chicken in the bowls was steaming, and smelled really good. She slid the plates in front of them with a smile.

A small slip of paper was on Brannigan's plate, wedged under the bowl. He returned the waitress's smile and pulled the paper out as she turned back toward the kitchen.

Finish your meal, and then meet me at the north side of Santa Matilde Park.

Flanagan had started in on his food, though he was watching Brannigan with a raised eyebrow. Brannigan tucked the paper into his shirt pocket and picked up his fork. "Looks like we're in business."

***

Three pickups came out of the night and screeched to a halt in front of the small, red-painted bungalow. Gunmen in green shirts, carrying AK-47s, G3s, and Galils, piled out of the beds and converged on the front door.

No one was awake inside, at least not at first. A single light burned above the door, but it did nothing to deter the men who kicked the door to splinters and rushed inside. They were in power. What was to deter them?

Diego Galvez stepped out of the lead truck's cab rather more sedately than his barely-leashed killers. Dressed in the same green shirt, but with a black beret on his head, his wolfish, sharp-edged features only serving to accentuate the feverish burning of his dark eyes as he watched the house, lighting a cigarette while he waited.

The Green Shirts were not expert tacticians. They didn't carefully clear each room—they smashed in doors and rushed toward the nearest figure that caught their eye. If they'd been up against trained soldiers—even some of the FARC's best fighters—they'd have been cut to pieces in moments.

Galvez didn't especially care. He had his special troops. They were assigned elsewhere for tonight. He'd needed knee-breakers for this, so he had picked these men carefully.

He could trust them to do two things—to be as violent as he needed them to be, and never to cross him. Every one of them had reason to fear Galvez.

To fear him more than any of the other leaders. Even Clemente.

Shouts and *thuds* reverberated through the open door. Galvez stood there, smoking, until matters had calmed down a little, then he started inside, flicking the still-burning cigarette into the garden out front. It was still too damp for the plants to burn—not that he would have cared.

He stepped through the door, looking around at the wreckage his men had left. They had not been gentle. The door itself hung on by one hinge, the jamb splintered and cracked where the latch and deadbolt had been smashed inward by a heavy boot. Plants were scattered amidst the potting soil and the fragments of their pots on the tiled floor.

More smashed furniture, including a shattered floor lamp, traced the trail his men had forced into the house. A mirror had been thrown on the floor, and Galvez's polished black boots crunched in the fragments as he stepped into the living room.

Fabian Camacho and his family knelt on the floor in front of the smashed remains of their coffee table, their arms cruelly twisted behind their backs. Blood ran down the side of Camacho's head—he'd been struck by a rifle butt. Galvez had seen that before. He'd received such a wound himself, long ago. The scar still ran through one eyebrow.

Camacho had had nothing to do with that. It had been a long time ago, and far from San Tabal. But Galvez looked down at the slightly paunchy financial tycoon, and his lip curled. It was just such men as Camacho who had paid the soldiers who had beaten him and left him for dead on the side of the road outside of Mocoa.

"Did they give you any trouble?" Galvez already knew the answer, as his eyes were drawn to Lorenzo's split lip.

Lorenzo pointed to Camacho's oldest, a boy of about fourteen. "That one tried to fight."

Galvez looked at Camacho. "Kill him."

Lorenzo didn't hesitate. He shifted his rifle to one side and shot the boy in the back of the head, almost before the Green Shirt holding him could get out of the way. The bullet blasted out through his mouth with a spray of red, blood and bits of shattered bone and teeth spattering the rug. The teenager fell on his face with an awful *thump*. His mother screamed in anguish.

The sound would have been heart-rending, if Galvez had not long ago extinguished any weak human feelings.

A rifle butt to the skull silenced the woman. She slumped to the floor beside her murdered son, whimpering.

Galvez lit another cigarette as he met Camacho's burning eyes. "You have been helping enemies of the people escape, Fabian Camacho. That alone is a crime worthy of death." He took a deep drag and blew it in Camacho's face. The man blinked, his eyes smarting from the smoke, but he refused to flinch. "The only reason that you are still alive is because I need information. You are going to tell me everything you know about your counter-revolutionary friends." He smiled, but there was no warmth in the expression, nothing human at all. "If you do, you will die quickly.

55

If not…" He took another drag on the cigarette and then dropped the still-glowing coal on Señora Camacho's back. She was still too dazed from the blow that had laid her out to react. "Then you will watch your family die slowly and in a great deal of pain before we even get to you."

Camacho glared daggers at him. "You are going to kill us anyway."

"Indeed. You are already condemned by your own actions. The only question is, will it be quick and relatively painless?" Galvez stepped closer and smiled down at the financier. "I can make each one of you last *days* if I want to." In truth, he'd never quite managed that feat, though it was something he'd always wanted to accomplish. They usually died after a few hours.

"Go to hell."

Galvez drew the knife he always carried opposite his pistol. "If there is any such thing as hell, Fabian Camacho, the closest to it will be what you witness and endure here tonight."

***

It was almost dawn. Camacho's face was a mask of blood, what remained of his clothes soaked in it. Not all of it was his own. The beatings had been savage and there had been spatter. Several of the Green Shirts were splashed with it, and they joked under their breath as they watched Galvez work on Camacho.

"You can kill me, Diego Galvez, but it won't stop God's wrath from finding you." Camacho's voice was a hoarse gurgle. His throat had been damaged, and the blood and phlegm running down into his lungs wasn't helping. "Clemente will fall."

Somehow, Galvez couldn't help but grin as he straightened. He hadn't gotten the information he wanted, at least not all of it. Camacho was tougher than he'd expected.

"I know." He drew his pistol and shot Fabian Camacho between the eyes.

CHAPTER 7

It was getting dark by the time they reached the park. There were a decent number of people on the street and strolling through the park, young and old, and they got some looks, being two big gringos, but not as many as they might have expected. Bogota was not an insular Middle Eastern city—there was still a respectable tourist industry in Colombia, especially since the drug wars had migrated north. The Colombian cartels were still involved, but they had mostly become suppliers to the far more savage and violent Mexican cartels. So, there were usually a fair number of white faces to be found, especially in large cities like Bogota.

Of course, those white faces were usually seen in more crowded places, rather than down here in the poorer part of town.

The two of them kept to the shadows as best they could, and tried to stay inconspicuous. That was more easily said than done, but as the sun went down and they kept to the trees on the edge of the park, near the street, the shadows made it slightly less obvious that they were two white men waiting for someone.

They hadn't been there long when a newish silver Nissan pulled up to the curb. "Get in." The thickset man from the restaurant was behind the wheel. He appeared to be alone.

Keeping his hand near his knife, Flanagan led the way, opening the back door and checking both the back seat itself and the cargo area behind it. Both were empty, so he slid inside, making room for Brannigan, who joined him and pulled the door shut.

No sooner had it latched than the man was pulling away from the curb, smoothly accelerating down the street.

"I don't know who you are, but you used a recognition signal I arranged years ago with someone I trust implicitly." The thickset man didn't look back as he spoke, but kept his eyes on the road. "I haven't seen him in a very long time, but he was never the kind who would give up a secret under duress. So, I will consider you his friends, until you prove otherwise."

"You're David Cruz, then?" Brannigan was watching their driver as much as he was watching where they were going.

"I am. Who are you, and how do you know Ignatius Kirk?"

"I'm John. This is Joe." Brannigan relaxed ever so slightly. Cruz had used Kirk's name, and his demeanor was more a combination of curiosity and wariness than the kind of affected friendliness that might herald a double-cross. "We've worked with Kirk recently. He'd be here himself, but he's a bit stove up."

"Business or pleasure?" From the tone and the faint glint in Cruz's eye in the rearview mirror, Brannigan caught what he meant.

"Business, I'm afraid. Work-related accident."

That did prompt Cruz to glance back at them in the mirror, his brow furrowed. "How bad?"

"This was, what? His third surgery? Or forth?" Brannigan glanced at Flanagan.

"Third, I think." Flanagan was still watching the buildings slide by, his eyes following anyone on foot or in a vehicle that might seem to be giving them a bit too much attention.

"That bad?" Cruz's frown deepened. "What happened? He didn't pay the girl?" Despite the flippant words, he was clearly probing for somewhat more detailed information, and not just because he was curious or playing a role. There was genuine worry for a friend in his voice.

"Like I said, it was work-related. Doing some of the same sort of stuff he used to before he retired." Brannigan didn't know Kirk well on a personal level, but he knew enough about the man's past—and Kirk had told them about his connection with the former *Sargento Mayor de Comando* Cruz of the *Agrupación de Fuerzas Especiales Antiterroristas Urbanas*, or AFEAU—that he was pretty sure the message would come through without giving away too much detail at the outset.

But Cruz clearly wasn't that worried about subtlety—or a bug in his car. "Did he get shot? Or blown up?"

"Sucking chest wound." Flanagan had decided that the extra detail might just buy a bit more of Cruz's trust. "Missed his heart, but it nicked a lung. He's taken some patching up."

"*Juepucha.*" Brannigan didn't know that particular curse, but he got the idea. "So, he couldn't come, but he sent you to meet with me." He squinted into the rearview mirror again. "You know what? Let's wait until we get to the house."

"Some reason you don't really want to talk in the car?" Brannigan didn't know what kind of surveillance they might need to watch for in Colombia, but if a former AFEAU operative was being cagey, he was inclined to pay attention.

"Just being a little paranoid. Kirk and I got into some interesting scrapes when he was down here—and not just the ones with the senoritas, either. If he was just sending someone who wanted to see the sights, he wouldn't have used the *Chuleta Valluna* signal." He turned toward the darkened hills above the city. "We'll talk when we get there."

***

"There" turned out to be a pretty nice house, up in the woods and scrub in the hills to the east of Bogota, surrounded by a thick hedge of tall pines. There was no sign of the city from up there—even if the hilltops they'd driven over hadn't been wreathed in mist at the time, they'd descended far enough onto the other side of the ridge that they might as well have been miles out in the country.

The fence around the property was barbed wire, and more barbed wire topped the green-painted gate at the front of the driveway. The gate was considerably taller than the rest of the fence, which was about the right height for livestock, so the barbed wire atop that was probably just for show. Brannigan didn't ask.

Cruz pulled the Nissan up the weed-choked driveway and parked it alongside the house, getting out and fending off the small mob of kids and dogs that came pouring out of the front door. He yelled up at the house in Spanish, and a plump, matronly woman appeared on the porch. She took a look at Brannigan and Flanagan where they stood near the vehicle, then yelled at the kids in a tone that brooked no argument. Cruz shooed the children toward their mother, then waved at the two Blackhearts to follow him.

He led the way back to a shed or garage in the back. Less fancy than the yellow-plastered house, it was a simple cinderblock construct with a corrugated metal roof and a dirt floor. He pulled several plastic lawn chairs out of the corner and lit a Coleman lantern. It hissed as he set it on the floor between the chairs.

"So. What brings friends of Ignatius Kirk out to Colombia?" He sat down in one of the chairs, crossing his beefy arms in front of his chest. "I would think that counter-drug operations would have most of you gringos up in Mexico."

"We suspect that there's some drug involvement, but that's not all." Brannigan eased himself down into another chair, wary of how well it was going to handle his weight. He'd seen chairs just like this one break under him before. But while the plastic creaked a little, it held. "What do you know about a place called San Tabal?"

Cruz went very still for a moment, but his expression was thoughtful rather than alarmed. "More than I'd like to. What's your interest there?"

"What can you tell us about the situation?" Brannigan wanted as much information as he could get. He also wanted to feel Cruz out about it. Kirk might trust him, but as Flanagan had pointed out, it had been a long time, and this was his country. He might not be quite as ambivalent about having American freelancers working in his own backyard. *Especially* if the situation wasn't as clear-cut as their limited briefing had made it sound.

Cruz leaned back in his chair a little. "About a month and a half ago, San Tabal became its own independent city-state. Not that the Colombian government agreed to any such thing, but as with most things in that part of the country, it's complicated. Even after the cease-fire with the FARC, it's been hard for Bogota to enforce its will up there."

"FARC and ELN camps in the jungle are one thing. This sounds like an entire city going over." Brannigan stroked his mustache as he watched Cruz carefully.

The former Colombian Sergeant Major snorted. "This *is* a bit of a unique situation, but since it's on a far smaller scale than, say, Pablo Escobar laying siege to the capitol, a lot of people are brushing it off."

Brannigan's eyes narrowed. "Seems a bit of a big deal to be brushed off."

"And it should be." Cruz shrugged. "But look where it sits. Right smack between the FARC—which is still a pain in the ass—and Venezuela."

"So." Brannigan nodded. "Venezuela."

Cruz made a "maybe" sort of gesture. "They're the most obvious backer. Clemente always was chummy with the Venezuelans before he was forced to retire. And there are definitely Venezuelan forces poised on the other side of the border. They're running 'exercises,' but they haven't actually done much. Of course, being Venezuela, that might be all the training they're capable of." Colombia had been fighting Marxist guerrillas for decades—it stood to reason that an AFEAU operative might not have a high opinion of the Communist country next door.

"But there's still something weird about all of it. Sure, Bogota hasn't been eager to fight the FARC or the ELN lately, and so locking horns with the Venezuelans might not be high on their to-do list, but for some reason they seem even more shy about

61

Clemente and his Green Shirts. And most of them are the same people who threw him out two years ago." Cruz shook his head thoughtfully. "No, I think there's more to this."

"What can you tell us about Clemente?" Brannigan asked.

"He's a thug." Cruz snorted. "Always has been. He comes from a decently connected family, and he always seemed to think that was enough to cover his ass. He's been corrupt from the beginning, and got in trouble a lot for abusing his subordinates. Of course, he really *was* connected enough to keep getting promoted for all those years, but he finally got in bed with the wrong people, pissed off the wrong politicians, and got stripped of his rank and thrown out of the Army on his ear two years ago. Then he shows up with a small army, takes over San Tabal, starts tearing down the nearby farms to convert them to coca production, and nobody will lift a finger."

"Well, nobody until now." Brannigan let the words hang in the air for a moment.

Cruz studied the two Blackhearts for a long moment, his expression unreadable. "Maybe this is where you tell me exactly why you're here, and what you think you need from me."

Brannigan leaned forward, his elbows on his knees. "Someone wants Clemente dead. They also want it to happen in a very specific place, at a very specific time. We're here to do some preliminary reconnaissance, to see if it's feasible to off Clemente and see this whole 'Green Shirt' thing you mentioned go away."

But Cruz was already shaking his head. "Clemente's the figurehead, and maybe something of a leader, but he doesn't have the charisma to have pulled this all together by himself. He might think he did, and someone might be using him as a commander, but he doesn't have the kind of personality that men will follow without an established rank structure having put him in command." His eyes narrowed as he stared into the dark, thinking.

"You think that if we off him, somebody else in his organization will just take his place?" Flanagan's voice was low and quiet. He hadn't said much since they'd arrived, and now he was sitting back from the lantern, letting Brannigan take most of the attention and ask most of the questions.

Cruz nodded. "Either that, or the Venezuelans will move in to 'restore order.'" He grimaced. "They're a lot closer than the Army right now."

The two Blackhearts traded a look. They didn't know who in Washington DC had ordered this mission, but it was getting sketchier and more suspicious by the minute.

Cruz rubbed his chin. "I will be honest, *amigos*, this sounds like one of those bright ideas that a politician thought up to buy himself some glory, all without putting in the effort. Even the cartels with flashy *capos* in charge don't disintegrate overnight when the *capo* gets killed or captured. And these Green Shirts, from what I've heard, are even more fanatical than any regular *narcos*. Many of them were *narcos*, but a lot more were FARC. Diego Galvez, Clemente's right hand? He was a FARC revolutionary, one of the ones who denounced the organization for caving to the government when the ceasefire was signed, no matter that the ceasefire has benefited the FARC a lot more than it has the rest of Colombia."

"You think he'd take over if Clemente bit it?" Brannigan mused.

"It's possible. He's got the force of personality, even if he's more feared than respected." Cruz didn't bother to hide his disgust. "The man wants to top Che Guevara. And he just might do it, if he gets the chance."

Brannigan watched Cruz, his own expression unreadable, slowly stroking his mustache as he thought.

This could be any number of things. The easy interpretation is exactly what Cruz thinks—that somebody high up wants to score some points and thinks that he can defuse this situation with one ambush, then reap the rewards as Clemente's little coup crumbles. We've certainly seen it before. Most of the people making decisions in DC that lead to these little deniable operations don't have the experience or the knowledge to know

63

what they're doing. A combination of hubris and naivete. Dangerous as hell.

But Cruz is right. Something's even more off about this. Unfortunately, I can't tell exactly what it is.

We need more intel.

"What kind of information is actually getting out of San Tabal?" he asked. "If the takeover is as thorough as you say it is…"

"Not a lot. That's not helping to expedite any response, either." Cruz was watching Brannigan carefully, though. He could tell where this was going.

"So, since you've got as much knowledge about Clemente and his cabal as you do, can I assume that means you have contacts in the area?" Brannigan studied Cruz with equal intensity, and saw the faint glint in his eyes.

"I might." A faint, hard grin spread across the other man's face. "Are you going to need weapons and gear, too?"

Brannigan returned the grin. "I believe we have an understanding, Señor Cruz."

CHAPTER 8

Galvez could hear Clemente before he even got into the office. The swearing echoed down the hallway outside.

Diego Galvez was not perturbed by Clemente's ranting. Even as several of the younger Green Shirts who had been assigned to guard the Leader tried very hard not to look through the door, Galvez strode past them, carefully smoothing the expression of contempt that threatened to overtake his features.

The Green Shirts had converted Jurado's entertainment room into Clemente's office. It was well-placed, opening up onto the balcony that overlooked the plaza. From there, Clemente could give his speeches and "inspire" the people the Green Shirts had "liberated" from their capitalist oppressors.

In truth, while Galvez believed strongly in the goal of eventual global Communism, far more than Clemente did, he had nothing but contempt for "the people." They were small-minded, hidebound, and far too religious for their own good. Even those who weren't religious were still too obsessed with "morality." They were good for nothing but forced labor.

Much like Clemente himself. The people were only tools to be used—and used up—in service to The Cause.

Clemente turned as Galvez stepped inside the office, clasping his hands behind his back. The Leader—clad in the pseudo-uniform that he had spent entirely too much time and energy working up after Jurado's hanging—stared at him, his face flushed.

"You! Tell me you didn't know that the Americans have sent operatives into Bogota!" Clemente stabbed a finger at Galvez, and the Green Shirts' chosen killer had to briefly bite back the white-hot flare of rage that tempted him to draw the Jericho 941 from its patent leather holster at his belt and finish Clemente early.

Who does this corrupt bastard think he is? He'd be nothing without us. A puppet in a uniform.

But the plan was too well-thought-out to abandon it now. There was too much to gain. Even at the expense of some of its chief players.

"What is surprising about Americans in Bogota?" Galvez kept his voice level and calm. "They have been working with their puppets there for decades. Their special operations troops come to Colombia every year. Even their Secret Service trains here. What would make you think that Americans in Bogota have anything to do with us here in San Tabal?"

What would *make you think that? Has someone talked? Has that fat fool, Ballesteros, given something away? If he has, I'll kill him just after you make your ultimate sacrifice for the Revolution.*

"I have my spies in Bogota," Clemente snapped. "Spies you know nothing about. Not everyone went along with those bastards when they stripped me of my position. They know the American special forces, they know where they come from and where they go. These men were like them, but they came by charter flight and then disappeared into the city."

That *did* sound strange, but Galvez didn't react. "Many of those special forces troops take lovers here in Colombia. It was probably only a couple of them on vacation." Things were too far along for Clemente, already paranoid, to begin to suspect that the noose was tightening. He would need to find out who Clemente's spies were and have them arrested or eliminated.

Clemente eyed him with naked hostility. Galvez met his gaze with a blank expression, well-practiced from years of circulating through revolutionary and criminal circles—there was a considerable overlap there—that were never entirely trustworthy.

"General." Galvez spread his hands. "Two Americans coming into Bogota means nothing. They are far from here, and our partners in Washington would have warned us if any moves against us were afoot."

"We have everything under control, General." Ballesteros probably thought he was being soothing, but his unctuous tone grated on Galvez's nerves. He could only imagine how much more it was going to infuriate Clemente. "This has been long in the planning, and we were prepared for many of these eventualities when we seized the city. The Americans have their own problems, and enough lobbyists to bog down any response for months, at least. The presence of the Venezuelans so close by will keep the Colombians in check. We are safe here, General."

Galvez watched Clemente carefully, waiting for the outburst. But the expected temper tantrum didn't materialize. Instead, Clemente looked with narrowed eyes from one to the other of them, clearly weighing their words in his head with what he'd already found out, not to mention the endless planning meetings they'd had in ELN camps and several official—if clandestine—buildings in Caracas.

He suspects something. But such is the nature of the Revolution. We must always suspect those around us. He does not know our plans. At least, Galvez hoped not. That would mean he would have to move the schedule up, and he didn't want to do that. Not all the pieces were in place. Not yet.

"Of course. You are right." Clemente leaned on the table with a sigh, one that Galvez suspected was more than slightly affected. "Forgive me, comrades. The strain of dealing with the resistance to the people's will has weighed on me." Clemente was mouthing the right words, but Galvez could hear the insincerity there. No matter. He knew where they all stood. "What did you find at Camacho's house?"

"Very little. He wouldn't talk, no matter what we did to him and his family. I executed them all and burned their house. The photos will be distributed and posted up in the plaza in the morning, as a warning to the rest." He poured a glass of Jurado's *aguardiente*. Enjoying the mayor's luxuries was one of the perks of being a leader of the revolution. "Do not worry. Camacho was always going to be a hard case. We will root them out." *You might not live to see it, but it will happen.*

"See to it that you do. We have already had problems with the farmers." That was no great surprise. Most of the farmers in those mountains who weren't already growing coca had made the conscious decision not to. Being forced to convert their fields of corn, beans, and coffee to coca would naturally be met with a certain degree of resistance—especially when they realized, accurately, that they would see none of the profit from the refined cocaine.

"Everything is under control, General." Galvez sipped the *aguardiente* and savored it for a moment before swallowing. "In six months, no one will be able to touch us."

***

Brannigan was waiting by the airstrip at Palonegro Airport, on the high tableland above Bucaramanga, as the charter plane taxied off the runway and toward the hangars and the civil air terminal. A plain, white, unmarked Learjet, it wouldn't stand out to anyone, not even the Colombian Army security posted around the airport.

Of course, the short, stocky man next to him helped with that, too.

Alejandro Pacheco was not a young man. His hair was solid silver, turning white. There was still a hard gleam in his eye, though, the gleam of a man who'd seen a lot of death, and dealt out his share, too. He was a veteran of the Search Bloc, the special operations unit formed from the Colombian Army and police to hunt down Pablo Escobar, years ago. Many of the Search Bloc were dead, and few of them of old age. That Pacheco was still around spoke volumes about him.

He also had contacts. It seemed he had not been idle in the years since the wars with the Medellin and Cali cartels. Cruz had introduced him to Brannigan, and he was going to be their primary supplier going into the mountains. He'd provided the two trucks that they'd driven to the airport. Neither was anything special— ancient, creaky diesels with covered beds. But they ran well, and they'd had no trouble with the mountain roads from Pacheco's farm.

The Learjet slowed and came to a stop, the engines winding down before the door opened, the stairs lowering toward the tarmac. Wade stepped out, scanning their surroundings carefully before his eyes lit on Brannigan and his companion.

Wade was too far away for Brannigan to read his expression very well, but he knew the other man enough to see the thought process well enough, anyway. *Okay, no armored vehicles or men with guns. The Colonel looks relaxed. Two trucks, no other security presence. We should be okay.*

He saw Wade turn inside and say something, then the big man started down the steps, his duffel over one shoulder. Bianco and Burgess followed, with Jenkins, Hank, Curtis, Gomez, and Javakhishvili coming after. They crossed quickly to where Brannigan waited.

"Welcome to Colombia, gents." Brannigan jerked a thumb toward the trucks behind them. "It's not a long drive to our staging point, which is Señor Pacheco's farm, about ten miles outside of town. We'll go over what Joe and I found out and get kitted up once we get there."

"I take it that this is still just as sketchy as we thought?" Wade asked.

Brannigan just waved toward the trucks again. "Like I said, we'll talk once we get there. The trucks are too noisy to carry on much of a conversation, anyway. Load up."

***

"So, where's Joe?" Curtis asked as he dropped down out of the back of the truck. He looked around at the farm, the modest, stuccoed house with cracking paint around the slightly ill-fitting

69

window frames, the fields with a few cows and a fair bit of corn just reaching knee height, and the rough stables built of wire, sticks, and corrugated sheet metal. "I can't imagine that you introduced him to a Colombian beauty hot enough to pry him away from Rachel."

"He's already up in the mountains, with Cruz." Brannigan was already leading the way toward the house. Pacheco had disappeared inside. "We need more information, so they're running some early reconnaissance. Once they get back, hopefully we'll have enough pieces of the puzzle to know where we need to dig deeper."

"So, this *is* still sketchy as hell." Wade's assessment wasn't a question.

"Always was. So was Azerbaijan." Brannigan led the way inside, and Pacheco waved them toward the back. "The implicit blackmail was the first red flag, and there haven't been many signals since that led me to think otherwise."

"I think it might be getting time to send a message." Wade's growl made it obvious what kind of "message" he had in mind. "I'm getting a little tired of this catspaw bullshit."

"You and me both, brother." The Blackhearts followed Pacheco into a relatively large living room in the back, with windows looking out on a garden that was already a riot of color, the mountains and the jungle looming beyond.

The living room was a little crowded at the moment. Nearly a dozen plastic storm cases lined the walls, and the furniture had been pushed toward the middle of the room to make space. Most of the Blackhearts eyed the cases with a glint of interest as Pacheco waved them to seats on the well-worn chairs and sofa.

"Coffee? Or maybe something a little stronger?" Pacheco's English was pretty good, and most of the Blackhearts probably couldn't have distinguished his accent from any other Spanish speaker, though Gomez cocked his head slightly, as if trying to place it. Half Texican, half Mescalero Apache, he was a fluent Spanish speaker, and was fairly familiar with a lot of

Central and South American dialects. More so than most Southwesterners might be. For all his silence and capacity for horrific violence, Gomez was a thinker, and he liked to learn.

"Coffee's fine." Brannigan wasn't worried about any of the Blackhearts getting drunk—well, maybe Curtis and Jenkins— but the last thing they needed right then was alcohol to cloud the planning process. And he'd heard good things about Colombian coffee for most of his life.

As Pacheco called to his wife to get some coffee brewing, Brannigan laid out what he and Flanagan had learned from Cruz. It really wasn't much, only some slight clarification of the already slim information they'd gotten from Van Zandt. "I've been on the horn with Carlo—he's digging. But he's got even less in the way of information that we can use on the ground. He's pressing Van Zandt, but so far, Mark's been reluctant to disclose much about our employer." When expressions turned dark, he held up his hands. "That doesn't mean he's stonewalling, not exactly." He momentarily reflected on the fact that there had definitely been a time when he would have expected Van Zandt to do exactly that. Maybe things had changed. Maybe they hadn't. "If the client is a senator, then he's got some serious resources to keep his skeletons in the closet, especially when someone like Van Zandt goes sniffing around.

"That said, Cruz told us that *someone* has given Clemente backing. He couldn't have pulled this off without it. Now, that might just mean the Venezuelans—they've certainly funneled FARC and ELN plenty of support since Chavez took over in Caracas. But…"

"*But* the strange interest in just taking out Clemente, no questions asked, means that somebody on our side of the fence is dirty." Burgess wasn't asking a question, either.

"It would hardly be the first time, would it?" Brannigan had seen plenty of instances of American politicians with their hands in the cookie jar of drug dealers and human traffickers— and worse.

71

"At any rate, Cruz doesn't think that just offing Clemente's going to do much. I'm inclined to agree with him. So, depending on what intel Joe and Cruz can bring back, we're going to see if we can set up the whole cabal to go down."

There was some silence after that. "And what happens to us when our employer knows we've gone off the reservation?" Bianco sounded a little perturbed. And well he might. Most of them had lives outside of the mercenary profession, and while they often lived for the fight, the consequences if their employers turned on them could be disastrous.

"I'm working on that." Actually, Santelli was working on their cover story more than he was, but that was part of why he'd had Santelli stay home. He and Hector Chavez were good at that particular dance, and they'd have a plan by the time the Blackhearts were ready to go loud on the ground. "We'll be ready if they try something. And if I have anything to say about it, if they do, we're going to turn their plan around and cram it right back down their throats."

There wasn't a whole lot more to say after that. They'd have to wait for Cruz and Flanagan. But in the meantime, as they sipped the scalding coffee that Pacheco's wife had brought in for them, their host started opening the equipment cases. They needed to be ready to roll as soon as the time came.

Pacheco had amassed quite an arsenal. It couldn't be legal—they'd all read up on Colombia's strict gun laws before heading down there—but he was close enough to FARC/ELN territory, and probably had greased more than a few palms, not to mention wielded his Search Bloc history like a club, that plenty of the local authorities were probably turning a blind eye. Brannigan certainly hoped so.

Most of the rifles were Galil SARs, the old standard weapon of the *Ejército Nacional de Colombia*'s infantry. The Colombians had transitioned to the newer Galil ACE or the bullpup IWI Tavor, but there were plenty of the older Israeli weapons still floating around. These weren't the modified

72

versions with adaptors to take STANAG magazines, so there were plenty of the older, AK-style mags to go with them.

Curtis's eyes gleamed as he hauled an IWI Negev light machinegun out of one of the bigger cases. "Ohh. I always wanted to give one of these a spin." He looked down into the case. "Hey, Vinnie! There's two of 'em, so you don't get stuck with a peashooter."

"That's assuming I didn't just take that one." Bianco was a good head taller than Curtis.

"Ha! You wish, nerd. I'd break your fingers." He put the 5.56 belt fed down and rummaged through the ammo case. "Looks like we've got plenty of ammo, too." He looked up at Pacheco. "You've got some serious balls, man."

Pacheco just smiled.

Wade and Hank were pulling more gear out. "Looks like we're going to be running old school. I don't see any body armor." Hank sounded a little uncomfortable at that, but Wade snorted.

"Body armor's going to be more of a liability in the jungle and the mountains than a help, Junior." He lifted one of the old, '90s-era load bearing vests. "These will do fine, as long as the mags fit." That took a brief experiment that confirmed that the mags did, indeed, fit.

"Damn. Even night vision." Burgess had opened yet another case. This one was full of old Pro-Tec bump helmets with NVG mounts and the green bags that carried PVS-14 night vision goggles and the necessary attachments. He looked up at Pacheco and frowned. "You've been ready for something like this for a long time."

Pacheco just shrugged as he sipped his own coffee. "We live in a country that is plagued by corruption, where the central government often as not would rather bow to the guerrillas and the *narcos* for a false 'peace' than fight for a real one. The drug wars against Medellin, Cali, and Norte del Valle might be over, but only on the surface. There might be a truce with the FARC, but only on the surface. Things have been getting much worse as time goes on, and it pays to be ready." There was an enigmatic look in his eyes as he took another sip. "I am not the only one."

"Well, I'm just as glad you had this stuff. Getting it by other means could have gotten messy." Wade was loading magazines.

Brannigan caught a glance from Curtis. With a bit of a pang, he realized that he and Curtis were the only ones in the room who remembered the fight with the Suleiman Syndicate in Dubai. Flanagan was out in the weeds with Cruz, but of the original seven Blackhearts, only Brannigan, Santelli, Flanagan, and Curtis were still alive.

He snatched up an ammo can and a handful of Galil magazines and got to loading. They needed to be ready when Flanagan and Cruz returned.

CHAPTER 9

Flanagan and Cruz were both wearing old tiger stripe camouflage—perhaps not the end-all, be-all of camouflage patterns, but it had been what Cruz had had on hand. It actually worked really well in the Colombian jungle—the play of light and shadow, not to mention all the thick vegetation, meant that they almost disappeared whenever they got far enough away from each other.

The sweat was threatening to cut through the camouflage face paint that he'd carefully applied before they'd stepped off, but so long as they stayed deep in the weeds, they should be okay, even if some of it wore off.

Both men were carrying Galil SARs and had three-day rucks on. They didn't plan on being out there that long, but sometimes it paid to be prepared.

Cruz was on point. He knew the area far better than Flanagan could hope to figure out just from studying the map, and the map was probably more than a little off in the first place. That was always a problem with jungle terrain—there was a lot on the ground that the map makers simply couldn't see.

Flanagan watched Cruz move through the bush carefully. The other man was a veteran, but he wasn't *quite* as good in the weeds as Flanagan. That said, he was still pretty good. There wasn't a lot of open-source information on the AFEAU, but rumor had it that they'd gone into the mountains after FARC, ELN, and various other guerrilla and *narco* groups more than once. They were supposed to be good, and if Cruz was representative of the unit as a whole, Flanagan believed it.

Cruz slowed, holding up a hand to signal a halt, then sank down to a knee behind a screen of thick bushes and trees. Flanagan moved up to join him, placing each step carefully to avoid making noise, and then took a knee beside the other man, turning to check their six and scan the woods around them before he did so.

They were still deep in the woods. Nothing but the jungle met his eyes, and he heard nothing but the birds, insects, and various other wildlife moving through the bush. He wasn't sure why they'd stopped, but he had to trust Cruz.

The two of them stayed put for a while, silent and listening. Flanagan was used to security halts on patrol—they'd already stopped several times since they'd left Cruz's truck and started their seven-kilometer hike through the hills to the southwest of San Tabal. But this one went on longer than any others they'd done.

He'd been doing his best to keep track of their general route, direction, and distance. It was difficult—pace counts got sketchy on mountainous terrain, and he'd had to keep checking his compass to be sure which direction they were going in the thick vegetation. It was possible that they were closer to their objective than he'd thought, but when he peered ahead of them, the slope of the mountain just kept going up, disappearing into the trees and the undergrowth, with no brighter light where the crest might be.

Finally, Cruz seemed satisfied. "We are about three hundred meters from our observation point." His voice was a low murmur, barely audible even from a couple feet away. "We need to be very careful from here on out. My sources tell me that the Green Shirts have been stepping up their patrols around the city, moving a lot farther out than they were just after the coup."

"How professional are they in the bush?"

"Not very. From what I've heard, the FARC and ELN are better. But even thugs can still kill us if they catch us, and they only have to get lucky once." Cruz hauled himself to his feet. "We will have to move more slowly and halt more often."

Flanagan just nodded. *Not my first rodeo, buddy.* But Cruz didn't know him any more than he knew Cruz, so it paid for both of them to communicate as carefully as possible. They were in enemy territory. Ego had no place here.

They kept climbing, moving with ever more caution. Each step was planted deliberately, testing for dead branches or loose rocks underfoot before putting weight down. Scanning was constant, and not only for the enemy. Flanagan had already seen more than a few snakes in the trees that he didn't want to tangle with, and he could have sworn he'd heard a jaguar all too close for comfort.

I preferred the woods in Azerbaijan. To hell with the jungle.

It took a long time to finish that last three hundred meters. The terrain, the vegetation, and the need for stealth slowed their advance to a crawl. But Flanagan was a hunter. Patience was something he'd cultivated since he'd been a kid.

Finally, they reached the crest, the slope falling away below them, so steep that any attempt to go down without ropes would probably lead to a nasty fall. The valley opened up beneath as they moved into position under a towering brazil nut tree, careful to keep to the shadows and the deeper undergrowth. They were most of a kilometer from their objective, but a trained observer could still pick them out if they exposed themselves.

They settled in, once again waiting, watching, and listening for several minutes to make sure that they were alone and unlikely to be stumbled upon by any Green Shirt patrols. Flanagan stayed still and sweated, as the bugs started trying to eat him alive.

Once they were reasonably sure that they hadn't been detected—or had picked a position right on a patrol route—they settled in and Flanagan pulled his borrowed binoculars out of his pack, getting down in the prone beside the tree, bracing the optics with his elbows planted against the roots, cupping his hands around the eyepieces.

A medium-sized farm spread across the slopes on the far side of the valley below. Cruz had given him the rundown before they'd inserted. This farm, originally belonging to one Diego Fuentes, had always grown mostly beans and corn, feeding not only the Fuentes family but a good chunk of the locals around San Tabal. The fields sprawled over several cleared hillsides, stretching from just short of the crest of the ridge clear down to the narrow creek that ran through the bottom of the valley. The house, two stories tall with a red tile roof and the stucco walls painted green and yellow, sat about two-thirds of the way up the slope, surrounded by trees.

Flanagan began his study with the house. A couple of ancient farm trucks were parked nearby, but they were outnumbered by the green-painted technicals that stood at all four corners, the machineguns in the beds manned by Green Shirts. He could see the source of the nickname—the dark green field shirts were the only uniform that Clemente's fighters seemed to have. They wore khakis, jeans, or camouflage trousers. Their gear was every bit as eclectic, running the gamut from plate carriers to ill-fitting load bearing harnesses to simple bandoliers full of magazines. A couple had belts of machinegun ammo draped around their torsos—mostly without a machinegun that would take that ammo in sight.

It became clear within a few minutes that the technicals and their crews weren't just there to guard the farm from outside interlopers. They were there to keep the farmers in check.

Most of the dozen or so Green Shirts he could see around the house were mostly lounging and smoking. Once, a young woman came out of the kitchen and onto the porch to throw something out. He could see from her body language that she was nervous, and the attention she was getting from several of the Green Shirts outside easily explained why.

He scanned down the main dirt road leading to the fields. Laborers were working out there, even though it was still far from harvest time. There's always work that needs doing on a farm, even while the crops grow.

But the strange thing was that there were no overseers out in the fields. All the Green Shirts were up by the house.

"You're sure Fuentes wouldn't willingly cooperate?" He kept his voice low and didn't take his eyes away from the optics as he asked the question.

"As certain as I am that the sun rises in the east." There was no doubt in Cruz's voice. "If he didn't have a family to worry about—and a lot of his workers are practically family—then he'd rather die."

"Hmm." Flanagan widened his scan, but he didn't see anything new. "There don't seem to be enough Green Shirts down there to act as overseers. I'm only seeing about a dozen near the house and the barn."

"Watch the barn closely." Cruz had clearly gotten eyes on this place already, but he wanted Flanagan to see it for himself.

He shifted the binoculars to watch the barn. It was a low, rough, cinderblock structure with a corrugated metal roof. A lot more care had gone into the house than the barn. The door was open, but it was dark inside, and he couldn't see much past the doorway itself.

Then there was movement. For a moment, a small face peered out before quickly vanishing back into the shadows. He shifted his gaze to see one of the Green Shirts, carrying an AK-47, striding quickly over to the barn. The skinny man leaned into the doorway for a moment before turning away and swaggering back toward his compatriots.

"They're holding hostages."

"The Green Shirts don't have the numbers to directly control everyone, so they take hostages to keep people in line. It's a time-honored technique." Cruz's voice was as flat and casual as if he were talking about ordering lunch. Flanagan still didn't have a great read on the other man. He couldn't tell if he was just that callous—there were a few stories about AFEAU—or if he had simply distanced his own mind from it for the sake of his own sanity.

Maybe it was a little of both.

"This is one of the few farms they've kept for food." A little bit of contempt leaked into Cruz's voice. "They're more concerned with the others. So, the more they can control these farms with threats against their loved ones, the more resources they can devote to the coca farms."

"Were any of these places coca farms before?" Flanagan knew that might be a loaded question, but he needed as much information as possible.

"No. There were grow areas nearby, but they've always been small. Clemente is trying to convert entire farms into an industrial-scale operation." Cruz might have snorted a little. "It's not clear what his endgame is, but if he can force some of the other cartels to their knees by undercutting them, he will have a bottomless source of funding to maintain his Communist hellhole."

"Not much you can do with money when there's no food to buy." While Flanagan had spent most of his career in the Middle East, the Blackhearts had seen some Communist hellholes, most notably in northern Burma. Plus, Flanagan, for all his backwoods manner and quiet demeanor, was an educated man. He knew Communism's long, bloody, and nightmarish history.

"There's always someone who will do business with them." Apparently, Cruz was a student of history, too.

"So, will Fuentes help us if we retake his farm?" Flanagan got back to business.

"I'm sure he will, if he survives and doesn't do anything stupid. There's a reason I showed you this farm first. Fuentes and his family have been part of the bedrock of this area for decades. He has never been aristocracy, but he is respected. If he isn't already part of a resistance, he'll still bring many out of the shadows to help if he stands up to Clemente." Cruz sighed. "I suspect that the only reason he hasn't already is that he knows he's alone and Clemente has a gun to his family's heads."

Flanagan took that in as he continued to scan the farm. He didn't see any more Green Shirts, despite Cruz's cautions about patrols. "Looks like it shouldn't be too difficult, if we can get close enough. Those technicals are a threat, but these guys don't look like they're all that alert or disciplined." He finally came off glass. "Are any of those coca farms nearby?"

"Yes. We can get there before dark."

***

The movement to the next objective was every bit as punishing as the first, especially given the fact that their muscles had had time to relax and start to stiffen up while they'd been lying there observing the Fuentes farm. But Flanagan was used to elk hunting in the high country, and so he adapted. He was probably having an easier time of it than Cruz—the other man might have been a veteran of one of Colombia's hardest units of trained killers, but he was getting older and probably wasn't spending much of his time out in the bush anymore. The skills came back, but conditioning was something else altogether.

It was indeed getting close to sunset by the time they neared their next OP. The terrain wasn't as conducive to standoff this time—they had to get a lot closer. And that nearness brought new dangers with it.

Flanagan could see the flicker of lights through the trees ahead and downhill, though they only occasionally penetrated the thick vegetation. It was already getting dark enough under the jungle canopy that he was starting to think about calling a halt to dig out the old PVS-14s that Cruz had brought, but it would be better to get into position while they still had some daylight to see by.

Cruz suddenly froze, putting up a clenched fist. Flanagan didn't bother to ask why; he just froze in turn. When you're in the bush and in hostile territory, you don't question the point man, even if he's a partisan contact. Kirk trusted Cruz, and that was going to have to be enough—at least, until the man tried to sell them out.

After a brief moment, Cruz sank to the forest floor, going prone with his rifle still held ready. Flanagan followed suit, still scanning and listening for whatever had alerted his companion.

That didn't take long. He could hear the rustle of movement through the trees and the sound of low voices. Someone was coming. And they were already close.

He'd slipped under a bush, hoping and praying that he wasn't about to lie down on a snake, or centipede, or anything else poisonous. Keeping his own Galil ready, he peered through the leaves, searching for the source of the noises.

The three Green Shirts appeared a few minutes later. They were dressed similarly to the ones he'd watched through the binoculars back at the Fuentes place, two of them wearing ill-fitting load bearing vests, one carrying a Galil and the other an AKM. The third was wearing an ancient belt and Y-harness and carrying an old M16A2 with almost all the bluing worn off.

It was his first up-close encounter with the Green Shirts, and if anything, he was even less impressed than he had been watching the group guarding the Fuentes farm from a distance. They weren't in anything approaching a tactical formation, simply clumped together and strolling through the jungle, chatting and laughing. They barely glanced to their left or right, and never checked behind them.

The three of them passed a few yards away from where the mercenary and his Colombian contact lay in the weeds. None of them so much as glanced in Flanagan's direction as they went past, all far too absorbed in their conversation. Though he couldn't understand most of the Spanish, the coarse tone and harsh, gloating laughter put his teeth on edge.

Flanagan knew what kind of men the likes of Clemente would surround himself with. Some of them might be naïve idealists, but those were actually very rare in real guerrilla movements. Most of them were unrepentant, vicious thugs, and from what he could see, these three definitely fit that description.

Not that it mattered that much in the long run. The naïve idealists quickly became the most bloodthirsty killers.

He didn't let himself slip into a dangerous contempt that would make him underestimate the threat they posed, even given their unprofessional behavior in the bush. They thought they were secure, believed that they had no enemies close enough to worry about. He was sure that if they'd believed there was a threat nearby, they would have been much more watchful.

Flanagan had learned a long time ago never to underestimate how dangerous an undertrained but cunning enemy could be. They might not be good, but a spray of automatic weapons fire can still kill you just as dead if you get sloppy through contempt.

They waited, still and silent, until the Green Shirt patrol had passed and was out of sight and out of earshot. Only then did the pair of them get to their feet and continue on toward their objective.

The farm's position and the lack of commanding terrain around it meant they had to move right up to the treeline. The sun was already behind the mountains to the west, but between the dying light of early evening and the spotlights set up around the farmhouse, they could see well enough.

There were a *lot* more Green Shirts here. Flanagan counted easily twice the numbers that had been at the Fuentes farm in the first few minutes. And instead of lounging around in a central location, they were spread out across the farm.

Several of the Green Shirts were posted up on hastily-erected guard towers, overlooking the laborers who were planting coca plants in place of whatever crops had previously been grown here. Several of them were armed with PKMs or M60s. The rest carried the same polyglot mix of M16s, AKs, and Galils that he'd seen at Fuentes's place.

The farmhouse itself was similarly surrounded by technicals and guards. But something else drew his gaze after a moment.

A spike had been driven into a tree just in front of the farmhouse. A man hung from the spike by his shackled wrists, his head bowed to his chest, dressed in only shorts and a white t-shirt. At least, it had been a white t-shirt. It was drenched in blood. The man wasn't moving.

Bright lights shone from a hastily erected shelter off to one side of the farmhouse. More laborers worked in there, unloading chemicals from a truck parked just outside. The coca crop wasn't remotely ready for harvest yet, but it appeared that they were preparing the processing facility already. More armed Green Shirts watched the unloading, hands on their weapons.

The coca farms were going to be tougher nuts to crack. But Flanagan didn't think that they'd be the first targets. Or even actionable targets at all. If they could break the Green Shirts, this might go away in the aftermath.

But there was a lot of work to be done before that could happen.

He watched as one of the laborers—little more than a kid—dropped one of the bags of chemicals as he tried to carry it from the back of the truck. The bag looked like it weighed more than half what he did. But the nearest Green Shirt guard stepped in and hit the kid in the kidney with his rifle butt as he bent over the fallen sack. When he didn't get the reaction he wanted, he hit the kid again. The boy crumpled, and the Green Shirt started kicking him.

Flanagan was aimed in, gritting his teeth, his finger hovering near the trigger, but he forced himself to lower his weapon. Engaging now meant compromise, and they couldn't afford that. As much as he wanted to save the kid, he wouldn't do any of the enslaved citizens of San Tabal and its environs any good if he got them all killed.

He'd seen enough. Together, he and Cruz faded back into the jungle.

CHAPTER 10

Galvez didn't usually carry a cell phone with him. He had a radio if any of his Green Shirts—he already thought of them as *his* Green Shirts; they answered to him before Clemente, anyway—needed to contact him. But he had this particular phone for certain special purposes. He only powered it up once every few days.

This time, there was a text message waiting once the old phone finished booting up and found the weak cell signal in San Tabal. Several of the local cell companies had cut off their service to the area after the Green Shirts' revolution.

He'd find a way to make them pay for that. Once the revolution was established and impregnable.

The message was short and succinct. *There's a problem. Contact me ASAP.*

Galvez's English was better than he liked most people to believe. It seemed somehow to clash with his image as a *revolucionario* to speak the language of the hated *Estados Unidos*. He played up that image deliberately, even as he held those who thought it important in contempt. Power and the ultimate triumph of the revolution were his goals. The little ideological purity tests that most revolutionaries got wrapped up in only infuriated him.

There was only one phone number programmed into the little Nokia. It took a couple seconds before it was ringing.

"You need to take some extra security steps." The American didn't bother with pleasantries. He never had. Galvez didn't especially care, though he still bristled slightly at this gringo's arrogance. "I've received indicators that my instructions might not have been followed to the letter."

"How so?" Galvez kept his own voice flat, even as his mind raced. Had Clemente's suspicions been right? The arrangement had been that the American would send a small, deniable team that would play its part in the plan and ask no questions. The American's cousin would then receive a greater cut of the cocaine profits, while the American himself would be able to play up his reputation as being tough on terrorism, at least behind closed doors. Galvez and Ballesteros would still rule San Tabal with an iron fist, all the while pretending to be more reasonable than Clemente.

But if the Americans were digging…

"The team might have left early. They were given a strict timeline, but one of the coordinator's assets went south only a few days ago. It's possible that they're sniffing around instead of just doing what they're told." The annoyance in the American's voice was obvious. Killers were supposed to do what he told them to, not think for themselves.

"And how do I know that you didn't send them ahead, and are warning me only to put my mind at ease, to assure me that you have not decided to go back on our arrangement?" Galvez was thinking hard. If the gringo had double-crossed them, he might have to take drastic steps, more quickly than he'd anticipated. "How do I know that this call is not simply intended to make me think that your subordinates disobeyed you when we find evidence of American special forces moving on San Tabal?"

"Don't be ridiculous. We have an arrangement."

"Which might be inconvenient for you in the future. But I warn you, American, that the revolution is not easily betrayed. We will find these Americans, if they are here. And when we interrogate them, and find out that you sent them to undermine us, then we will make sure that you pay the price. That might only require a release of information. Or it might cost you much, much more." He hung up.

Frowning, he stared at the phone for a moment. He would have to proceed carefully. Clemente still had a certain hold over many of the Green Shirts, and he was already paranoid. Admitting that the Americans had, in fact, infiltrated their territory, after assuring the disgraced general that he was jumping at shadows, might easily backfire. At best, Clemente would accuse him—*him*—of incompetence. At worst, he would see a betrayal.

The fact that betrayal was, in fact, in motion only made his situation that much more dangerous.

He returned the phone to its hiding place and picked up his radio. "Avispa, this is Galvez. Come to my quarters." He didn't wait for an acknowledgement, but put the radio back on his desk and paced the room, tapping his fingers against the butt of the Jericho on his hip.

The small man known as Avispa, or "Wasp," knocked on his door a few minutes later. "You wanted to see me, *Compadre?*" The gimlet-eyed little man had been by Galvez's side through battles across Central and South America for the last decade. He'd killed more men—and women—than Galvez, though he held that lead by only a few.

"We might have some trouble coming." Galvez stopped his pacing and moved to the map he'd pinned up on the wall. "We'll have to step up our patrols in the hinterlands around the city."

Avispa's eyes narrowed. "We only have so many men, and we haven't gotten as many recruits from the slums as we'd hoped. Increasing the patrols will cut down on the forces we have available to maintain our hold on the city."

"I know." Galvez's eyes were hard as flint. "So, before we send them out, we will have to make some examples." He smiled, the expression as dead and predatory as a shark's. "Terror has a quantitative quality all its own."

***

"If they're holding hostages, we're going to have to move fast, once this starts." Brannigan frowned down at the map that Flanagan had marked up following their reconnaissance. The black-bearded man still had camouflage facepaint on, and looked exhausted. He and Cruz had just gotten back to Pacheco's farm less than an hour before. It was well past midnight.

"There's only so fast we'll be able to move without overextending ourselves." Wade stood at the other side of the table, his icy blue eyes fixed on the same markings. "I think that taking one farm at a time might be our best bet."

"The people in the city will suffer for it." Pacheco wasn't arguing from where he stood, his arms crossed. He was simply stating facts. "The Green Shirts will not let such a challenge go unanswered."

"I didn't figure they would, but we don't have a lot of options, at least not until we can recruit and equip more of a local force. Unless the National Army wants to step in, but if they're more worried about the Venezuelans intervening..." Brannigan glowered at the map as if the entire situation offended him. That was another problem. He was worried about the Colombians. They hadn't interfered with Clemente's seizure of the city, but that kind of indecision could only last so long. A shooting war in their own backyard might just stir some Colombian politicians to action, and then the Blackhearts could end up caught between the hammer and the anvil.

"Fuentes is one of the bigger farmers around here, right?" Burgess had been quiet so far, but there was one thing Brannigan had learned about the quiet man. He was always listening and thinking. That was in marked contrast to their other SEAL, Jenkins, but Burgess was older, and had been around the block. "If they're keeping such a small security element on his place and focusing more on the new coca farms, might there be some smaller farmers who've gone relatively untouched?"

"There should be." Cruz sounded as tired as he looked. Despite his background, like Pacheco, he was no spring chicken. "We didn't have time to check on any of them. They'll be afraid, though. Most of them have nowhere to flee if the Green Shirts come burn them out, and I'm sure the threat has been put out there. Clemente doesn't have the men to rule except through terror."

"We'd have to be careful, then, but I'd be willing to bet that we can find a few who might lend a hand." Brannigan was thinking in terms not only of manpower and firepower—the latter would necessarily be limited, at least at first. Pacheco had a surprising amount of weapons, ammunition, and gear squirreled away, but it wouldn't be enough to arm and equip more than a handful. They'd have to capture some from the Green Shirts. But more importantly, the local farmers would know the ground. "Even if we can recruit ones and twos, get them to drift away into the jungle where we can stage for a follow-on attack, it'll help."

"I still think that Fuentes's farm would be the best starting place." Flanagan had seen the place, but more importantly, he was a thinker, too. "If Fuentes is the pillar of the community that Cruz says he is, then freeing him and his family will give the locals a leader to rally around. Especially if most of the high-profile citizens in San Tabal itself have been executed or imprisoned. And I think that we can fortify his house and use it as a better—and closer—base of operations."

"There's one problem in all of this." Bianco sounded almost apologetic. "And that's our original mission. We've been approaching this as if we've got to liberate San Tabal all by ourselves, but what if we're really just one piece of the puzzle? I mean, we got a time and a place that the target's supposed to be, along with a description to make sure we whack the right guy." He looked around at the rest of the team. "Are we really that sure that we should be going off the reservation already? What if there really is another unit here, ready to move in as soon as Clemente gets taken off the board?"

Flanagan looked at Pacheco. "If there was another unit in the area, there should be some indicators. Have you seen any?"

The older man shook his head. "No. You're the first. And yes, I'd hear if anyone were sniffing around, unless they were very, very stealthy. Which isn't impossible, but it seems a little unlikely."

Brannigan's frown deepened, and he stroked his mustache. "Unfortunately, Vinnie's got a point. We don't *know* what's supposed to happen after we kill Clemente. There might be a follow-on plan. Or, this might be one of those Good Idea Fairy ops, where somebody picks the figurehead whose death is supposed to end everything magically, just assuming that the rest of the bad guys will just kind of fade away after their leader goes down." He grimaced. "We've only seen that a few dozen times before."

His eyes narrowed as he thought. "H-Hour is coming up fast." He checked his watch. "We've got just over a week before the hit's supposed to go down."

Wade looked thoughtful. He glanced at Pacheco. "How much have you found out about the Green Shirts' leadership, aside from Clemente? Does he have mid-level cronies, or is this a one-man, cult of personality sort of thing?"

"He's got at least two lieutenants." Pacheco didn't sound entirely certain. "At least, he's been seen with Diego Galvez and Julio Ballesteros. Ballesteros is a local rancher and sometime politician. The man doesn't have an honest bone in his body. Galvez is another matter. He's a foreigner—some say he's Panamanian, others Argentinian. He has a reputation, though. He's a killer. He's wanted from Mexico to Brazil."

"Regular murderer kind of killer, or 'revolutionary' kind of killer?" Brannigan suspected he knew, but he had to ask the question.

"The man's a terrorist and a professional revolutionary. He's been involved with FARC and ELN in the past. As far as anyone knows, he had actually assumed a fairly high-level leadership position in the FARC just before the peace deal." From the tone of Cruz's voice, Brannigan suspected that Galvez had been on the AFEAU's target deck more than once.

"Men like that don't usually get involved in cult of personality operations." Wade spoke with dead certainty. "Hell, he's probably waiting in the wings to take over if Clemente gets killed. He might even have a plan to do it himself."

Brannigan thought hard. Finally, he leaned on the table, making the entire thing creak with his weight. "Okay, as I see it, we've got two options. We can continue to run recon, develop the situation, and see if we can recruit a few of the locals so we can get a better grasp on the situation and get into a better position to take down the Green Shirts as a whole and secure the city. Or, we can go with the plan we were handed at the outset, set up as instructed, off Clemente, and fade, hoping that there is, in fact, a follow-on plan." He sighed. "I can get in touch with Carlo and see if he can get Van Zandt to discreetly inquire about any such follow-on. It might not work, but it's better than sitting here in the dark, assuming."

"There's a third option," Flanagan pointed out. "We prep for both. It shouldn't take all of us to spring an ambush on a motorcade, especially not if we can get some explosives." He glanced at Pacheco, who nodded. He had some, or else he knew how to get them.

"That might be our best bet." Brannigan looked around at the rest of the team. "All right. George, Vinnie, Herc, and I will prep for the ambush. In the meantime, the rest of you keep running recon and see if you can get a few of the smaller local farmers on board, with an eye on liberating the Fuentes farm as a central base for the resistance.

"In the meantime, I've got a call to make."

CHAPTER 11

The sun was just coming up when the Green Shirts stormed the little shop. The colorful sign plastered to the white stucco advertised "*Productos de Limpieza.*" Flowers bloomed in the blue-painted window boxes above the street.

Galvez climbed out of his truck and stood by the hood, his Jericho still in its holster, as his gunmen smashed the door in and rushed inside. The sounds of shouts, thumps, and breaking glass resounded from the interior of the store as the Green Shirts smashed things randomly on the way toward the stairs at the back, which would lead them up to the apartment above.

Screams had already begun to resound from the upper windows as boots clattered on the stairs. More rough shouts followed, and a female voice was raised in a wail, suddenly cut off. Galvez took a long pull on his cigarette as he glanced up at the darkened windows on the second story. He hoped that they hadn't killed anyone yet. This needed to be public.

It took several minutes for the Green Shirts to drag the storekeeper and his family out onto the street. The storekeeper stumbled between two of them, in his t-shirt and shorts, looking a little dazed. Two men dragged the wife between them, her head hanging, blood dripping from her face. She was alive, but a blow from a rifle butt had silenced her screaming, at least for the moment.

The children were crying, but they'd quieted a little after their mother had been struck down. They whimpered as they were hauled out onto the street, their arms held cruelly by Green Shirts who shoved them down into the gutter.

Galvez finished his cigarette in silence as his men forced the storekeeper to his knees in front of him. He studied the man disinterestedly for a while, taking some pleasure in the fear manifest in the storekeeper's wide, bloodshot eyes.

"Please, Señor..." A rifle butt to the kidneys silenced the storekeeper. Galvez just watched, taking a final drag off the cigarette before dropping it to the street and crushing it out with his boot. Then he looked up and around at the surrounding houses. The windows were dark and empty. He knew that they were being watched, but none of the locals wanted to risk showing their faces.

That would change.

He picked up the bullhorn. It was a quiet, misty morning, the sun turning the humid air gold as it topped the ridge to the east. Lifting the megaphone, he triggered it with a faint squeal of feedback.

"Everyone come out of your houses! Now!" He waited a moment, the hesitation on the street palpable. "If you do not, I will be forced to send my men to drag you out! Everyone will witness what happens here this morning! Anyone who resists will join this cringing running dog for the *Capitalistas*!"

For a moment, he was met with silence and stillness, as fear battled with fear. Finally, though, Jimenez's neighbors started to come out or come to their windows. Galvez swept the street with his eyes, deliberately making eye contact, as if to ensure that each man and woman knew that the right hand of the revolution had his eye on them, personally.

"Today, you will witness the price of treason!" He could easily have made himself heard with only his voice, but he chose to use the megaphone, blasting the street with his amplified voice. "This rat, this *worm*, has sold out the revolution! He has bowed and scraped to the imperialists and the exploiters! He has betrayed you as he has betrayed the Leader, General Clemente!" He looked

94

down at the weeping storeowner with undisguised contempt—contempt that he held toward the frightened faces in windows and doorways all around them, as well. "He has spied and reported to the Americans and their puppets in Bogota!"

"No!" The storekeeper looked up at Galvez through his tears. "No, Señor, I have done nothing! I have only tried to run my store and feed my children!"

Galvez spat in his face. "Run your store? Driving your neighbors to poverty, for what? And your filthy profits weren't enough for you, were they? You had to communicate with the Army." He bent low over the weeping man. "What did you tell them? Did you tell them how many of us are here? Where our supplies are kept? *What did you tell them?*"

He knew he would get no answer from the terrified shopkeeper. There was no answer to give. The man had sent no messages, had no contacts in Bogota that Galvez knew of. The store had been chosen completely at random. It had looked clean and well-kept-up enough to make it a likely target. The somewhat better off were always the best targets for this sort of thing.

Galvez needed an example. The storeowner and his family would provide as good a sacrificial victim as any. After what was about to happen on this street, any of the locals would be too afraid to take advantage of the lessened numbers as he pushed more of his Green Shirts out into the jungle to patrol the area.

Vladimir Lenin, one of his heroes, had said it best. "The purpose of terror is to terrorize."

"Please," The shopkeeper begged, sobbing. "We've done nothing…"

Galvez kicked him in the face. He collapsed onto his back, still weeping.

"Now watch what happens to traitors and capitalist exploiters!" Galvez motioned to the Green Shirts who held the wife.

The violence that followed was not quick. The storeowner's wife came out of her daze as the rifle butts broke her shins. Her screams echoed up and down the street as they systematically broke her bones, while her husband was held up by his hair and forced to watch. She fell silent again when her skull was cracked. The beating continued until no sign of life remained.

The shopkeeper's weeping hadn't stopped through the entire ordeal. Galvez remained unmoved. He'd killed any sentimental part of his soul—which he would have denied existed in the first place—a long time ago.

Still, while he had originally planned to kill the entire family, he'd eventually decided that the children would serve as a terrified reminder of what had happened here. The other families might have been able to put it out of their minds. But to leave the storeowner's children alive, they would have to look at them and take care of them, making the deaths constantly present.

"See what happens to all spies, traitors, and wreckers!" The Green Shirts hauled the already broken man to his feet, while a third man prepared a noose at the end of an electrical cable, throwing the running end over the lamppost on the corner. The shopkeeper wept, his eyes still fixed on his wife's corpse, as they dragged him under the lamppost and looped the noose around his neck.

There was no short drop and broken neck for the storeowner. He was hauled, hand-over-hand, into the air, kicking and strangling. The Green Shirts hadn't tied his hands, so he tried to haul himself up, scrabbling at the cable as it dug into his throat, but to no avail. He was not a particularly fit man, and even if he managed to pull himself up with sweaty hands on the slick cable, there was no way he would be able to do so indefinitely.

They stood there, Galvez sweeping the bystanders with burning eyes, as the storeowner slowly strangled to death. The pained, gurgling sounds of his struggle slowly faded, until finally he hung, limp and lifeless, slowly swinging and rotating under the streetlight.

The Green Shirts left him there, as they left his wife in the street, their children weeping in shock and horror at the murders, as Galvez climbed back into his truck and waved at the driver. There was work to be done.

***

Flanagan thought he was getting more familiar with the terrain. He knew it was an illusion—he and Cruz hadn't covered nearly enough of the ground around San Tabal for him to have truly learned it—but they were close enough to the Fuentes place that he thought he recognized a few landmarks, whenever they became visible through the mist and the trees. Which was not often.

He was following Cruz again, though this time Gomez was taking up the rear. Wade and Burgess had both offered to come along, but there were still other preparations to make, and Flanagan had wanted to keep their footprint small, especially as they were on their way to one of the smaller farms, owned by a man named Otero. If this worked, they'd be heading back with new recruits, and he didn't want to be trooping through the woods that close to San Tabal with a full squad or more.

He also realized he was perhaps being over-optimistic. They didn't even know if Otero had enough workers or sons to commit to the resistance. Or that he wasn't so over-cowed by the Green Shirts—or even sympathetic—that he'd refuse to step up.

Cruz halted, sinking to a knee just behind a fallen tree. Flanagan moved up to join him and Gomez settled in to watch their six a moment later.

"We are about two hundred meters away from the edge of Otero's fields." Cruz kept his voice low. They couldn't see more than a dozen yards in any direction, and that was only in certain places. "I think it would be best if we stay hidden until we can observe the situation before we move in and try to make contact."

"Agreed." Flanagan had been on more than a few partisan linkups during this new career as a mercenary, to include their recent meeting with Cruz. Caution was always called for.

With that settled, they waited a few more moments to listen and watch for the enemy before getting up and moving on.

Movement in the jungle always takes longer than anywhere else. The limited visibility mandates a greater degree of caution, and the thickness of the vegetation is an obstacle as well. Not only that, but there are innumerable dangerous animals that must be watched for as well as enemy fighters, and they could be above as well as in front, behind, or to either side. It takes longer to move when you're trying to scan seven hundred twenty degrees.

So, it took most of an hour and a half to cover that last two hundred meters to the Otero farm. Once again, they got low and stayed within the shadows of the treeline as they took in the farm and its surroundings.

Otero was clearly a lot poorer than Fuentes. His fields were smaller, and his house was a tiny block of plastered concrete with a corrugated metal roof. A single, skinny cow cropped grass next to a lean-to shelter that looked like it was about ready to fall over.

There was no one in sight.

Flanagan frowned. "Something's not right."

"What?" Cruz hadn't noticed. Maybe it was Flanagan just being paranoid.

"There's no one outside. No one in the fields. No movement at all." He watched the trees and the narrow road leading off down the hillside, disappearing around a turn and into the woods.

"It's the middle of the afternoon. This is usually siesta time. I'd be surprised if anyone was out working for another hour."

Flanagan frowned. He hadn't thought of that. They hadn't had a chance to slow down enough since they'd gotten in country. He'd forgotten about the generally different schedules in Latin America.

Cruz was probably right. But something had his hackles up. And Flanagan had learned long before to pay attention when he got the heebie-jeebies.

"Let's move carefully. Cruz, you're on point. Mario, stay here for the moment, until we get to the house and I signal that it's all clear." Flanagan wanted some overwatch set in before he crossed that open field to the house, which was out in the middle of the cleared ground, unlike Fuentes's house, which had been surrounded by shade trees.

Gomez faded into the brush, bracing his Galil against a tree and going completely still. Flanagan nodded to Cruz, who stepped out into the fields and started toward the farmhouse.

Flanagan let him get a few yards away before following. He took one step out of the trees and froze.

Six Green Shirts, talking and bitching in Spanish, one of them trying to shake leaves out of his collar, had just stepped out of the woods on the far side of the field.

Cruz was already halfway to the house—the fields weren't all that big, at least not on this side of the farm. He froze for a second, then tried to dash for the house.

Unfortunately, the sudden movement drew one of the Green Shirts' eye. He shouted, lifting his AK-47 and opening fire.

It wasn't a good shot. He wasn't even aiming, really. He'd just pointed and mashed the trigger, the rifle already on full auto. The Kalashnikov chattered, the muzzle climbing as the long burst forced it up and back, until the Green Shirt was drilling holes in the sky, spewing little more than flame and noise.

Flanagan had thrown himself flat in the dirt, getting down among the seedlings that had just started coming up out of the soil, yanking his own Galil to his shoulder and searching for the sights. A bullet *crack*ed overhead and one of the Green Shirts dropped. Gomez was doing work.

Cruz was still moving, rushing toward the house, but there was something a little wrong with his stride. Flanagan didn't have time to worry about it, but found one of the Green Shirts that was advancing across the field, firing from the hip. The kid—he looked like he was about seventeen—was getting his ass kicked by the recoil, but he was still holding the trigger down, even as the M16 bounced and jumped in his hands.

Flanagan resisted the urgency that clawed at him as bullets *snap*ped overhead and smacked plaster off the farmhouse.

He let his breath out as the Galil's sights settled, and he shot the kid twice in the chest.

Suppressive fire only works if it's close enough to force the enemy to keep his head down. Volume of fire can't always make up for poor marksmanship.

The Green Shirt stopped dead in his tracks, the twin hammer blows to his chest halting his forward progress even before it penetrated to his brain that he was dead. The M16 slid out of suddenly nerveless hands as he fell over onto his back, staring sightlessly at the sky.

Flanagan had already shifted targets as soon as he'd been sure that the shot was good. His next pair were a little high, the follow-up shot climbing to smash the second Green Shirt's collarbone, but that one was already choking on his own blood, as the first bullet had pulped a lung. Pink foam frothed out of his mouth and nose as he collapsed, his fall pushing the muzzle of his AK into the damp earth.

Gomez had already killed another one. The last two turned and ran back into the woods.

Flanagan was up and moving. He dashed forward a few steps before dropping to an almost perfect kneeling position, letting his breath out again before he got a single shot off. One of the Green Shirts had already disappeared into the jungle, but his shot took the second one high in the back. The man's back arched as he was jerked up on his toes by the impact, and he stumbled a little farther on before he collapsed against a tree, sliding down the rough bark and leaving blood and skin behind. It didn't matter much to him. He would be dead in the next few seconds.

Then Flanagan was running, passing the bodies, one of which was still twitching, and plunging into the woods after the sole survivor. They couldn't afford to let word of this fight get back to Clemente.

The jungle was thick, the density of the undergrowth made worse by how close some of the trees were. The Green Shirt was thrashing through the vegetation ahead of him, making enough noise to follow easily.

Flanagan didn't really like the jungle—he was far more at home in the high alpine woods back home. But he was good in the bush, whatever form that bush took. He knew better than to try to crash through the bushes—instead he sort of "swam" through the vegetation, ducking and weaving around the thickest branches, picking his footing as carefully as he could without slowing down too much.

He wasn't running, but he was catching up with the fleeing Green Shirt quickly.

In a moment, he caught a glimpse of the other man, just as the Green Shirt glanced over his shoulder, his eyes widening as he realized that he hadn't escaped after all. He tried to run faster, but only succeeded in tripping over a tree root and going sprawling. He rolled onto his back, scrambling to bring his shorty AR pistol around.

Flanagan was almost on top of him. He realized that a prisoner might be useful, but after a split second he knew he was just a little bit too far away. The Green Shirt got his hand on his AR's pistol grip and snatched it up, whipping the muzzle toward Flanagan's face as his finger tightened on the trigger, his teeth bared and a curse in Spanish on his lips.

Flanagan snapped his own rifle to his shoulder and double-tapped the Green Shirt from six feet away. He didn't even bother to use the sights. The first bullet was slightly low, punching into the man's solar plexus. The second one hit just above his sternum. The man grunted and jerked under the sharp blows as the bullets tore through his vitals, but he wasn't out of the fight yet. His finger yanked spasmodically at the trigger, even though he only had one hand on the weapon, and it wasn't *quite* pointed at his target yet. A burst of three rounds ripped past Flanagan's ear and almost tore the AR out of the Green Shirt's grip.

Flanagan had barely let the trigger reset from his second shot as he found the sights, put the front sight on the bridge of the Green Shirt's nose, and squeezed the trigger.

The single shot echoed through the jungle with a deafening finality as the Green Shirt's head bounced, blood spattering from the bullet hole and covering his suddenly fixed and staring eyes.

Flanagan lowered his rifle, his heart thumping and his breath rasping in his suddenly dry throat. He scanned the woods one last time before he turned back toward the farm. They'd have to move fast, now. There was no telling how far the sounds of the firefight had traveled.

There was one thing for certain, though. *Someone* would know that Clemente and his Green Shirts no longer held uncontested control of these hills.

CHAPTER 12

Flanagan came out of the trees to see Gomez crouched by the house and several of the farmer's family emerging into the open. He frowned as he took in the scene. Something was wrong.

Gomez didn't relax as Flanagan came closer, but Gomez wasn't the laid-back type, anyway. There was always a coiled-spring readiness about the man. He was a killer to his bones, and he carried himself accordingly.

Cruz was next to him. He was slumped against the farmhouse wall, his head bowed to his chest. He wasn't moving. Flanagan made sure Gomez was covering security, then bent to check on Cruz.

Their primary contact was dead. He'd taken a bullet to the leg, which was completely soaked in blood. He'd taken a hit that had clipped his femoral, and he'd bled out in the next couple of minutes.

Flanagan looked down at the body for a long moment. This was bad. Without Cruz, this whole op could easily fall apart.

A small, wiry man with a machete in his hand came around the corner from the front door. Flanagan hadn't seen a photo yet, but this had to be Otero. He stood up and stepped back, his hand still on his Galil, just in case. Cruz had been relatively certain of Otero's reaction, but Cruz was dead.

"Mario." Flanagan didn't trust his own meager Spanish in this situation. Gomez rose and turned toward Otero, who was staring at Cruz's body. Several children peeked around the corner, and Otero barked at them. They vanished.

Flanagan took over security while Gomez spoke to Otero. Flanagan couldn't quite follow the conversation—both men were talking too fast, and with contrasting accents. They might speak the same language generally, but there were distinct differences between the Spanish spoken in Colombia and that spoken in the American Southwest.

He scanned the woods, careful not to get too sucked into one particular sector. Otero's kids—skinny, dirty, and clearly as scared as they were curious—kept peeking around the corner, but this time their father was too absorbed in the conversation with Gomez to yell at them.

The jungle stayed quiet—as quiet as the jungle ever could be, anyway—but Flanagan was already starting to get antsy. They needed to move. Two guns would not be enough if the Green Shirts showed up in force to investigate the gunfire.

"Well, he won't join us without assurances that we've got more people with us." Gomez turned back to Flanagan without quite turning his back on Otero. "He's got a wife and kids, and he's way out here in the hinterlands. He's already worried as hell about retribution for this fight."

Flanagan eyed Otero and the machete in his hand. "He's not thinking about proving himself harmless to the Green Shirts, is he?"

Gomez shook his head. "I'm pretty sure he hates them as much as he's scared of them. But he's afraid that they're going to come looking for the assholes we just killed. And that they'll find Cruz's body, too."

"Well, we'll do what we can to protect him, then." Flanagan glanced at Otero, who was staring at the bodies with a blank, haunted look on his face. He didn't doubt that the little man was seeing visions of reprisals, in all their gory horror. "We'll need some help, but I think we can get the bodies hidden in the jungle in a few minutes." He looked down at Cruz's corpse with a frown. "And as much as I hate to say it, we're going to have to hide Cruz, too. We can't carry him back with us." They had too far to go to carry a body and hold security at the same time.

"Going to be interesting to see what Pacheco has to say about this." Gomez was already stripping Cruz's weapons and equipment.

"Yeah." They hadn't learned much about Pacheco, except that he was old-school Search Bloc. And what he'd had to do to survive that meant that he had to have a certain degree of moral flexibility.

With his rifle set aside and his gear off, any identifying papers collected and shoved into a cargo pocket, Gomez hefted the body under the arms and started to drag Cruz across the fields toward the woodline, careful to keep from leaving too many incriminating prints in the tilled earth.

Flanagan stayed where he was, scanning their surroundings, his rifle at the ready. They couldn't afford to drop security altogether while they hid the corpses. They'd have to switch off.

He glanced up. The vultures were already starting to circle overhead. They didn't have a lot of time.

***

It took nearly an hour to get Cruz and the dead Green Shirts hidden, well back into the jungle and covered in leaves against a massive fallen tree. There wasn't time to bury them, and it was conceivably possible that an animal might drag them out into the open to be found, but there was a lot of jungle, and there wasn't a lot of traffic in that area. Otero had assured them of that. He'd even helped them move the bodies, once Gomez had convinced him that they were trying to protect him and his family, and that they meant him and his no harm.

Finally, they faded into the jungle, heading back toward Pacheco's farm. The plan had to change. Provided that Cruz's death hadn't just destroyed it completely.

***

"Joe and Mario are coming back." Burgess frowned. He was on watch at the window, keeping an eye on the long dirt road that led to Pacheco's house. "Colonel? I think they've got bad news."

Brannigan joined him. "What makes you say that?"

He didn't need to hear what Burgess said next. He could see for himself. "Cruz isn't with them, and Joe's got a spare rifle slung on his back."

Brannigan turned and left the window, grabbing his own Galil from where it leaned against Pacheco's couch before he strode out the door, moving to meet Flanagan and Gomez. "What happened?"

"We took contact at Otero's farm." Flanagan's voice was even and matter of fact. The black-bearded man had always been known for his calm in stressful situations. "Six Green Shirts came out of the weeds just as we were about halfway to the house." He shrugged. "Cruz took a round to the leg and bled out before the fight was over. I couldn't have gotten to him in time, even if I'd known." He tilted his head toward Gomez. "Mario was on overwatch. He was even farther away."

"Where is the body?" Brannigan hadn't even noticed that Pacheco had come with him. The older man was *quiet*.

"We hid it in the jungle, with Otero's help." Flanagan sounded apologetic. "There wasn't time to bury him. I'm sorry."

"It's war." Pacheco didn't seem all that bothered. He took a deep breath. "He won't be the first or the last Colombian soldier to go unrecovered in these mountains. I know who to talk to so that his family is taken care of." His eyes narrowed as he shifted mental gears back to the fight. "We'll have to move quickly. Even if they never find the bodies, Clemente will know that he lost a patrol, sooner or later."

"Do you think he has a target list already worked up?" Brannigan wasn't happy about the prospect of rushing a guerrilla resistance. It was largely going to depend on just how much Clemente and his Green Shirts knew, and how quickly they reacted. Not to mention what form that reaction took.

"I don't doubt it. People like Clemente always do." Pacheco started back toward the house. "What about Otero?"

Brannigan, Gomez, and Flanagan followed him. Flanagan and Gomez looked exhausted—and no wonder; they'd covered a lot of miles through the jungle since that morning.

"He won't be the first one to join up. He needs to know that he's not going to be the nail that gets hammered down," Flanagan said grimly. "Can't say as I blame him."

"He might be that nail anyway, if Clemente and Galvez realize that their patrol disappeared near his farm. They don't necessarily need to find the bodies." Pacheco stepped through the door and into the living room, where most of the rest of the team was gathered, their weapons in their hands. "From what they've done already, they'll make an example out of Otero and his family if we don't give them something else to focus on."

"You've got an idea." Brannigan wasn't asking.

Pacheco nodded as he pulled a map out and spread it on the table. "We could hit one of the coca farms." He pointed. "One of these, maybe, on the far side of the city."

"That might buy us time, or it might get a whole lot of civilians killed in reprisals." Brannigan frowned down at the map. He wasn't seeing a lot of options. He sighed and ran a hand over his face. "We've got eight more days before the ambush was supposed to go down." He glanced up at Bianco. "I don't think the 'wait and see' plan is going to work anymore. We're going to have to push the 'liberation' plan."

"And if there *is* a backup force?" Bianco still sounded a little uncertain.

"We'll deal with that problem when we come to it." He grimaced. "No, I don't like it, either. But we're kind of stuck at this point. That fight and Cruz's death committed us." He looked down at the table and sighed. "Look, it's entirely possible that Bianco's worries are justified. We're used to 'give us the job and let us handle it.' We don't do well with the kind of limited, 'don't ask questions' info we got for this mission. In fact, if not for the implied blackmail, I would have turned this down flat." He looked up at Pacheco. "No offense." The other man just spread his hands and shrugged. Brannigan looked around at the rest. "It's *possible* that our paranoia led us into a mistake. I don't think that's the case, mind you. But we need to be ready to roll with the punches if we just threw a wrench into a carefully coordinated plan."

Wade just snorted to express his opinion of that possibility.

Brannigan looked up at Pacheco again. "I'm going to call back home and see if I can dig up any more information. But lacking that, I think that Fuentes needs to be our next step. And if we're going to try to liberate his farm and bring him in, I'm pretty sure we're going to need to move fast." He turned toward the packs at the back of the room. "Everybody get ready to move. I've got a call to make."

***

Santelli hung up the phone. It was a little odd, playing a support role back in the States, and even odder to be almost on the same time schedule. Decades of focus on the Eastern Hemisphere—and the Blackhearts had done more missions on the east side of the Atlantic than the west—had accustomed him to a significant time difference. He'd halfway been mentally expecting a lot of calls in the middle of the night.

Looking down at the phone, he took a deep breath. His teammates were in a bit of a crack, possibly of their own making, though he didn't think so. They needed more information. The situation, however, required some care.

He finally dialed and put the phone to his ear. Van Zandt would ordinarily be their first contact, but Van Zandt was probably as much in the dark as the rest of them. Santelli was sure that the retired general would be doing some digging of his own, but while Santelli didn't share the adversarial history that Brannigan had with Van Zandt, he didn't have a terrifically high opinion of the other man's ability to dig into the deeper, darker seams of the irregular world that the Blackhearts worked in.

The man he was calling? He might not know *everything*, but he came awfully close. Building connections for forty years tended to expand a man's understanding of the shape of the world. Both in the light, and in the shadows.

The phone rang for several minutes, then went to voicemail. Santelli hung up without saying anything. He trusted the other man, but this wasn't something he wanted committed to a recording.

He was considering the next call when the phone rang. Looking down, he recognized the number and answered it. "Master Guns Drake."

"Long time, Carlo." Santelli had never served with Ben Drake in the Marine Corps, like Brannigan had, but he'd certainly known of him. Drake had been a fixture, a modern "Grand Old Man of the Marine Corps," until his retirement after thirty years in uniform. But he'd had a bit of a hand in the Blackhearts—his recommendation had led to Javakhishvili's recruitment—and the partnership with Drake's "Old Fogies" network had been a close one ever since the Humanity Front's hired killers had gone after Childress. "What do you need?"

"Information, Master Guns." Santelli leaned back in his chair as he spoke. He was in his garage, so he wasn't too worried about Melissa coming in and overhearing anything. She didn't want to know details about the Blackhearts' work, anyway. "Information of a rather sensitive nature. I need to know if there are any ops happening down in Colombia, particularly near the Venezuelan border. Even deep, dark, non-official ops."

"Hmm. I take it you're circuitously talking about that little coup and declaration of an independent city-state in San Tabal?" Naturally, Drake had already figured most of it out. "I haven't heard about anything beyond the rumor that a small, deniable PMC might have been hired to intervene." It was unlikely, given their connections, that anyone was listening in, but both men tended to be cautious when it came to this sort of thing. "I can do some more digging, but if it's classified highly enough, I might not be able to find out."

"If you can't find anything, there's a mutual acquaintance that I don't have contact information for that you might ask. An older gent, name of Abernathy."

"I know him." Drake didn't sound surprised. "I'll see what I can find out. I take it this is somewhat time-sensitive?"

"It is." The phone vibrated in Santelli's hand and he took it from his ear to look at the screen with a frown. "Master Guns, I've got to go. Van Zandt's calling."

"I'll get back with you as soon as I've got anything, Carlo. Have a good one."

Santelli hit the button to answer Van Zandt's call. "Talk to me."

"This just got a lot more interesting." From the tone in Van Zandt's voice, it wasn't a good kind of *interesting*, either. "John hasn't contacted anyone but you, correct?"

"Not so far as I know. At least, no one but their contact on the ground." That was getting more complicated by the minute, too, but Santelli didn't consider that relevant to the conversation at hand. Not at the moment.

"I didn't think so. And yet, I got a phone call from the client not long ago, demanding to know why the team had already left and made a Green Shirt patrol disappear in the jungle."

Santelli's eyebrows climbed toward his receding hairline. "Your client's talking to someone else on the ground."

"Yep. And as far as I can tell, it's not our people. I can't find any comms with any special mission units or paramilitary spooks down there. Hell, I can't find any indication that we've *got* any special mission units or paramilitary operators in the vicinity, aside from the handful on liaison with the National Army in Bogota." Van Zandt wasn't known among the Blackhearts for his suspicious nature, but this was getting too blatant for even him to ignore.

"So, our client's talking to the bad guys." It wasn't a question.

"That's not entirely certain, but it sure sounds suspicious, doesn't it?" Van Zandt sighed, his breath rasping over the mic.

"I'm going to keep digging, but let John know that I'm pretty much ninety percent sure that the canned plan we got is a setup."

"I think he was already assuming that, sir." Santelli knew that *he* sure had been. Van Zandt signed off unceremoniously, and Santelli put the phone down on his workbench, thinking.

He ground a meaty fist into his palm. For all his worries about his family, for all the remembered heebie-jeebies he'd endured in Azerbaijan, he hated sitting back here while the rest of the team was in harm's way. Sure, Brannigan needed someone to coordinate, but couldn't Chavez do that? There was only so much he could do. He didn't have Drake's connections, never mind Abernathy's insider information. All he could do was contact those who did have such connections and information, and then wait.

All the same, as he glanced at the garage door, he knew that he wasn't getting any younger, and that while he worried about the other Blackhearts, he didn't have to worry about leaving Melissa and Carlo Jr. alone and wondering, anymore. That was a relief.

He just wished that he didn't hate himself for feeling that relief.

The phone rang again. He didn't recognize the number, but after a moment, he snatched it up and answered it. "Santelli."

"Santelli, this is Abernathy. I understand you've got an op going on down south?"

"Something like that." Santelli, like most of the Blackhearts, was still unsure just who Clayton Abernathy was, or what his interest was. That he had connections—and was most likely either in command of, or otherwise involved in, some kind of covert unit of his own—was undisputed. And he'd helped them several times already. "We need to know if there are any others working the same vicinity—and possibly the same mission set."

"No." Abernathy was usually a man of few words, and this was no exception. "You can take that to the bank. Your boys are the only ones working down there at the moment. That answer your questions?"

"It does." It didn't solve the problems, not really. But it answered many of the questions, as long as they weren't looking for specifics. "Thank you, sir."

"Don't thank me until your team is out of harm's way." Santelli had gathered that Abernathy was a hard old man, and his words this time didn't change that assessment. "I'll have some of my intel people do some digging. If they come up with anything that might help, I'll pass it along. But that's all I can do. My people are mostly committed at the moment."

"We'll take whatever you can give us, sir." Santelli meant that. He might not know what Abernathy's real angle was, but he'd demonstrated that he was a formidable ally.

"I'll be in touch." The enigmatic old man hung up. Santelli reached for the satellite phone. Brannigan needed to hear this, and quickly.

CHAPTER 13

Galvez scowled at the valley below as he thought, standing next to the ancient Jeep that had taken him up to the top of the ridge overlooking San Tabal. They still hadn't found the missing patrol, and he seriously doubted that they would. It had been almost a day before anyone had noticed they hadn't returned. Clemente had flown into a fury, and it had been all that he and Ballesteros could do to avoid being shot.

It was clear that Clemente suspected something. His paranoia was getting worse by the day. Galvez was seriously considering scrapping the plan and simply killing the man himself. But that would signal weakness, not only to the Colombians, but to the Venezuelans, who might not support them anymore. The Cartel de los Soles had other sources of drugs, and despite their connections with the *Chavistas* and the Venezuelan socialists in general, they were hardly ideologically pure. They wouldn't care about the potential for revolution if they couldn't make a profit off the flood of cocaine that Clemente had promised.

And if their American ally didn't get some minor victory to point to, then they could count on that support evaporating, as well. Never mind the drug money in the background.

He was going to have to decide. And while Ballesteros was a part of the conspiracy, Galvez was not interested in the fat rancher's input. He would decide this himself.

Finding the patrol was next to impossible, so finding who had killed them was also next to impossible. They'd been somewhere to the west of the city—that was about the extent of their information. They hadn't reported in for almost twelve hours before anyone had noticed anything amiss. It had been assumed that they were having fun at the local farmers' expense—and that had not been an unreasonable assumption.

Galvez had encouraged that, himself. It was necessary, so that the farmers understood who was now in charge. He wasn't so much regretting it, now, as he was furious at the patrol that had gone astray and disappeared.

It was possible that they'd defected. He doubted it, though. So far, most of the farmers they'd "interviewed" on the west side had been remarkably stupid when asked if they'd seen the missing Green Shirts.

If the American is betraying us, then his operatives will need local support. So, who could be giving that support?

"Give me your map." He held out a hand to the Green Shirt subcommander standing next to him. The man gaped at him stupidly for a moment, and then fumbled at his shirt pockets before his hands fell to his sides and he looked around, as if searching for someone else to blame for the fact that he didn't have a map.

Galvez fumed, and his hand twitched toward the Jericho in his waistband. The subcommander saw it, and blanched.

Galvez forced himself to reconsider. The man probably couldn't have read the map in the first place. So he turned away, furious, and scanned the valley below once again, trying to remember more of the surrounding area. *Who might be providing them support? Not the government—we would have heard already. So, it must be someone local. Who could it be?*

His scowl deepened. He couldn't remember enough detail. He needed to get back to San Tabal—and do it without Clemente suspecting what was happening.

It raised, once again, the question of what to do. It was apparent that the Americans were probably already on the ground, and that that part of the plan was going awry. Their ally's phone call had warned them of it, but now the threat was far more immediate. Did he dare try to go forward with the original plan?

Maybe he could. An idea started to form. But he needed to buy time. He turned to the subcommander. "I want as many of our men as possible to move into the hills. A full sweep to the west. Find that patrol, or else find what happened to them, and punish whoever did it." Without waiting for a reply, he turned and headed back toward his Jeep. "I will send more detailed instructions later."

Perhaps if he removed some of their support, he could slow the Americans down until he could put Clemente in their sights.

***

Javakhishvili had finished prepping his gear—including the unfortunately limited medical gear that Pacheco had been able to provide—and had taken his turn on watch to allow Bianco to go down and get his own gear ready. He sighed as he scanned the jungle around them.

While he understood some of the reasoning, Javakhishvili wasn't as stirred up about this plan as Brannigan and some of the others were. As far as he was concerned, if killing Clemente hadn't done the job, they could have followed up to knock off whoever replaced him afterward.

Javakhishvili had to allow that he never had considered himself any kind of strategic genius. He was a simple man, and he liked simple solutions. If they could break the Green Shirts by killing their leadership one at a time, he was fine with that. He wasn't sure if all this skullduggery and wondering about their client was justified. Maybe it really was a simple matter of trying for a solution on the cheap, and that was it. They could always follow up and charge more later.

Brannigan didn't seem to think so, and that was his call. Javakhishvili wasn't going to get too worked up about it. He was there to kill bad guys and get paid. He had no pretentions of leadership, and if Brannigan ever called it quits, he'd probably go find another PMC to take up with. They wouldn't get the kind of missions that the Blackhearts did—and wouldn't pay nearly as well—but the work was the work.

Movement caught his eye and ended his woolgathering. He was up on the hillside above Pacheco's farm, with a pretty good view across the fields, clear out to the road. The slope of the hill thinned the jungle growth enough that he could see through the trees easily without sacrificing concealment.

Two pickup trucks had stopped on the road, a few hundred yards short of Pacheco's driveway. They were still a couple of miles from the house, but they wouldn't stop there for nothing. There was nothing else nearby.

At least, he didn't think so. He might be a simple man at heart, but he'd survived far too many wars to take anything for granted. He didn't believe in coincidences.

Bracing his binoculars against a tree, he studied the trucks. Sure enough, they were Green Shirt vehicles—two each in the cabs, and three to four riding in back of each. They were all armed, too.

As he watched, they split into three groups and spread out, moving into the trees to either side of the fields. They were moving roughly toward Pacheco's farm, too.

It didn't take a genius to see what was happening. Either they were made, or they were about to be. He scooped up the radio and keyed it. "Kodiak, Shady Slav. We're about to have company."

***

Pacheco might have had a history, and training, but his farm was still a farm rather than a fortress. Given Colombia's laws, and the closeness of the FARC—peace deal or no peace deal—visible defenses might have drawn too much scrutiny. Remaining covert was the best way to survive in South America— or anywhere else, really.

So, there were no fighting holes, no bunkers, and very little cover to be had. But the Blackhearts spread out and got ready to ambush the Green Shirts as best they could.

Flanagan was puffing a little, sweat already staining his tiger stripes dark as he struggled up the steep hill behind the house. He was carrying his Galil in his hands, but he also had Pacheco's IWI Galatz, the 7.62 NATO sniper variant of the Galil slung across his back. It made for more weight as he made his way through the vegetation, but if he was going to hold overwatch for the rest of the team, he needed the range.

He got up on a narrow shelf, lined with slender trees clinging to the shallow soil between the rocks, and took a knee. "Herc! It's Joe. I'm coming in on your right." He didn't like just hissing at the other man, but they only had a couple of radios. Flying in through Customs with military radios for each man would have raised some eyebrows.

He really had to wonder what the client had hoped to accomplish with this mission. Deniability was one thing. Refusing to equip your deniable hitters—with the subsequent risk of mission failure because of it—was something else.

"Bring it in."

Flanagan rose and slipped through the trees. Javakhishvili was still watching the scene unfolding below through his binoculars, though he turned to look as Flanagan approached, then twisted to check the hillside above him. It had been a risk, setting out a one-man outpost, but the Blackhearts were all experienced enough and savvy enough to be careful of their own security.

Flanagan had always just thought of it in terms of the old mountain men. They'd rarely had a partner to watch their backs. They'd had to keep their eyes and ears open all the time.

He moved in behind Javakhishvili, leaning his Galil carefully against the rocky slope before unslinging the Galatz, flipping out the bipods, and looking for a good window to set up.

Unfortunately, the shelf was too narrow for him to stretch out and get all the way behind the weapon. So, he had to kind of angle himself, adjusting his position behind the weapon to keep it steady without muscling it.

It seemed like a lot of effort for a semi-auto sniper rifle, but it was what they had, and the less his position affected the flight of the round, the better.

The window he found through the foliage was relatively narrow, but with some work and creative readjustment, he found positions that would give him overlapping fields of fire to cover the entire farm. "Any newcomers?"

"Not yet." Javakhishvili had his eyes back to the binoculars. "I counted eleven, total. Looks like they're just scouting so far. No sign that they know we're here."

"They've got to be this far out for a reason." Flanagan tracked his scope carefully across the woodline, looking for targets. He'd have to rely on Javakhishvili to spot for him—the scope's field of view was too narrow. "We're a good way outside their sphere of influence."

"Got to be because of that patrol you and Mario disappeared." Javakhishvili took another break to sweep their surroundings. The ridge above them was steep enough that it wasn't *likely* than an enemy would come at them from that direction, but it wasn't *impossible*, either. "You put the fear of God into them, and now they're trying to find whoever killed their buddies." He frowned and got thoughtful. "You think they know about Pacheco?"

"Who knows? I don't have a crystal ball that lets me sit in on their planning sessions." Flanagan stopped, peering through the scope, then lifted his head and scanned above it. "Check about…five fingers over to the right from the house, just past that really tall tree."

Javakhishvili shifted the binoculars. "I got nothing."

Flanagan had lowered his cheek to the Galatz's buttstock again, and was once again searching the vegetation. "I saw movement, almost like somebody had just stuck their head out to take a look at the farmhouse. It's gone now."

"I saw one of the bigger fire teams go in there earlier, so there's probably someone there." Javakhishvili grunted. "They're hunting, all right. If they were just patrolling, they would have come up the drive already."

"They've got to know something about Pacheco, then. They wouldn't be so cautious otherwise. Not thugs like these."

"Maybe. Maybe they're just nervous. How many of them did you and Mario kill, anyway?"

"Six." That wasn't a brag. Flanagan knew how many men he'd killed—well, those he could confirm that he had, anyway. Some would have seen that as slightly psycho, but again, Flanagan didn't keep track for bragging rights. He felt he had a responsibility to know what he had done. The weight of the dead never quite left him. That was deliberate. It was too easy to make it into a game, otherwise.

Flanagan knew himself. He knew that siren song of combat and killing. It was a song that he'd answered many times, but he also knew that if he lost himself in it, he'd never quite find his soul ever again.

"Six of their *compadres* disappearing into the jungle without a trace will tend to make even the nastiest of these bastards nervous." Javakhishvili paused, and something about that sudden silence made Flanagan lift his head.

"Here we go." Several of the Green Shirts had emerged onto the dirt road leading to Pacheco's front door. They were openly armed, and while they were looking around carefully, there was still that thuggish swagger to their movements.

"They don't know we're here." Flanagan shifted his position behind the gun to get his sights on the two in the lead. "They wouldn't come traipsing right up to the front door like that if they did."

"Or maybe they're just that stupid." Javakhishvili shifted his Galil to make sure it was within easy reach. "Maybe they think that the guys you scragged weren't as good as they are."

"Maybe." Flanagan followed the lead Green Shirt with his crosshairs. It was a head-on shot, though the increasing angle between his elevated position and the target meant he was going to have to aim a little low. The wind was negligible, even at the eight hundred yards between him and the target. "If they don't know about us, though, Pacheco might be able to play this cool."

The six Green Shirts spread out as they approached Pacheco's lawn. Most of them held their weapons loosely but somewhat ready, though the one in the lead had thrown his over his shoulder. He probably thought it made him look tough and cool, but it would take him an extra couple of precious seconds to get it down and into action.

He looked up at the house and called out in Spanish. Flanagan couldn't make out the words, especially at that distance, but the tone was arrogant, almost mocking. They were outside of their seized territory, they knew it, and they knew that nobody was going to cross them anyway.

Something made Flanagan shift his aim back to the treeline along the edge of the southern field, where he'd seen movement before. Sure enough, he spotted a Green Shirt aiming in at the house. The slightly pudgy man was screened from the house by a bush, but Flanagan had a clear shot from up on the hillside.

That explained the apparent confidence. They were nervous, all right, but they thought they were being clever, keeping a team back on overwatch. It said something about their training level. Like Javakhishvili had noted, these were thugs, not soldiers. They considered the most basic tactical measures a masterclass level advantage.

They were about to learn the hard way, unless Pacheco talked fast.

Apparently, the group out front didn't get a response, at least not the response they were looking for. The man with his rifle on his shoulder yelled again, his voice even more strident. He was met with further silence.

Flanagan carefully scanned the woods around the first Green Shirt he'd spotted. Where there was one, there would be more.

There. That one was even less concealed than the first, his rifle in the fork in a tree, but he was a little bit farther back in the shadows, which was why Flanagan hadn't seen him right off. That, and the limited field of view he had through the twelve-power scope.

From there, it got easier to spot the other five. "How many did you say there were?" He kept his voice down, even though it was next to impossible for the bad guys to be able to hear them from down there.

"I counted eleven."

"So, unless they got some reinforcements that we didn't see, they regrouped to come in on the farmhouse." Flanagan moved his sights back to the first man he'd spotted. "Which means they've got radios."

"Yeah. So, we got to get them all real quick, don't we?" Javakhishvili was ordinarily fairly blasé when it came to the killing part of the job, and this time was no exception.

"Yes, we do. *If* it comes to that. More killing at this point is probably just going to show our hand."

"That's why you and John do all the thinking and planning." Javakhishvili put his binoculars down and picked up his rifle. "I'm just here to do the grunt work. Seems to me that killing them all quick, before they can send a message, will just take eleven more obstacles out of the way."

"I'd rather we do that on our terms." But the words had hardly left Flanagan's mouth when the decision was taken out of their hands.

The Green Shirts who had moved up to Pacheco's porch were apparently unsatisfied with whatever Pacheco or his wife had told them. The man in the lead brought his rifle down off his shoulder and stepped up on the porch, clearly intending to shove his way inside.

He got Mozambiqued from point blank range, the three shots coming so fast that they almost blended together into a single, rolling, thunderous report. He crashed onto his back halfway off the porch, dark red spreading across his chest and the contents of his skull spilling out onto the ground.

A split second later, a rattling volley of gunfire ripped out from the front of the house, smashing the other five off their feet in a welter of blood and flying metal.

As soon as the first shots were fired, Flanagan let out his breath and tightened his finger on the trigger. The Galatz's trigger wasn't as crisp as he might have wanted on a long-range rifle, but it still broke cleanly, and his round took the Green Shirt in the woods high in the chest. The man staggered, looking down at the bloody hole in his torso before he slumped.

Flanagan had called the shot as soon as it had broken, and just barely registered the hit before he was shifting to the next one. That man was staring at the falling body in shock, his head turned away from his rifle.

The shot broke slightly low, and the angle of the man's body and the nearby trees made it a difficult shot as it was. The bullet clipped the tree trunk and ricocheted, but the man was right up against the trunk, so it went into his side, though Flanagan could already tell that it had been deflected enough to keep the hit from being lethal.

The follow-up shot came as soon as the trigger reset, as he held the reticle just slightly higher, and put the next round through the man's left lung and into his heart. The Green Shirt fell out of sight.

Flanagan was transitioning to the third man when Javakhishvili opened fire.

They were a good eight hundred yards away, much too far for the Galil to be reliably, lethally accurate. But Javakhishvili was a good shot, and he wasn't relying on single shots like Flanagan was. He braced the rifle against the log that was his cover, making sure to breathe between shots, and started dropping steady, constant fire on the Green Shirts' position.

Flanagan worried for a second that the Green Shirts would drop to the ground and he'd lose them, but one of them broke cover instead and tried to run, thrashing through the brush. Flanagan's shot was slightly too high as he tried to lead the fleeing killer, but it smashed into the back of his skull and he went head-over-heels into the dirt.

The fourth Green Shirt promptly freaked out and started shooting. He was probably trying to aim for the house, but his fire was going wild, some of the bullets hitting the dirt not far in front of him.

Flanagan moved in on the muzzle blast where he could see it violently shaking and shredding the vegetation in front of the Green Shirt's muzzle, judged roughly where he probably was, and aimed slightly low. The first shot silenced the gunfire and made the man jerk hard enough that Flanagan knew exactly where he was. The second shot finished it. There was no more movement.

He was searching for the last one, but Javakhishvili had stopped shooting. The echoes of gunfire faded away across the valley, and Flanagan spotted the fifth man, sprawled on his face, halfway into the field.

"I'll be damned. Didn't think I'd manage to do anything but suppress him." Javakhishvili sounded surprised and proud all at the same time.

"Let's move." Flanagan got up and slung the Galatz. "We're going to have to hit them hard and fast, now, before word about this gets too far."

CHAPTER 14

The clouds had rolled in, and the jungle was pitch black under the trees. Even the PVS-14s couldn't do much to mitigate the darkness.

Fortunately, Mario Gomez was used to working in the dark. What was more, he was used to hunting men in the dark.

He'd known that Brannigan had wondered about the recent troubles down on the border. The truth was, there were always troubles where the Gomez ranch was situated. Perhaps not to the extent they'd faced when the Espino-Gallo Cartel had invaded and taken the ranch, murdering most of the family in the process. But the Gomez boys had always needed to be somewhat proactive when dealing with the cartels and the coyotes trying to use their land as an illegal superhighway.

Mario had grown up stalking other human beings as much as the four-legged coyotes and wolves who preyed on the livestock. There were more bodies out in that desert than even Brannigan guessed. And much of that had been before he'd ever had access to NVGs, and on moonless nights when the *narcos* thought no one could find them. He'd learned a lot from Marine Recon, but much of it had simply sharpened skills he'd already possessed.

Gomez didn't need a lot of light to do this kind of work. He'd honed his other senses to make up for the lack of vision—and his night eyes were remarkably good, anyway.

Movement was still achingly slow. It had to be, even if he'd been able to see more clearly. The vegetation was thick, and that meant there were a lot of roots and fallen branches on the forest floor, not to mention vines, snakes, spiders, and all the other hazards of the jungle. The need for stealth made patience an absolute must. And that stealth wasn't just to prevent the Green Shirt sentry ahead from hearing him. He also needed to be able to hear the Green Shirt.

The man who was about to die wasn't staying still or particularly alert. Even though he could just make out the Green Shirt's silhouette in his NVGs, Gomez could tell from the amount of noise he was making as he fidgeted, muttered to himself, cursed, and finally lit a cigarette. A whiff of the smoke told Gomez that it wasn't tobacco, either. So much the better. While smoking destroys night vision—and is therefore a bad idea when on security, even aside from the fact that the ember blazes like the sun in night vision goggles—at least tobacco makes a man somewhat more alert. Marijuana was not recommended for sentry duty at night.

Gomez just hoped he could avoid a contact high while he dealt with this one. He wasn't too worried about it—they were outside, and he was barely five yards away from his target. This would be over very quickly.

He wasn't crawling—that would have been *too* slow, and up close it made too much noise. Instead, while he was low to the ground, he was in a predatory crouch, his Galil slung across his back and cinched down tightly, a long knife in his hand.

This wouldn't have been something that he'd ever have done in the Marine Corps. While there wasn't a Recon Marine alive who didn't wax rhapsodic about the dream of getting that knife kill, for the most part, the Marine Corps still believed in standoff whenever possible. Going to a knife meant your rifle was down, all your team's rifles were down, and either nobody had a pistol, or all of those had gone down, too.

But Mario Gomez's combat experience had spanned a great deal more than just his time in the Marine Corps.

He placed each foot with exaggerated care, feeling his way with his toes before putting his weight down. He was also careful to keep at least one tree between him and his quarry as he moved closer. The jungle was thick enough that he could move from tree to tree with relative ease, and with that glowing ember of burning marijuana right in front of the man's face, it wasn't as if he was going to be able to see more than three feet in front of him in the dark, if that.

The sentry looked back at the lights of the house, further damaging what night adaptation he might have left, and cursed. From some of the noise up that way—pounding music and harsh laughter—Gomez could imagine why he was upset. The Green Shirts were having some fun.

Gomez's jaw clenched. If they were having the sort of fun he thought, they were about to pay dearly for it.

Then he was at the last tree. His target was just over an arm's length away, and still had no idea he was there. Gomez had circled around until he was behind the sentry, freezing whenever the Green Shirt had turned toward him, especially as he'd gotten closer. Now, as the frustrated young man turned back toward the jungle while taking another deep drag on his joint, Gomez moved.

The slow, deliberate movement he'd maintained for the last two hours was no more. He moved like a striking snake, knocking the Green Shirt's rifle out of his slack hand with his own free hand before he grabbed him, almost burning his hand on the joint as he clapped a palm over the suddenly frightened and confused thug's mouth and nose.

A second later, he brought the knife down, stabbing deep into the hollow between the Green Shirt's neck and his clavicle. Hot blood gushed out onto his hand, and he twisted the knife, doing as much damage as possible as he held the sentry tightly, squeezing his nose and mouth shut with an iron grip.

The Green Shirt tried to struggle, but he was already dead. It took just over three seconds for him to bleed out from the cut subclavian artery, and he went limp in Gomez's grip.

Easing the body to the forest floor, he turned toward the house, unslinging his rifle and bringing it around to the ready.

The music still thumped in the house, and hoarse, harsh voices were still raised, but not with alarm. He hadn't heard a gunshot yet. Which meant that they hadn't been made yet.

He would have been willing to bet that he had more knife kills than any of the other Blackhearts, but they were all deadly, and with only a couple of exceptions, he didn't doubt that they could sneak up on a bunch of distracted, stoned thugs.

Moving through the brush like a panther, his rifle up and ready, he crept toward the fields.

***

Vincent Bianco wasn't a stealthy man. He knew that all too well. Oh, he could move through the brush smoothly—compared to many of the grunts he'd served with back in the day, he was a ghost in the woods. But compared to the likes of Flanagan, Gomez, or the man that Childress had been, he was a blundering ox, and he knew it.

He'd never wanted to be that guy who snuck up on sentries and knifed them. If he was being honest—though he'd never admit this around the rest of the team—the idea of ending a man's life so up close and personal made him a little ill. He'd much rather have that standoff, and the IWI Negev in his hands as he crept forward to the edge of Fuentes's upper field, where he had a good view and field of fire down toward the house and the road below, was emblematic of the way he preferred to do his killing.

The light machinegun didn't have an optic, but Bianco had come up before optics on machineguns had been common, so that didn't bother him. There were enough tracers in the belts he'd brought that he would be able to direct his fire easily enough once things started off.

He scanned the farm below him carefully before checking his left and right. The Blackhearts didn't have IR strobes for this, but Pacheco had had a few IR chemlights, so those had been cracked and tucked into shoulder or cargo pockets. He spotted the small IR light creeping out of the trees off to the right. That would be Curtis, with the other Negev. The base of fire was in place.

He settled in behind the Negev and waited for Brannigan to open the ball.

***

Brannigan and Pacheco came up from the south, with Wade, Javakhishvili, and Hank in tow. The rest were either finishing off the outer security up ahead or getting into position up above.

They moved to the edge of the fields and spotted a small IR light ahead, shielded by the trees from the house. They hadn't seen any evidence that the Green Shirts had night vision, but it never paid to get overconfident and sloppy.

Flanagan was down on a knee behind the tree, his Galil leveled at the two Green Shirts on the porch. Additional tiny gleams of IR light to the right and left pointed out Burgess and Gomez. They'd moved in toward the central assault lane after eliminating their sentries.

Brannigan would have preferred to take all of the outer security down before moving in, but that wasn't practical with the numbers they had, never mind the timing. Opening a hole that they could drive through to get to the house—where most of the Green Shirts were apparently sleeping—was the best they could do.

Brannigan got down next to Flanagan, sighting in on the man leaning against the M60 machinegun mounted in the back of one of the pickups stationed around the house. The others found their own firing positions, mostly kneeling. They'd have to move fast once the first shot was fired.

He let out his breath, flipping the selector lever to "R" as he slipped his finger inside the trigger guard.

The shot echoed across the valley, the shock of it almost seeming louder than the actual sound of the report and the *crack* of the bullet. The bullet hit the gunner in the shoulder or side of the chest, spinning him halfway around as it knocked him away from the machinegun—which he hadn't been holding onto.

Under other circumstances, the stoned and/or drunk Green Shirts might have stared in shock at the man groaning in the bed of the truck, or else immediately started blazing away at the jungle in reaction. But they didn't have the chance.

Both Negevs opened fire from uphill, glowing red tracers reaching out toward the technicals. The first rounds missed, one gun's going over, the other landing short. But the tracers quickly corrected, walking into the armed pickups and hammering holes through sheet metal, glass, fiberglass, and human flesh.

The assault element was already up and moving as the machinegun fire tore the dazed gunners to shreds. Bianco lifted his fire as they moved up toward the porch. They pushed past the bullet-riddled pickup trucks, the shattered glass and holed bodies splashed with blood, weapons up and searching for targets.

The two Green Shirts on the porch were staring at the carnage, and probably didn't even see the dark figures coming out of the shadows beyond the trucks before they died. Each one got at least six rounds as the wedge of Blackhearts closed in and hammered them off their feet before they could even make a move for the weapons they'd left just out of reach.

None of the Blackhearts bothered to kick the weapons away from twitching fingers. Both men had taken at least two rounds each to the skull from about ten yards away. Blood and brains dripped slowly down the plastered wall as Wade moved up and, almost without pausing, kicked in the door.

He went left, riding the door, as Flanagan went right. Brannigan had been a half a step behind his second, so he followed Wade.

They spread out into the living room, which was still lit by several propane lanterns. Half a dozen Green Shirts were trying to scramble for weapons, but they were far too slow and far too late. They had clearly already gotten deep into the liquor bottles and marijuana, judging by the sickly-sweet smoke that filled the room.

Six Galils thundered and spat flame in the confines of the house, bullets tearing through flesh and bone and spattering blood and less wholesome debris across the furniture and the detritus of their partying.

It was all over very quickly.

Without a word, the Blackhearts spread out, clearing the dead spaces and checking the bodies, while Brannigan and Wade moved to the next door to continue clearing the house. It wasn't really over until they'd accounted for every Green Shirt and found Fuentes and his family.

***

The house was large for a Colombian farmhouse out in the sticks, but it wasn't so large that it took a long time to clear. After only a few minutes, they were back in the living room with Fuentes, his family huddled in the kitchen. The only Green Shirts in the house had been drinking and smoking in the living room, and they were all now rapidly assuming room temperature.

Fuentes was white as a sheet. "What have you done?" He wrung his hands as he stared at the corpses. "Do you have any idea what they will do now? How many people they will kill in retaliation? They've shot and hanged people just to send a message! They hanged Raul Jimenez as a spy, for nothing! Now..."

"That alone should tell you that you can't stay on the sidelines anymore, Fuentes." Pacheco's voice was cold. He stood next to the door, his Galil cradled in his hands, leaning against the wall. "The longer you bow to these people, the more they will take, and torture, and kill. There is no end to it. There is no 'enough' for them. Just like the FARC."

"There's a peace deal with the FARC!" Fuentes's eyes were wide, and there was a note of desperation in his voice.

"And what has that deal accomplished? Has the violence stopped?" Pacheco stabbed a finger in the direction of San Tabal.

"No, it hasn't. In fact, I'd be willing to bet that a lot of those bastards squatting in San Tabal were FARC before."

"What do you want from me?" It was almost a scream.

Pacheco stared at him grimly. "You are an important man among the farmers around San Tabal, Señor Fuentes. If you stand up, others will follow."

"I'm a farmer. Only a farmer."

"You were in the Army once. I seem to remember your name being connected with that fight outside of Ocaña." Pacheco was relentless.

"That was a long time ago," Fuentes protested. "I only want to feed my family, give them a better life. I haven't even shot a gun in years."

Pacheco waved to indicate the Blackhearts. "That's why they're here. They know how to fight. They can lead the fight. But the others won't fight without someone like you to rally around."

"Diego."

Fuentes turned to look at his wife, who had stepped out of the kitchen, facing him with her face composed and calm, though she pointedly didn't look at the corpses sprawled in her living room. She was a small, slightly plump woman, her hair still dark.

Neither of them said anything. Fuentes was older than his wife, but not by that much. The crow's feet around his wife's eyes belied her age. The two of them had clearly been married long enough that they didn't need to speak to communicate. She held his gaze, her expression frightened and yet defiant, her face pale yet her back straight and her head held high. And after a moment, he cast his eyes down at the floor, then turned back to Pacheco.

"What is the plan?"

***

The roads were narrow and treacherous, as they twisted back and forth through the mountains. The clouds lowered over the peaks, and a faint drizzle had started to make it even harder to see, even with the headlights on.

Galvez fumed in the passenger seat of the lead Nissan Frontier. This was taking too long. It had already taken him far too

132

long to realize that a former Search Bloc operator lived entirely too close to San Tabal for comfort. Then gathering up enough Green Shirts who hadn't already drunk or smoked themselves into uselessness as the evening got older had taken even more time. Now it was past midnight, and they still had over ten miles to go to get to Pacheco's farm.

He didn't *know* that Alejandro Pacheco had been behind the loss of his patrol. Finding out that the man had been in the Search Bloc had meant calling in favors with certain people in Bogota. It wasn't something that was widely advertised or recorded. Families were always targets in Colombia, going back to the days of *La Violencia.*

The convoy struggled up toward the bend around the next finger. Only when they rounded the tight, hairpin turn and started up the other side of the ridge did Galvez's radio start squawking.

"…alvez, come in!"

He lifted the radio to his lips. "This is Commander Galvez."

The incoming transmission was scratchy and broken. "Some…attacked the Fuentes farm. Only a… survivors. They have control of…farm now."

He cursed. "Stop the vehicles!" He searched the dark ahead of the headlights as the driver stomped on the brake, bringing them to a halt with a lurch, but the slope of the ridge was sheer to either side. He punched the dashboard. "Keep going. Find us a place to turn around." They were several miles past the Fuentes farm. It would take well over an hour to reach it, and something told him that they did not have that much time. If Pacheco—or whoever was moving against the Green Shirt revolution—had struck that quickly, they would be moving while he tried to get turned around.

He was behind, he knew it, and someone was going to pay in blood.

CHAPTER 15

"We don't have enough time to harden this place." Brannigan stood by Fuentes's kitchen table, his arms folded and his Galil hanging by its sling around his neck. Flanagan, Wade, and Pacheco stood with him and Fuentes, as the rest of the Blackhearts helped Fuentes's hands haul the bodies out of the living room.

Brannigan suspected that the family wasn't going to be able to live in that house for a little while.

"We don't have the time, and we don't have the manpower," he continued. "We'll have to move you and your family somewhere safer—I should say, we'll have to have Pacheco and his network get you moved somewhere safer. We need to move before the Green Shirts can get their act together." He stroked his mustache as he looked down at the map he'd spread over the table. "Since we can't turn this place into the Alamo, we'll have to move fast and hit them hard, keep them off balance." He glanced over at Pacheco. "Any suggestions?"

Pacheco, for his part, looked at Fuentes. "You know the people here better than I do. What do you think?"

Fuentes still looked a little green around the gills. While Pacheco had assured Brannigan that the farmer had done a stint in the National Army, and had even fought the ELN once or twice, he was hardly a seasoned veteran, and he was still working through his shock at the bloodshed in his own living room. But he'd had a little time to adjust, and his mind was working through things. Brannigan could see him start to harden as he thought.

"A lot of the farmers are not happy, and I'm sure that if we can give them some kind of substantial plan—and a way to make it work without charging machineguns with machetes and bare hands—more of them will be willing to rise up. Especially some of those who have had their farms turned into cocaine labs." Fuentes was soft-spoken and his English was halting and thickly accented. He grimaced. "Not all of them. There are a few, I think, who would have gladly turned their farms to growing coca if they thought they could get away with it. Serra, Nieto, and Zamora, especially, I think will probably resist if we try to turn them against the Green Shirts. We might even... no."

"We might have to deal with them." Pacheco didn't share Fuentes's reticence. "Sooner or later, we *will* have to deal with them. If any of the Green Shirts make it out of San Tabal alive, it will be a bad idea to leave sympathizers behind. And if they're willingly cooperating with these *pendejos*, then they need to pay the price, anyway."

Pacheco had a ruthless streak. Given his history, that shouldn't have come as a surprise.

"We don't have the time to go after the small fry first." Brannigan was firm. "We can mop them up after we've torn down the Green Shirts and gotten the National Army to move in and keep the Venezuelans from crossing the border." Of course, the Blackhearts would need to be long gone by then. Regardless of the nobility of the mission, the National Army would not react well to American mercenaries on the ground in their country.

He looked at Fuentes. "Part of why we came to clear them out here first was because Pacheco said you're a bit of a pillar of the community among the farmers here. Which means you know who else we should go after first."

"That is easy. Clemente, Ballesteros, and that wolf, Galvez. Kill them, and the rest will crumble." There was a note of both trepidation and bloodthirst in Fuentes's voice. Brannigan studied him closely for a moment.

The farmer wasn't looking at him, but was still staring at the map. He was still pale, and his hands were shaking a little, but increasingly not because of fear. He was dealing with the reaction of a sane man turned into a prisoner in his own home, his own country. He wanted to lash out and see the people who killed his neighbors and turned him into a slave humbled, hurt, killed.

But at the same time, even if he had seen combat back in the day, time tended to make those memories and reactions fade. He might have been hardened once, but it had been a long time since he'd had to face the sort of real, intense violence that had been unleashed on San Tabal since Clemente's coming. A small voice in the back of his head had to be reminding him of that. And it was making him a little shaky.

Brannigan leaned in a little, lowering his voice. "I'm afraid a target list isn't going to be enough. We don't have the numbers to secure the whole city and its environs, and we can't just leave the aftermath to chance. If we're reading the situation right, the Venezuelans might just roll right in if things turn to crap around here, and then you're just as bad off, if not worse." He shook his head. "We need to organize, and we need to do it fast. They have a small army. Since I don't imagine we'll have time for a lot of in-depth training, we're going to need a bigger one. That means mobilizing a good chunk of the local population, and that means starting with people they'll follow." He gestured to himself and the rest of the Blackhearts, including Pacheco. "They don't know us from Adam. But they know you. And I think you know who else might be able to help."

Fuentes's brow furrowed. "I had not thought of that." His frown deepened. "You really think the Venezuelans will move against us?"

"We had reporting before we came down here that they had army units on the border, just waiting. In fact, we have some information suggesting that they're the reason Bogota hasn't intervened here."

"That, and the fear of making it look like the peace deal with the FARC is a sham." Pacheco had his arms folded, a scowl on his face.

Fuentes looked even more spooked at that, and Brannigan briefly wondered if telling him had been the best idea. If he decided that the devil they knew was better than the devil they didn't…

But he swallowed, and bent his head, thinking. "I think I might know a few names. I don't know for sure how any of them will react, but you are right. We need to try."

***

"I'm not sure about this one." Jenkins had generally kept his head down and his mouth shut lately. Brannigan hadn't gotten the full story about what had happened before the Azerbaijan mission, but something Santelli had said to him had definitely deflated some of his ego. This was probably the first time he'd ventured an opinion on anything since they'd left the States.

"Why is that?" Brannigan was in the front seat of the truck with Pacheco, while Jenkins was crammed into the back.

"Fuentes didn't seem to have too high an opinion of this guy. I mean, he survived the coup because he played along, and it doesn't sound like he was all that great a guy *before* Clemente took over."

"He kept his head down, that's correct." Pacheco kept his eyes on the road as he spoke over his shoulder. "But I've heard a few things that back Fuentes up. I think he'll join us."

"If you say so." Then there wasn't time for further discussion.

Pacheco pulled over onto the side of the road and then drove a little bit farther off into the trees. They couldn't see the enemy yet, but if Fuentes had been right, there should be a Green Shirt checkpoint on the way into San Tabal just around the bend. It was a minor miracle that they hadn't already run into a patrol, but Brannigan was hoping that they'd already disrupted things a bit, between wiping out the group that had showed up at Pacheco's farm, and then hitting the Fuentes place less than two hours later.

Pacheco shut the truck down, and they got out, in their tiger stripe fatigues, load bearing gear, and wearing camouflage face paint under their ProTec helmets and NVGs. All three pulled their Galils out with them, but they hoped to avoid using them, at least for the next couple of hours.

"Pacheco's on point. Jenkins, watch our six." They crossed the road and faded into the jungle that lined the ridge that pointed toward San Tabal, where it nestled in a hanging valley less than a mile away.

The slope was steep and rough, and the vegetation made it even worse. They'd barely gotten five hundred yards and Brannigan was starting to wonder about the wisdom of taking this approach. He couldn't check his watch on the move, if only because he didn't want to risk the light in the dark under the trees, just in case the Green Shirts had patrols out. But they were already behind schedule, he was sure of that.

They needed to pick up the pace. He hadn't seen anything to suggest that the Green Shirts were professional enough that they'd brave the jungle and the terrain. Most of those they'd encountered so far had been little more than enforcers, far from trained infantrymen, never mind the kind of hard-core light infantry who would see a nasty piece of ground like this ridgeline and say, "Let's go up there." So, noise was probably less of an issue than they were assuming.

The next time Pacheco looked back at him, Brannigan pumped his fist up and down. *Speed up.* Pacheco acknowledged, and they were soon moving at a better clip, making slightly more noise but covering ground more quickly. Still, getting into the city this way was going to take hours. The veg was just too thick.

Nothing for it. Forcing the checkpoint would be far too loud, alerting every Green Shirt in the valley. They had to take the long, difficult, exhausting way.

Time stretched as they hacked their way through the undergrowth, Pacheco leading with a machete. Every few minutes, they had to stop, crouching down and listening for any movement that wasn't one of the myriad nocturnal animals moving through the jungle. The night noises were almost deafening, and Brannigan could only hope that they'd hear any Green Shirts before they were right on top of them.

He really hoped they weren't in some jaguar's night hunting ground. He was consistently looking up as well as side to side and behind them, but he wasn't sure he could spot one of the big cats before it dropped onto his head.

Finally, somewhere around three in the morning, they got to the edge of the city. Pacheco held up a hand to call a halt, sinking to a knee behind a tree, just behind a low, white-plastered brick house with barred windows and a Spanish-style fluted tile roof. A single light out front cast a dim glow around the corner, giving them just enough illum to see the street clearly through their PVS-14s.

Brannigan moved out onto Pacheco's flank, his Galil held ready as he found his own vantage point, and Jenkins took up a position behind them, leaning against a tree, panting and sweating, watching their six. Brannigan had half expected to have to tell the former SEAL to watch the hill behind them, but he hadn't.

Santelli must have really put the fear into him.

He scanned what he could see of the street below through the narrow gap between the single-story whitewashed house and the darker, two story place next door. It appeared to be empty, and he strained his ears but couldn't hear engines or any other movement over the chirping, shrieking, and buzzing of the jungle night life behind him.

Pacheco apparently thought it was clear. He rose slowly, but instead of moving down into the neighborhood just below them, he moved over and joined Brannigan.

"You know where we are?" Brannigan kept his voice pitched as low as he could while still being able to hear himself.

"We're about half a kilometer from Quintana's house—unless he's moved. Fuentes might be reasonably confident that he'll join us, but he's been a prisoner in his own house for the last couple of weeks, at least. He hasn't been in town to see what Quintana's been up to. That said, I don't think Quintana would

140

have moved. It doesn't fit the role he's picked out for himself in the new order."

"Well, let's go, before a patrol decides to come down the street." Brannigan rose and started toward the gap between the houses.

Pacheco put out a hand to stop him. "Try not to look sneaky. If we swagger a little and act like we belong here, like we own the city, any Green Shirt patrols might mistake us for some of their own, especially at a distance and in the dark."

"Good thinking." It was too easy, especially under these circumstances, to get so wrapped up in not being seen that sometimes the simplest and most straightforward solutions got lost. There's no way to be completely invisible in an urban setting, so you settle for the next best thing—blending in with the population. If the population's locked down, try to blend in with the forces holding the area.

Their tiger stripe camouflage, face paint, and NVGs wouldn't fool anyone up close, but they hoped that they could keep their distance and avoid the Green Shirts altogether.

Pacheco took lead again, letting his rifle hang on its sling, walking casually out into the street. He didn't silhouette himself under the streetlight, but he strolled up the street as if he didn't have a care in the world. Brannigan didn't know if that was really the way the Green Shirts acted in the city, but it was probably a close enough approximation, especially if the patrols that were actually on the streets had taken a bit of the edge off to make up for being on night patrol.

Of course, the other possibility was that they might be a bit extra aggressive in the hopes of getting some action to make up for being on the streets at that hour. There were a couple different ways that thugs might react to extra duty, neither of them particularly professional. The latter was certainly the most dangerous.

The night was quiet and still as they moved up the street. It was late enough that none of the locals would be out and about, especially not since the Green Shirts' presence had all but obliterated the city's night life—what there ever had been of it. They didn't really have to worry about cameras, either. San Tabal was too far out in the boonies, too small and too poor, to merit the effort of putting a CCTV system in.

Brannigan had more than half expected to at least see *some* kind of open force on the streets, though. They didn't have a good estimate of the Green Shirts' numbers, but if they were holding a city by fear, he would have assumed that they'd see more of a presence. But the streets were deserted, at least the parts they could see as they worked their way toward Quintana's house.

It didn't take long. Without sneaking and moving from shadow to shadow, they reached the place in a matter of a few minutes. Pacheco slowed as they got closer. They didn't want to blunder into anything.

The house itself was a small, two-story block of poorly fitted brick with a shallowly slanted roof, wedged between two more similar houses. Once they'd gotten deeper into the city, even the tiny yards of the outer houses had disappeared. Most of the people of San Tabal lived practically on top of each other, tenements and houses crammed wall-to-wall along narrow streets terraced into the hillside. It meant that if they did get spotted, their escape routes were necessarily limited, but there was nothing they could do about it. They needed to secure or turn Quintana, and they needed to do it tonight.

Scanning the street, they saw no one. A mangy dog trotted across from alley to alley about a hundred yards away, but it paid them no mind. Pacheco and Brannigan moved to the door, while Jenkins held security.

Now they had to break character slightly. Small, barred windows flanked the similarly barred front door. While everything was quiet and dark on the street, they couldn't be entirely sure that no one was watching the windows. So, Pacheco and Brannigan ducked beneath the window as they moved to the door.

It was locked. Pacheco, however, had come prepared, and dropped to a knee, pulling a set of lockpicks out of his own vest and going to work.

Brannigan semi-shielded Pacheco from the street, trying to stay casual, letting his Galil hang from its sling while he tried to simultaneously watch the street, the door, and the windows. Pacheco was muttering under his breath as he worked the lock. The time ticked past, and Brannigan found himself getting anxious. This was taking too long. The street was still empty, but sunrise was coming fast.

Finally, the lock gave up, opening with a rasping scrape, and the door swung open with a faint creak. Pacheco stood, bringing his rifle up, and then the three of them moved inside. It wasn't nearly as smooth as some of the Blackhearts' entries had been in the past, but it was about as good as they could expect beside an old-school narco hunter they hadn't trained with.

The tiny living room was spare and backed up against an equally tiny kitchen. Stairs in the back led up to the second floor. A small couch and a pair of chairs faced an old TV in the corner. The TV was off, and two Green Shirts were sprawled on the couch and one of the chairs.

Brannigan moved to one of them, while Pacheco took the other. Brannigan put his muzzle against the snoring man's forehead, and gave him a light tap.

The Green Shirt's eyes flew open, and the first thing he saw was a looming shadow pointing a rifle at his face. He froze, and, judging by the acrid odor that met Brannigan's nose, he'd lost control of his bladder.

The other made a grab for Pacheco's weapon, opening his mouth to yell. Pacheco yanked his Galil back, flipped it around, and savagely buttstroked the man in the head. The impact snapped the Green Shirt's head back with a *crack*, and he slumped, then started to twitch.

"Holy shit." Jenkins was looking over his shoulder at the spasming Green Shirt, just before the man shuddered one more time and went still, blood trickling from his ear.

"Keep your eye on the door, George." Brannigan understood Jenkins' reaction, to some extent. No one necessarily expects to watch a man die from a simple blow to the head. But blunt force trauma can do that.

He quickly tied and gagged the surviving Green Shirt. He wasn't going to murder the man, though they were going to have to take him with them when they left, in case he talked. Then he turned toward the staircase, his rifle back in his hands. "Going upstairs."

Pacheco just fell in behind him without a word. The former Search Bloc operator's face was impassive, as if he'd just done nothing more intense than swatting a fly. Brannigan briefly wondered a bit at some of the stories about the Search Bloc. When fighting those with no morals or restraints, a man gets hardened to some things.

The house was still quiet as they climbed the stairs. The death had been almost completely silent. Pacheco had hit the man before he could make a sound.

The upper floor was divided into two rooms. Brannigan took the right, Pacheco the left.

The right-hand room was the children's room. Three of them slept on two beds, still sound asleep, unaware that there was anyone in their house. He quietly closed the door and moved to join Pacheco, who had already moved into Quintana's room.

Pacheco was already looming over Quintana. It was easy enough to identify the man—his wife was about half his size. Pacheco kept his rifle out of reach and put a hand over Quintana's mouth.

The former deputy police chief of San Tabal's eyes flew open. Pacheco put a finger to his lips. "Get out of bed, very quietly, and no one gets hurt. We need you to come downstairs where we can have a talk without waking your wife."

Quintana's eyes flicked from Pacheco to Brannigan, looming in the doorway and then nodded carefully. Pacheco stepped back, lifting his Galil just in case, and let him up.

There was no yelling, no protest. Quintana, a man of medium height with a slowly expanding waistline and a thick mustache, padded meekly toward the door. Brannigan moved aside and let him lead the way downstairs. Jenkins was down there. If Quintana tried to bolt, he didn't doubt that Jenkins could stop him.

"Sit down." Pacheco turned on the kitchen light and pointed to the kitchen table. Quintana's eyes flicked toward the couch, where the dead Green Shirt was assuming room temperature. "Don't worry about them. They won't interfere."

One of them wouldn't interfere with anything ever again.

"What do you want?" Quintana sat down, the old metal chair creaking under his weight, and folded his hands nervously on the table.

Pacheco sat across from him, while Brannigan stood nearby. "You don't know us, but we've talked with one of your neighbors, and he told us some interesting things about you."

Quintana's eyes would not stay still. The man was scared out of his mind. Brannigan was wondering about the wisdom of this little meeting. "What neighbor is that?"

"Diego Fuentes." Pacheco leaned his elbows on the table. "He told us that you were the deputy police chief until Chief Inspector Manzano was put up against the police station wall and shot. He also told us that you had the spine of a jellyfish and the moral compass of a windsock."

If Quintana felt insulted, he didn't dare show it.

"Under the circumstances, we might have expected you to willingly do everything that Clemente and his Green Shirts told you to, even accept a promotion to take Manzano's place." He raised an eyebrow. "But you didn't. You even took a demotion. It would *seem* like you did that to save your skin, except for one little detail. He says that you've been so incompetent as a police officer since the 'revolution' that several of the Green Shirts' targets have mysteriously gotten away before they could be arrested."

Quintana's face had gone utterly still. He tore his eyes away from Pacheco to look at Brannigan. For the first time, it

145

seemed, he took in their camouflage, gear, and the fact that Brannigan was a huge Anglo with a handlebar mustache and icy blue eyes.

"Who are you?"

"We're friends... *if* you are willing to act against the Green Shirts."

"I thought you *were* the Green Shirts, here to kill me." He ran a beefy hand over his face. "I thought that they had figured out what I was doing." Then he froze again. "Unless this is a ploy, and you *are* working for Clemente." His hand started to shake.

"We are here to help liberate San Tabal from the Green Shirts." Pacheco's voice was still low, flat, and hard. "Are you going to help? Or do we have to make you disappear, like your two guards?"

Quintana looked back at the body of the guard, noticing the blood, and he was clearly thinking. Then he lowered his hand, which had stopped shaking. He looked from Pacheco to Brannigan one more time, then folded his arms.

For the first time, Quintana didn't look like a frightened man waiting to learn he was going to die. He leaned back in his chair, making it creak even more alarmingly. "If you're serious, then yes." His expression was somewhat inscrutable. "How many have you recruited so far?"

"You're one of the first." Pacheco wasn't going to give everything away.

Quintana nodded. "If we move fast, we can have at least a dozen people ready to act by morning."

Pacheco raised that eyebrow again. "Really? You're part of the underground already?"

"Not directly. But I imagine that the list of those I'm supposed to be watching will be useful to form such an underground." He sat up a little straighter. "Let me go upstairs and get dressed. We need to move quickly."

CHAPTER 16

Wade held up a fist and immediately dropped to a knee, making sure he was concealed from multiple directions. He wasn't entirely sure where the road or the checkpoint were, but he knew they were far too close.

Night land nav can be difficult under the best of conditions. In the dark, in the jungle, on unfamiliar terrain, it can become a nightmare. And one of Wade's nightmares looked like it might just come true.

He'd been walking point, taking his cues from Fuentes, who was behind him with Hank Brannigan staying close, just in case the farmer freaked out under stress. So far, both of them were doing all right, but Wade wasn't sure how they were going to react when they realized just how close to the enemy they'd strayed.

He'd halted at the first sound of an engine, which he shouldn't have been able to hear, not if they were on their planned route. They'd planned to stay well away from the single road leaving San Tabal to the north. So, when Wade had seen the flickering illumination of headlights and heard a vehicle motor, he knew they'd drifted east. And when the lights stopped, a door slammed, and he heard voices, he knew they were *much* too far east. They were almost on top of the northern checkpoint.

Though as he thought about it, even that was off. It should have taken them at least another thirty minutes to get that close to the city. And he didn't think that they'd sped up more than they should have, given the thickness of the jungle and the roughness of the terrain. If anything, they should be behind schedule.

He tried to peer through any gaps in the bush to see what they were up against, but all he could make out was the glow of one set of headlights. He frowned behind his NVGs. None of the Blackhearts had gotten close enough to the city to see one of the actual entry control points yet, but he would have expected more lights, especially since none of the Green Shirts they'd encountered so far had been using night vision goggles. If they didn't have night vision capability, they'd be almost blind without illumination. He would have expected them to have at least a couple of work lights set up with a generator. But the more he studied the situation, the more he was convinced that the vehicle was the only source of light. Which meant this *wasn't* one of the main checkpoints.

Still, the bad guys were right there, and from the sounds of things, they were sticking. The headlights didn't move, and after the initial sound of the vehicle's doors slamming, he'd heard nothing but the idling of the engine, the crunch of footsteps, and voices speaking Spanish.

He backed up cautiously, placing each step carefully so as to avoid breaking a branch—or stepping on a snake. Crouching down next to Fuentes and Hank, while Burgess watched their rear, he whispered, "We've got a vehicle and what sounds like a patrol immediately to our left. How close are we to the northern entry checkpoint?"

"We should still be two kilometers from the edge of the city." Fuentes sounded scared, though it was so dark under the trees that even on NVGs, Wade couldn't see his expression. He could, however, see the man gripping his shotgun—which he'd had buried behind his farmhouse—nervously. The weapon was *probably* already illegal under Colombian gun laws—he probably wouldn't have had time to bury it before the Green Shirts had descended on his farm. Not that Wade cared. But if Fuentes flipped out and started blasting, they'd be made, and this would get a *lot* more complicated.

"Maybe it's a patrol, then. Either way, we're *way* too close to the road." He looked around, though the jungle was so close that it was hard to see more than a couple of yards. But he knew which way the road was, so they needed to keep moving south while pushing west, away from the road and the headlights.

"Let's go." He led out, careful to move as slowly and smoothly as he could. Each step took longer than it felt like it should have. He had to look all around and test the ground with his boot before he put his weight down.

But while the three Blackhearts had NVGs, Fuentes did not. Nor was he well-practiced in moving through the bush in a combat situation. He put his foot down on a fallen branch, which *crack*ed loudly in the night.

Wade froze, swiveling his head to peer back toward the headlights. Maybe the sound of the engine and their conversation would mask the noise.

His hopes were dashed a moment later, as a voice was raised, calling out a challenge in Spanish. Someone had heard the branch break.

"Get down!" He kept his voice to a low hiss, quickly suiting actions to words and getting down into the roots of a towering tree, his Galil pointed back toward the glow of the headlights, now all but invisible through the vegetation. Burgess had done the same, but Fuentes was slow, and Hank grabbed him and dragged him down behind a fallen tree.

Flashlight beams flickered through the forest, and footsteps crunched in the undergrowth. More voices spoke up in rough Spanish, the Green Shirts calling to each other to ask if they'd seen anything. Wade shifted his position slightly and felt something beneath him start to give. He froze again. His weapon wasn't in a good position to shoot the closest Green Shirt, but if he moved any farther, he was going to make noise, and those flashlights were about twenty yards away and getting closer.

He stayed perfectly still, planning every move in his head, second by second, as the Green Shirts got closer. He'd have to roll onto his back and fire between his knees. He'd put a pair into the first man, then transition to the next one to his right.

Always have a plan.

The lead Green Shirt stopped a bare ten yards away, shining his flashlight around the jungle. The cone of illumination swept across the bush, passing right over where Hank and Fuentes lay in the undergrowth.

Wade braced himself. The Galils didn't have optics or laser sights, so he'd have to point shoot. He was offset far enough from the rest that he was confident he wouldn't hit either Fuentes or Hank. He eased the selector lever to "R," the semiautomatic setting.

Then another voice from back by the road called out, and the man in the lead answered with what sounded like a negative. The voice in the dark called again, sounding impatient.

The lead Green Shirt swept the undergrowth with his light once more, then turned away and headed back toward the road.

Wade let out a breath he hadn't quite realized he'd been holding and took his finger off the trigger. *That was close.*

He was going to wait until the Green Shirts got some distance, but Fuentes was already starting to get up. Hank dragged him back down, but he started to crawl away instead of lying low and waiting.

Wade bit back an angry curse. They'd just dodged a bullet, but if Fuentes got too frisky, they might still get compromised. He wanted to hiss at Hank to get the farmer under control, but even that seemed like it would be too loud. He shifted his muzzle back toward the receding lights, as the younger Brannigan lunged forward and all but tackled Fuentes, flattening him to the forest floor and whispering fiercely into his ear. Wade couldn't hear what he was saying, but whatever it was, it got Fuentes to freeze.

He waited, his Galil pointed toward the lights bobbing through the jungle. They didn't turn around, didn't come back to investigate. They headed back toward the road, the sound of their passage receding as they went.

Wade finally got up, slowly and carefully. A moment later, Hank did the same, helping Fuentes up. Wade made sure they were following, then turned back into the jungle. They needed to make tracks.

***

Over the next hour, he started to think that he'd figured out how they'd drifted so close to the road. The terrain was increasingly brutal, and the tendency to drift downhill had forced them closer and closer to the bottom of the valley. But he thought they were back on track. It was still hard to be sure in the blackness of the jungle at night, but they were heading back uphill and generally south.

He just hoped that they could get to their destination before the sun came up.

The slope ahead had gotten steeper and steeper as they climbed. He wasn't sure how far they were from the top, but he'd definitely slowed down. He stopped altogether when he heard a deep, grunting call off to his right, farther up the ridge.

Fuentes and Hank caught up to him while he stayed still and listened. "What the hell was that?"

"Jaguar." Fuentes' whisper was as nervous as ever. "That's their territorial call."

"Well, I'm not trying to challenge him." Wade kept scanning the jungle around them. "You know where we are?"

"Roughly. The Galán farm should be just over this ridge."

"And you're sure that's where Lara's hiding?"

He glanced back to see Fuentes's nod, though it was dark enough to only see the general shape of his head. Night vision goggles like the PVS-14 need some ambient light to work. "If he hasn't been killed, then he has to be here. Galán is his brother-in-law. And if he'd been killed, Clemente would have gloated about it weeks ago."

Wade had a few questions about that, but those could wait until they found Lara. He started back up the slope, his legs burning.

They reached the crest of the ridge without further incident, though he heard the jaguar a couple more times, raising his hackles each time. It sounded farther away, though, so that was a good sign.

The absolute last thing he wanted was to get in a fight with a jaguar in the dark. *Give me human enemies any day of the week.*

He would have slowed as he neared the crest, but the jungle was so thick and the night so dark that he was over it before he'd even realized that he'd reached it. He halted suddenly as the trees suddenly gave way to a terraced cornfield, leading down to a small stone house with a faint glow in the windows indicating that someone was probably still up with a light burning.

Hank and Fuentes joined him. A moment later, Burgess came down and knelt next to him, scanning the field below before turning back to cover the ridge behind them. "We're still clear."

"Well, Señor Fuentes, this is your game." Wade waved him down toward the house, about twenty yards away. "We'll cover you until you signal that it's clear to come down."

It was too dark to see what Fuentes thought of that. He didn't say anything. He just started down through the cornfield, his shotgun held up at the ready.

I hope he's not so jumpy that he shoots whoever opens the door. Or gets shot when they see he's got a shotgun.

The farmer approached the house warily. Wade watched him over his Galil's sights, shifting the rifle over so that he could use the eye not covered by his NVGs. The moon had risen, and the clouds were breaking up a little, so there was some illum now that they were out of the jungle. He'd at least be able to get a decent shot at the doorway, especially if there was light inside.

Fuentes knocked at the door. After a moment, he leaned toward it, as if he was speaking to someone inside, but Wade couldn't hear from up at the top of the cornfield. However, the door opened all the way after a moment, and then Fuentes was waving them down.

The three Blackhearts descended toward the house in a loose wedge, their weapons still up and ready. Hank had started with his weapon down at first—he probably had assumed that Fuentes's signal had meant they were really clear. Both Wade and Burgess knew better. They weren't going to be "clear" until they were out of Colombia and back in the States.

Fuentes waited for them at the door, accompanied by a small, wiry man with black eyes and graying hair. The black-eyed man stepped inside, briefly revealing the ancient, rusty AK, its stock held together with duct tape, that he'd held behind his back.

"This is Galán." Fuentes indicated the black-eyed man as they entered the tiny house. "And this is Rodrigo Lara."

Lara was probably in his sixties, tall and spare of frame, clean shaven with a prominent *Indio* nose and dark eyes. He was still fully dressed, despite the fact that it was late at night, in a light collared shirt and dark trousers.

"Señor Lara, we're here to help liberate San Tabal from the Green Shirts." Wade let his rifle hang as Galán shut the front door and Burgess took up security on the window next to it. "Well, technically we were hired just to kill Clemente, but my boss thinks that we should actually make it a proper liberation, which means taking control of the city instead of just killing the Green Shirts' leader and letting things sort themselves out. Since you're a former mayor, and according to Señor Fuentes here, one of the most respected men in the valley, we've come to secure your help."

"How many men have you brought?" Lara's English was accented but understandable. Wade had been somewhat surprised how many people in this remote corner of Colombia spoke English.

"We brought a small team of specialists." That sounded better than "mercenaries." "We're prepared to help train and lead your people against the Green Shirts. We have access to weapons—and we can get more from the Green Shirts as we proceed."

Lara, apparently deciding that they weren't, in fact, there to kill him, sat down at Galán's table. "You are asking a lot. The National Army should have come to intervene here. We sent messages when we could, both before and after the coup. There was no reply." He waved to indicate the whole valley. "These people are farmers and craftsmen. They're not soldiers."

Wade let that go, knowing how close they were to FARC and ELN territory. He'd be willing to bet that there were more killers in San Tabal than Lara wanted to admit.

"The National Army is worried about the Venezuelans. They've got a short brigade on the other side of the border." He hadn't heard solid numbers on the Venezuelan army presence, but that sounded about right for a small city in the jungle. "They don't want to risk a war with Venezuela, especially since they're pretty sure that the former FARC and ELN fighters will probably join the Venezuelans." He spread his hands. "You and the locals are going to have to step up, or else spend the rest of your lives toiling for Clemente and his cronies."

Lara glanced at Fuentes and spoke in Spanish. Fuentes replied calmly, motioning toward Wade and Hank. Wade couldn't make out all the Spanish, but he gathered that Fuentes was telling Lara how the Blackhearts had liberated his farm.

He'd barely finished when Burgess called out. "Hey, gents? I think we'd better get ready to move or fight, right now. We've got company coming."

CHAPTER 17

The mansion was lit up like a Christmas tree, complete with spotlights on every corner. Flanagan looked back at Gomez and Javakhishvili. "Looks like Ballesteros is getting paranoid."

"From what Fuentes told us, that's not that surprising. The man's an opportunist, not a true believer. If he thinks things are starting to get out of control..." Javakhishvili shrugged. "Guys like him might do some pretty bad shit when they think there's no risk to them, but as soon as the plan starts to go wrong, they freak out. If he's part of Clemente's inner circle, then he must have heard about the patrol we took out. That might be enough to spook him."

Flanagan nodded as he continued to study the mansion set into the hillside overlooking San Tabal. It was somewhat small for a "mansion," but it was obviously a particularly expensive house for that part of Colombia. A two-story block of whitewashed plaster and glass, it sat against the hillside, overlooking a wide, green lawn that was currently dotted with hasty defensive emplacements built from partially dug-in sandbags and barbed wire. The spotlights weren't well placed or aimed, and some of them backlit the defenses rather than shining out on the jungle at the periphery. Two trucks were parked on the driveway, where more Green Shirts with weapons leaned against the cabs or stood in the beds, looking out at the road. The whole compound was surrounded by a six-foot fence, topped with barbed wire angled outward forty-five degrees.

"I make about a heavy squad, and that's just outside." There were a couple of angles they couldn't see from up on the ridgetop, but most of those were alongside a nearly sheer drop on the other side of the house.

"If what Fuentes told us was right, he's not likely to have a lot of security on the inside. This guy's a bigwig, and apparently a high roller. He liked to flaunt his money and what it could get him before the revolution. He's not the kind to let the hoi polloi into his house." Javakhishvili snorted. "The gunmen might get his carpets dirty."

"That may be, but that's not something we can absolutely bank on if he's running scared. He might have decided that the extra security is worth it." Flanagan wasn't a believer in assuming that the enemy was going to be stupid. That was an assumption that usually resulted in an op going sideways before it had even begun. He got down below the ridge and looked at his little assault team.

Curtis and Bianco had humped their Negevs up the ridge, and Bianco was now covering back the way they'd come, while Curtis had joined Flanagan and Javakhishvili on the crest of the ridge. Gomez was slightly below, watching their flank.

"Okay. Machinegunners will stay up here on overwatch. Make sure you get some separation, so you can cover more ground, and one of you needs to have a good field of fire on that road leading up to the place. The rest of us are going to move down to that big clump of trees that they let grow right up to the fence." Flanagan couldn't quite keep the contempt out of his voice. Ballesteros might be paranoid enough that he'd called in a good-sized fraction of the Green Shirts to protect his personal hide, but he hadn't paid enough attention to fields of fire—or he'd just assumed that the jungle on the ridgeline would keep anyone from approaching the mansion from that direction. Not only did the trees and brush grow right up to the fence itself, but there were no spotlights directed at that area.

"We'll cut the fence and move through." He glanced over the crest of the ridge and reassessed for a moment. When he dropped back down, he grimaced. "There's too much light once we're past the fence to try to do this the sneaky way. We'll have to go loud immediately." There wasn't a lot of cover on the lawn. "Hit 'em hard, hit 'em fast, and move on the house. Don't slow down for anything. Speed, surprise, and violence of action are going to be the only things that get us through this." It was less than what he'd consider an ideal plan, but it was what they had.

No one had any objections or suggestions. Even Curtis was quiet, and he usually had something to say just for the sake of saying something. Flanagan nodded. "Let's move."

Bianco moved quickly up to the crest of the hill, looking for a good firing position. Curtis faded into the bush, following the crest of the ridgeline toward the north, looking for a better spot where he could fire on the trucks in the driveway—along with any reinforcements that might show up once the shooting started.

Flanagan, Gomez, and Javakhishvili slipped over the crest of the ridge and flowed through the vegetation toward the fence.

It was somewhat slow going, given the need for stealth. That close, they had to take extra care not to give themselves away before they could get through or over the fence. That meant placing each step carefully, pausing and listening often. Unfortunately, even at the late hour, music was still pounding and blaring from Ballesteros's house, potentially drowning out any of the auditory warnings they might have had that the enemy was closing in on them.

Hopefully, it would also disguise the sound of the fence being cut.

They slowed even more as they got closer to the fence. Flanagan peered through the undergrowth toward the nearest security position, a roughly sandbagged pit with a mounted M60 machinegun. He could see the rust on the weapon from yards away, thanks to the ill-aimed floodlight up on Ballesteros's roof.

The Green Shirts weren't happy about being on guard duty, and that had been obvious from up on the ridgeline. One of the two was smoking, and the other one was sitting with his back against the sandbags, facing the house, bitching in Spanish. Flanagan could hear him from the other side of the fence.

Unfortunately, the fact that he could hear the Green Shirt meant that, presuming the Green Shirts weren't high, they would be able to hear the wire cutters snapping through the fence. The music wasn't quite *that* loud.

This might get interesting faster than they'd hoped.

He pointed at the fence, in the deepest shadow available, where some of the undergrowth had already started to grow through the barrier. Gomez moved toward it, slinging his Galil onto his back and pulling the wire cutters. Flanagan and Javakhishvili got down and aimed in at the Green Shirts, just in case.

Gomez went to work, holding each wire carefully before he cut it. He took his time, working through each wire carefully, rather than snapping them, and since he was holding the wires, the breaks didn't reverberate down the length of the fence. Flanagan started to think that maybe they might get through the fence and onto the objective before they had to go loud.

Then the one who wasn't smoking got up, slung his AK, and started sauntering straight toward their hiding place, unbuttoning his fly as he came.

Oh, you've got to be kidding me.

Flanagan pivoted, his muzzle tracking the advancing Green Shirt. *Don't come all the way to the fence. Gomez needs five more minutes. Don't come all the way to the fence.*

But the Green Shirt must have really needed to piss. He threw a sarcastic bit of Spanish over his shoulder as he stepped within a yard of Gomez, who had frozen where he was.

Flanagan sized up the situation and made the decision. There was nothing for it. All that kid would have to do would be to look slightly to his left, and at the very least he'd see the growing hole in the fence.

The thunder of the shot echoed off the hillside, the Galil's muzzle flash lighting up the Green Shirt for a split second as the bullet tore through his side.

The Green Shirt stumbled, his knees giving way, and fell on his face. Unfortunately, he fell against the fence, and the undergrowth and the wire held him up, despite the fact that his weight started to push open the gap that Gomez had been cutting in the wire.

For a split second, everyone on that lawn stared in shock, as the echoes of the gunshot rolled across the city below.

Then all hell broke loose.

The M60 gunner grabbed for his weapon, and Javakhishvili shot him twice, the hammer pair tearing through his upper chest and ripping out his throat. He collapsed on top of the gun, choking and aspirating blood.

Gomez dropped to his belly and wormed his way through the hole he'd cut in the fence, leading with his rifle, while Flanagan hammered rounds at the farther security position. Bianco probably couldn't see a lot of what had happened, but he opened fire from up on top of the ridge, the Negev spitting tracers down to smash the other two Green Shirts to bloody doll rags in their fighting pit.

Gomez dashed to the first pit, though he didn't get into it, but grabbed the 60 and turned it toward the house as he dove behind the crumbling sandbag parapet. He got behind the machinegun while Javakhishvili cursed and tried to follow him, as muzzle flashes flickered from the roof, bullets shredding leaves and chopping into the trees overhead. The Green Shirts on Ballesteros's roof must not have seen Gomez move.

With a curse, Gomez racked the M60's charging handle. The Green Shirts had left the rounds on the tray, but they hadn't pulled back the bolt.

He leaned into the gun, opening up with a stuttering *thudthudthudthud* as he raked the rooftop with a long, roaring burst. The incoming fire fell silent, as Javakhishvili dashed to join him, and Flanagan crawled under the cut fencing.

Curtis had also opened fire, raking the vehicles at the front of the mansion. He was laying it on heavy, giving each vehicle long, stuttering bursts of fire. Flanagan couldn't see the vehicles as he wormed his way under the fence, the wire catching at his gear and his NVGs, but he could imagine the devastation that Curtis was sowing with that Negev. The man's personal life might be a train wreck, but he was an artist with a belt-fed.

Of course, he was also alone, and if they had a react force coming, his position would be easy enough to spot by the tracers and the Negev's muzzle blast. They had to move fast. This was already going sideways.

Flanagan got clear of the fence, though one wire tried to snatch at his trousers, and rolled over, pushed himself up, and ran—not for the sandbags where Javakhishvili and Gomez crouched, but for the covered patio and the door leading inside.

Not a moment too soon, either, as a machinegun opened up from inside the mansion, shattering the glass wall that opened up onto the southern patio, raking the defensive position where Gomez had turned the Green Shirts' own machinegun against them. Gomez and Javakhishvili hit the dirt as bullets chewed into the poorly secured sandbags that were all that stood between the two of them and imminent death.

Flanagan found himself alone, facing the door with a rifle and two frags.

Nothing for it. If I wait, we're all dead.

Generally speaking, trying to storm an enemy house solo is not recommended. Flanagan wouldn't have dreamed of it, if not for the fact that there was no other choice. Gomez and Javakhishvili were pinned, and Bianco and Curtis were too far away to help.

Quickly swiveling his rifle to check the front of the house and the bullet-riddled trucks in the driveway, he saw two corpses sprawled on the pavement, and one Green Shirt huddled behind an engine block. The Green Shirt saw him at the same moment, but Flanagan was faster. The pair of 5.56 rounds punched through the Green Shirt's clavicle and tore through his vitals before he could bring his own Galil to bear. He still had enough life left in him to trigger a burst into the pavement, kicking up bits of smashed asphalt before he fell on his face.

Flanagan had shot the man on the move as he glided toward the side door. A single kick slammed it open—it hadn't been locked. He found himself in a small entryway, and a half-step to his right put the two Green Shirts manning a MAG-58 in the living room right into his sights.

He might have trained to kill each with a controlled pair, but this wasn't training, and two of his teammates were under fire. He dumped about half the mag into the two of them, raking his fire across their bodies. Bloody holes blossomed in their shirts as they jerked under the impacts, and the gun fell silent.

He didn't dare stay put. To stay still was to die.

Taking a breath, he quickly rounded the corner, sweeping the living room to his right, where it faced the open patio and the lawn, where Gomez and Javakhishvili were already closing in, now that the machinegun fire had ceased. That side of the room was clear.

He snapped his muzzle back toward the back of the house, sweeping the rest of the room with his eyes just above his sights, feeling his back prickling at the thought of another Green Shirt back in that corner he'd just put his back to.

But the two on the machinegun had been the only ones in the room. The kitchen was empty, and the stairs leading up to the second floor lay just beyond.

He held his position, even as more full-auto 5.56 fire roared outside. One or both of their machinegunners were laying down some serious hate. But Flanagan had enough problems to solve inside the house, even as Javakhishvili and Gomez came through the shattered glass doors and joined him.

Without a word, Flanagan moved toward the stairs, even though he gave the door he'd made entry through a quick check as he passed. Even with three men, they still had to cover every angle.

The interior was strikingly modern. Everything was laid out in stark, straight lines and displaying a simple, minimalist design. The light wood floor and a few accents were the only parts of the interior that didn't seem to be white—except for the spreading pool of blood under the dead machinegunners.

Pointing his rifle up the stairs, Flanagan led the way up.

A short hallway opened on three doors. One was open, the room beyond it dark. The other two had been closed, but Flanagan could hear someone yelling behind the single door that led toward what had to be the master bedroom. It was in Spanish, but he was pretty sure he heard the name Clemente somewhere in the ranting tirade.

The open door presented the most immediate threat, even though he knew that there were people in the master bedroom. He pointed, even as he kept his eyes and muzzle on the master bedroom door, and Javakhishvili swept past him, moving to clear that room. Flanagan posted himself in the hallway, where he could see the other two doors, while Gomez and Javakhishvili cleared the darkened room. They were back out a moment later, without a shot being fired. Empty room.

The three of them moved on the master bedroom. They hadn't made a sound since mounting the stairs, and the stairs and the hallway floor were covered in a thick, cream-colored carpet that rendered their footfalls soundless—especially since whoever was on the other side of that door was making far too much noise to listen to what was happening in the hallway.

A single kick splintered the doorjamb and sent the door juddering inward. Flanagan rode it to the wall, quickly clearing the corner and pivoting toward the center of the room.

Ballesteros was on the bed, pointing what looked like a very expensive semiautomatic at the door, screaming in Spanish as he cranked rounds at the intruding figures, though he only succeeded in putting one bullet through the doorway, the rest climbing into the plaster overhead. *"¡No me matarás, Diego Galvez!"*

Gomez and Flanagan shot him at the same time. Their bullets crossed through his chest cavity, spattering blood on the white sheets behind him. The immensely fat man flopped backward, the chromed pistol falling from a suddenly nerveless hand to land on the carpet with a muted *thump*.

He had been the only one in the room. Javakhishvili moved quickly to the master bath, his weapon up and ready. Clearing that took a matter of moments.

From there, they rolled to the second bedroom. It was as empty as the first, but from the clothing and backpacks—and the obviously used bed—it appeared that some of Ballesteros's security had been sleeping there.

"Looks like he retreated alone here with his security. Wonder where he squirreled his family away." Javakhishvili rubbed his chin as he let his Galil hang.

Flanagan shrugged. "Not our targets, not our problem." He cocked his head and listened. The machinegun fire from outside had ceased. He keyed his radio. "Gambler, Woodsrunner. Status?"

"React force is Swiss cheese. I'm getting low on ammo, though. And I think I just heard something from Angry Ragnar. They might be under attack."

"Roger." Flanagan looked around. "Let's grab as much of the weapons and ammo as we can, load it into a truck that's *not* shot to crap, and get moving toward Wade's position.

"The night ain't over yet."

CHAPTER 18

Brannigan looked over at Quintana as the radio fell silent. "We don't have until morning. My guys have made contact with another potential ally, but they're under attack right now, and they don't have a lot of numbers."

"Who did they meet with?" Quintana asked.

Brannigan hesitated, just for a moment. He'd seen this go pear-shaped before. Old grudges often got in the way in an irregular warfare environment—in fact, they often just poured more fuel on the fire. More than once, American forces had been unknowingly turned into the instruments of local vendettas, as one man turned in his long-time rival as an insurgent, when the other man didn't necessarily have anything to do with the bad guys the Americans had been there to fight.

But they had little time, and sometimes risks had to be taken. *Especially* in unconventional warfare. That was a reality that many of his peers had had a hard time wrapping their heads around. "Rodrigo Lara."

Quintana nodded. "He is the man I would have suggested. He is near the top of the list of 'undesirables' that I am supposed to be hunting down. I do not know him well, myself." Brannigan's eyes narrowed slightly. Something about the way Quintana had said that suggested he wasn't telling the whole truth. "He is highly thought of, though, and Jurado already considered him a rival. Jurado did not have the cleanest hands, himself."

Ain't that always the story? There isn't a politician alive with clean hands. Brannigan rubbed the stubble on his chin. *I wonder what skeletons Lara has in his closet? Or Quintana, for that matter?*

The slightly pudgy former deputy police chief ran a hand over his face, thinking hard. "I think I can get about twelve of us together quickly. Mostly policemen." He sighed. "We might have to be…firm with some of them." His expression remained flat and emotionless as he met Pacheco's hard, icy stare. Then he shrugged. "They have stayed on in a police force that now answers to the Green Shirts. Most of them did so out of fear of repercussions against them and their families. Others…" He spread his hands. "Every man has his own reasons for doing things."

Brannigan could appreciate the diplomacy while still seeing the weasel words for what they were.

"Well, we need to move fast. Those boys can hold their own for a while, but unless Lara's got a hell of a security detachment, they're four men with four rifles against a dedicated hit team. They've only got so many bullets."

***

"Kid, take that window there." Wade pointed to the second window that flanked the main door while he peered over Burgess's shoulder. Sure enough, two trucks with what looked like about a dozen Green Shirts had pulled over on the side of the road at the base of the hill, and the Green Shirts were clambering out and spreading out across the fields below the house. "Hold your fire until I say."

If the younger Brannigan, who had been a Marine captain and a company commander, resented being ordered around by a retired E-8, he kept his mouth shut. Hank apparently understood that he was still the low man on the totem pole among the Blackhearts, not to mention that most of the rest of the mercenaries had a lot more combat experience than he did.

166

Wade turned his attention back to the enemy with a scowl. These Green Shirts had learned some caution. They weren't swaggering up to the house the way he'd halfway hoped they would. That would have been easy. Clumped up, overconfident thugs could have been mowed down relatively quickly. But these guys were spread out, crouched down, and advancing in some semblance of bounding overwatch. Furthermore, they'd left two of their buddies back on the guns mounted in the backs of the trucks to cover them.

Word must be getting out. There are scary monsters making Green Shirts disappear in the jungle.

He turned back to Fuentes, Lara, Galán, and the women and kids who had somehow all crammed themselves into the back rooms of the little house, and had now come out curiously to see what was happening. "Get everyone down on the floor, and have the kids cover their ears. This is gonna get loud." He started toward the back, but there were too many people. How had they gotten two rather large families into this tiny hovel? "Is there a back door?"

Fuentes asked Galán, and the little farmer pointed. "There is. It leads to the barn out back." The older farmer looked a little uncertain. "That's mostly sheet metal, though. Will it protect them from gunfire?"

"No, it won't." Wade looked around the tiny cinderblock house again. Cinderblock wasn't bulletproof, either, as several Rangers he'd known had found out the hard way in Iraq. But it was better than sheet metal. And he didn't think that trying to escape and evade in the jungle at night with a bunch of women and kids was going to be a recipe for survival. "Okay, then, get everybody down on the floor. We're going to have to defend this place." He turned back to the window, where Burgess was crouched so that he could just expose his weapon at the corner. The Green Shirts were getting closer, but still holding their fire and advancing cautiously. Wade brought his Galil up and wished that he'd had time to knock a murder hole in the wall down by the floor.

I hate *defense. Hurry up, Colonel.*

***

The first house was deeper inside the city than Brannigan was all that comfortable with. There didn't seem to be many Green Shirt patrols on the streets—Quintana had explained that the Green Shirts had murdered a storeowner's wife in the street before hanging him from a lamppost for talking to the National Army and the Americans, presumably to spread enough terror through the city that they could spare the manpower to go out and patrol the hinterlands more aggressively—but the deeper they got into town, the more likely it became that they would be spotted. *Especially* since the streets were all but completely deserted. It seemed like the Green Shirts' terror tactics were more successful than anyone might have hoped.

They'd moved on foot, even as Pacheco had slipped out of town to get the truck—and the deadly cargo in the two crates in the back. The police that Quintana was going to recruit probably had some of their own issue weapons, but even under the kind of regime the Green Shirts had put in place, regular police didn't carry infantry weapons.

Of course, that also meant that most of these policemen weren't going to be any great infantrymen, either. But you work with what you've got, especially in irregular warfare.

Quintana waved at the Blackhearts to stay in the alley, and stepped out onto the street. He was in uniform—the San Tabal police had maintained their police uniforms, differentiating themselves from the Green Shirts who were the real enforcement arm of the new state—and he potentially had an excuse for being out and about. The Blackhearts, in their green tiger stripes and carrying Galils, wouldn't.

Of course, they had to trust Quintana. The door he had pointed out on the way was about halfway down the block, and there were no other alleys or even gaps between the houses between the darkened alley where Brannigan and Jenkins waited in the shadows.

168

Quintana walked casually up the street, even though it was about four in the morning. Brannigan stayed back in the shadows, but close enough to the street that he could follow their contact and cover him, if need be.

Or shoot him, if that became necessary.

Quintana knocked on the door. After a moment, he spoke in Spanish, apparently in response to a query from inside. Then the door opened, and he disappeared into the house.

"I don't like this, Colonel." Jenkins hadn't watched the byplay—he was still watching the alley itself, in case the Green Shirts wandered through. "He's in there with nobody to watch him, and he knows exactly where we're hiding."

"I know." Brannigan kept his eyes on the house Quintana had disappeared into. "Which is why we're going to di di mau out of here if anything looks off. And I made sure Quintana understood that, too." He'd framed it more as a contingency plan, but he also hadn't told the former deputy police chief where they might be going if they faded into the night. They'd have to put the pieces back together afterward if it came to that.

They waited in silence. They didn't have comms with Quintana, either, and the only signal they'd have if the policeman he was trying to recruit turned on them would be when the shooting started, or Quintana busted out of the house and ran for it.

Then a Green Shirt patrol appeared around the corner, just up the street from where Quintana was trying to argue one of his fellow cops into rebelling.

Brannigan tensed, his rifle coming up fractionally, his finger hovering near the trigger. *That was fast*. Quintana must have called his new bosses right after he entered the house.

His eyes narrowed slightly, and he lowered the muzzle. There were only three of them. And they weren't acting like they were on a hit. They sauntered down the street, chatting in low Spanish, one of them with his AK-47 slung. One of the other two had his FNC dangling loosely from his right hand, and the third

169

had an M16 with all the bluing rubbed off carried over his shoulder by the barrel.

Brannigan eased back from the street, moving deeper into the shadows. Quintana hadn't sold them out. This was just bad timing. He didn't think even the Green Shirts, as savagely amateurish as they might be, would try to raid a potential rebel house with only three men.

He started to scan the adjacent rooftops, and he even circled around to the other side of the alley, where he couldn't see the patrol or the door Quintana had entered anymore, but he could see the other end of the street, and the intersection just beyond. No more foot mobiles. No gun trucks. The streets were as deserted as ever, except for those three.

Pure, dumb luck.

Now, just so long as Quintana doesn't decide to come out right now.

Even as he thought it, Brannigan knew they didn't have time for this. Especially not with Wade, Burgess, and—even as he thought it, he flinched a little—his own son pinned down with their best hope for a new leader to keep San Tabal from turning into a bloodbath. They had to move, and they had to move quickly.

But could he afford to get into a gunfight in central San Tabal? Even if the majority of the Green Shirts were out in the hills, there would still be enough of them in town to overwhelm two or three shooters, and they had to have loyalists on the police force. Quintana wouldn't be so careful as to who he'd picked out to contact otherwise.

Still, he crouched down in the alley, easing his Galil's selector lever to "R," and waited for the Green Shirts to come back into view. They might not have any choice.

He heard a door open. A voice called out in Spanish, and Quintana answered imperiously. Jenkins glanced toward the street, but neither Blackheart could see what was going on. Brannigan moved back to his previous vantage point, while pointing back down the alley with a stabbing finger. There were only two of them. Jenkins needed to be watching their six.

170

Easing one eye around the corner, he spotted the Green Shirts, their weapons now held somewhat more readily, facing Quintana and a skinny, short man, who was also wearing a police uniform, though it looked like he'd just put it on. His collar was still open, and his shirt was partially untucked under his duty belt. Quintana was arguing with one of the Green Shirts, his head held high and radiating every bit of officious self-importance he could muster.

Unfortunately, it didn't look like the Green Shirts were buying it. They were still the powers that be in San Tabal, and the police force were supposed to be their whipping boys. Brannigan couldn't really see facial expressions, but their body language was simultaneously confident and threatening. The one with the AK pointed toward the door and barked something in Spanish, while the man with the FNC reached for what must have been a radio. Brannigan lifted his rifle, careful to keep the movement smooth and relatively slow, trying to avoid attracting their eye with sudden movement.

The Green Shirts, however, were so focused on Quintana and the other policeman that they weren't paying any attention to their flanks. Or to the covered patio on the roof of the policeman's house.

Brannigan didn't see who threw it, but he saw the man with the FNC take a brick to the face from about five yards away. He didn't even make a sound but just collapsed like a sack of dirt, knocked cold. And then Quintana and his companion moved.

"On me." Brannigan was already moving, even as Quintana and the other policeman grappled with the two remaining Green Shirts. Brannigan was somewhat surprised that a shot hadn't been fired yet, even though Quintana and the other man had gone for the weapons first. He was pretty sure that trigger discipline wasn't a concern to the Communist thugs, so it was a minor miracle that one of them hadn't cranked off a round or a burst as they struggled for control of the weapons. Quintana had seized the AK, trying to wrench it up and out of the Green Shirt's hands. The other man had tackled his target, driving into his midsection and knocking both of them on top of the unconscious man, the M16 pinned between the two of them.

Brannigan got to Quintana and the man with the AK first, even as they turned away, still wrestling for the rifle. Slinging his Galil behind him, he stepped in quickly, wrapped one beefy arm around the Green Shirt's neck, and bore down on the back of his skull with the other, pressing the V of his upper and lower arm together on either side of the man's neck. The pressure mounted, cutting off the blood flow to the Green Shirt's brain, and he was unconscious in seconds.

Jenkins was standing over the other policeman and the Green Shirt with the M16, his rifle leveled, trying to get a shot.

"No shooting!" Brannigan hissed in some horror. If Jenkins shot the man, or worse, missed and shot the cop…

Jenkins snatched his finger off the trigger, as if he'd just then realized that firing a shot under these circumstances was going to bring half the city down on their heads. He stepped in, reversed the rifle, and in an eerie echo of what Pacheco had done before, he buttstroked the struggling Green Shirt in the head.

At least, he tried to. The buttstock skittered off the side of the man's skull, tearing skin and ripping off part of his ear. Blood welled from the wound, and the Green Shirt started to cry out, but the shock had given the policeman enough of an advantage that he got one hand on the M16 before rearing up and landing a vicious elbow strike to the Communist fighter's jaw.

The Green Shirt's head bounced, and he stopped struggling. He was still moving, so he was still alive, but he was dazed enough that the cop was able to rip the rifle from his suddenly slack fingers and stood up.

"We need to get these three secured and hidden and get moving," Brannigan told Quintana. "We don't have a lot of time."

"I know." Quintana looked up and down the street, then pointed. "That might be their vehicle up there. The Green Shirts are lazy. They don't like to patrol on foot for very far. We can stuff them in the back and hide the vehicle in the jungle on the way to the rendezvous point." He turned to the cop, and spoke quickly, pointing up toward the hills and the road where Pacheco was taking the truck with the weapons. The cop nodded, pulling his handcuffs out of his belt and flipping the stunned Green Shirt onto his back.

Quintana went to work on the one Brannigan had choked out, as Jenkins held security and Brannigan moved to the man who'd been hit in the head with a brick. A glance up at the balcony showed him a small head peering over the low wall, another brick held ready to throw. One of the cop's kids, more than likely.

It was a universal. Boys everywhere wanted to be resistance fighters. Few ever got the opportunity.

He checked the unconscious man's pulse. He was still bleeding from a cut on his forehead and what might very well be a broken nose. He had a pulse, though it was slow and thready. He was alive, but he wasn't in great shape. He'd probably be unconscious for quite some time. A concussion was a certainty.

Brannigan pulled a length of 550 cord out of his chest rig and tied the man's hands after dragging the FNC rifle out of reach anyway. Best not to take chances.

"George, you're on security." He hefted the unconscious Green Shirt into a fireman's carry, even as Quintana and the other cop started dragging their prisoners toward the vehicle, an old VW van.

It took seconds to get the incapacitated fighters into the back, check their bonds, and find the keys. Then the cop started the van and rolled out, waving to Quintana. He'd ditch the van and meet with Pacheco.

Provided he didn't turn on them. It was doubtful, given what had just happened, but Brannigan was long past trusting anyone in a situation like this.

"Come on." Quintana kept going up the street. "We have a few more to find. We should be able to speed things up after this next house—both brothers are policemen, and they both live in the same house." He glanced up at Brannigan. "And I trust them more than I do Abalos."

173

"Let's go, then. We're running out of time." He tried not to think too much about Hank as they hustled up the street.

CHAPTER 19

The gun trucks parked at the entrance to Ballesteros's house weren't in the greatest of shape anymore—Curtis was a good machinegunner, but machineguns aren't precision instruments. Most of the glass had been shattered and the driver's side was riddled with bullet holes. More rounds had punched into the bed, and the PKM mounted on top of the cab had taken a single round to the buttstock, shattering the wood and making it more than a little uncomfortable to shoot.

Curtis, currently in the back, was still bemoaning the damage to the gun. "I mean, we need all the firepower we can get, but I can't shoot that, not now!"

"Why not?" Flanagan saw Bianco wince in the rear-view mirror even as the words left his mouth. But it was too late.

"Can you imagine what that splintered buttstock would do to this face under sustained recoil?" Curtis managed to sound indignant even over the roar of the wind and the engine. "Do you have any idea how many women would be devastated at the damage to such a national treasure?"

Flanagan just rolled his eyes and kept driving. Javakhishvili didn't want to let it go, though. "Dude, chicks dig scars."

"*Some* chicks dig scars." Curtis wagged a finger as if he were giving a lecture. "Not as many do these days. And those who

175

do dig scars aren't necessarily turned off by a *lack* of scars. So, scarring up this handsome face will take more of the chicks out of the equation than will potentially be added." He folded his heavily-muscled arms in front of his chest. "It's simple math."

Flanagan knew better than to get involved in that conversation. Even less so when he thought he could hear gunfire over the noise the wind was making whistling through the remains of the windshield.

He sped up, hurtling along the narrow mountain road toward the Galán farm, where Wade and the others were under siege.

***

The women and children were down flat on the floor, and Galán had turned off the light. The advancing Green Shirts had noticed, too, and they'd gotten down and disappeared into the corn as soon as the house went dark. Wade, Burgess, and Hank dropped their PVS-14s and scanned the fields for their enemies. Wade really wished that he had an ATPIAL infrared laser right then, but wish in one hand…

For a long moment, the fields below were still, the only sign of the Green Shirts being the gunners on the two trucks on the side of the road. They were definitely getting more cautious.

Wade swept the cornfield with his muzzle, searching intently for any movement. He was beyond giving a damn about who engaged first—if he saw overhead movement in the corn, he was going to engage. He knew the best way to do it, too. The Rhodesians had developed "cover shooting" as a combination of a counter-ambush tactic and recon by fire, a pattern of finding likely bits of concealment in the bush when you knew that there were bad guys close and at the very least making anyone behind that concealment extremely uncomfortable. He'd aim low, below where he thought the movement was coming from. Most shots missed high, so the Rhodies had adjusted accordingly.

But the foot mobiles didn't show themselves first, not even by movement. The gunners changed the equation.

Both truck-mounted machineguns opened fire at the same time, their muzzle flashes flickering in the dark and tracers spewing up the hillside toward the house. The first rounds went high, but the gunners walked them down on target, and the three Blackhearts went flat as bullets punched through the window glass and chewed through the cinder block and plaster. Pulverized concrete, plaster, and bits of hot, spent lead and copper rained down on them as they tried to get as low to the floor as possible.

Wade cursed as the battering continued, dredging up obscenities he hadn't actually used in years. The Green Shirts might not have mortars, but the machinegun fire could keep them pinned in the tiny house until the foot mobiles could close in and toss grenades in the shattered windows, or just stick their muzzles inside and murder everyone that way.

And lying there, pinned down, waiting to die, was not John Wade's way.

Worming his way across the floor, he bumped into Hank, who was huddled underneath the window, and reached up toward the doorknob. He snatched his hand back with a curse as a burst of machinegun fire punched ragged holes through the flimsy metal door, scattering hot fragments across his forearm.

He gritted his teeth, then heaved himself up, grabbed the door handle, and yanked the door open. He could almost hear the gasp of fear behind him, but it wasn't as if that door was providing any of them any protection as it was.

He shifted his position, leaning out into the partially open door and sighting toward the enemy. Only to find that he couldn't see any of them.

The lay of the land was such that the top terrace was cutting off his line of sight—and field of fire—toward the machineguns and the gun trucks. The good news was that as long as they all stayed low, the machineguns couldn't hit them. The bad news was, as long as they stayed low, they couldn't shoot back, either, and the Green Shirts would be able to maneuver on them with impunity.

Wade still wasn't inclined to just lie there and wait to die.

Burgess had pulled the door farther open, and looked across at Wade. "On three?" He was clearly thinking along the same lines.

Wade nodded. "On three. One, two, *three!*"

The two of them had been shifting their positions, getting their feet under them even as Wade counted. Finally, they heaved themselves up to a low kneeling position, bracing their rifles against the doorjamb. Both men opened fire within a split second of each other, even though they didn't *quite* have targets yet.

Fire superiority has a value all its own.

But two rifles against two machineguns don't make for good odds. Wade was just high enough off the ground now that he could make out some of the muzzle flash down below, and apparently, the gunners could see his, too. A moment later, both he and Burgess were forced back down to the prone as streams of tracers reached out for them, some skipping off the edge of the terrace in front of them, tearing through cornstalks and hammering against the house. More concrete and plaster was pulverized, and more glass shattered and rained down onto the floor.

Wade lay on his side, his rifle still pointed out into the night but without targets to engage, cursing a continuous blue streak through clenched teeth.

Hurry up, guys.

***

Brannigan was getting more than a little anxious. They'd gathered about half a dozen of Quintana's loyal cops, and he had about half a dozen more on the list, but time was running out, and for all he knew, it may already have run out for Wade, Burgess, and Hank.

Finally, as the sixth man, Dominguez, hustled up the hill out of town toward the rendezvous with Pacheco, he couldn't wait anymore. "We need to go. I've got men under fire."

Quintana looked for a moment like he was going to argue. But he looked up at the towering, six-foot-four mercenary, and saw something in his face that made him shut his mouth with a snap and nod, jerkily. Together, he, Brannigan, and Jenkins headed for the hills.

They had to thread through several alleys and cross streets that were barely bigger than the alleys. They still moved carefully, muzzles pivoting to cover danger areas as they passed. They didn't move slowly, but they moved carefully.

At that point, Brannigan was perfectly willing to slaughter his way out of San Tabal if it meant getting to his boy before the Green Shirts murdered him.

He knew that his emotions were getting the better of him. He didn't care anymore. Hank was his flesh and blood, and he was already cursing himself for letting his son come on this mission. Never mind that Hank was already a combat veteran, and that Brannigan had encouraged him—even while warning him against certain mistakes—down that path. This was different. In the Marine Corps, Hank had had support waiting if he got into a situation like this. Out here, with the Blackhearts, there was nothing.

And Brannigan was out of position and behind the eight ball when it came to rescuing his own son.

They got out of the city proper and started struggling up the slope toward the road that ran along the ridgeline. There was another road leading up from the city itself, but Brannigan wasn't so far down the emotional slippery slope that he was willing to compromise good tactics *that* far. He wouldn't do Hank any good if he got himself and Jenkins killed because they took shortcuts.

But if Hank was dead by the time he got there, he'd never forgive himself.

Brannigan quickly outstripped Jenkins and the Colombians as he forged up the hill toward the ridge road. He could already hear Pacheco's truck idling up ahead.

He had to force himself to halt while he was still in the brush. *Won't do Hank any good if I get myself shot by friendly fire because I was too anxious to conduct a proper linkup.* He keyed his radio. "Pacheco, Kodiak. I'm directly to your right."

179

"Come ahead, Kodiak." Pacheco didn't waste time or breath on asking questions over the radio, especially since Brannigan loomed out of the jungle right outside the passenger side window. "What's going on? I thought we had at least six more coming."

"We'll have to gather them up later. Wade's element's in contact, and it sounds like they're pinned down." He really didn't have any more information than he'd had before, but his imagination was going strong, especially extrapolating from what Wade had said over the radio. Brannigan's Blackhearts were extremely efficient killers, but outnumbered was still outnumbered.

"Get in." Brannigan felt a wave of gratitude that Pacheco didn't feel like asking questions. He clambered into the bed even as Jenkins and Quintana came out of the jungle both of them sucking wind.

"Mount up! We've got a fight to get to!"

***

Flanagan could hear the gunfire up ahead, around the bend in the road. They were probably too close according to some tactical manual somewhere, but he'd spent enough time in warzones over the years that he'd developed a pretty finely tuned sense for when to throw the book out and when to stick with it. This was a time to throw it out. They still had concealment, and it didn't look like the Green Shirts had flankers out.

"Somebody get up on that gun! Somebody other than Kevin or Vinnie!" He hadn't quite stopped, but he'd slowed considerably, and now he crept forward, riding the clutch and the brake, determined not to over penetrate.

"See! He does care about what's important!" Curtis crowed.

"No, you and Vinnie already *have* machineguns," Flanagan retorted. "I want as much fire superiority as we can get right now."

Javakhishvili laughed. The sound was out of place, given the timing and the fact that he was preparing to lean out the side

180

window with a Galil, while Gomez had climbed up without a word, slinging his own rifle onto his back and taking hold of the PKM, ignoring the splintered stock. But adrenaline does weird things when it runs high, and something about Flanagan and Curtis sniping at each other had struck Javakhishvili's funny bone.

Their Georgian doc had a weird sense of humor, anyway.

They eased out into the curve in the road, slowly clearing the wall of trees and undergrowth. Flanagan craned his neck to see around the curve as far as he could.

Finally, with a muttered curse, he gunned the acclerator, clearing the trees and stomping on the brake as the two Green Shirt gun trucks came into clear view, their gunners crouched back behind their mounted PKM and M60, lit by the muzzle flashes as they poured fire up the terraced slope toward Galán's house.

The truck was still rocking on its shocks as he and Javakhishvili bailed, keeping their heads down to make sure that the other Blackhearts' fields of fire were clear. Gomez, up on the PKM, had already opened up, the stuttering roar shockingly loud up close, flame strobing from the muzzle brake as he leaned into the gun and raked the two gun trucks with a dashed stream of green tracers.

The first gunner went down immediately, smashed off his feet by a stream of flying metal that tore through his side and pulped his innards before ripping them out the exit wounds. The second started to pivot toward the new threat, saw his buddy get shredded, and tried to dive out of the truck.

He was too late by a second. Curtis had jumped out of the back of the truck as he'd realized that he didn't have a clear shot at the angle they'd stopped, dashed to the side of the road, dropped prone behind his Negev, and his first burst took the second gunner high in the chest. He toppled backward, his feet flying over his head as he hit the edge of the truck bed and went over, disappearing into the dark behind the vehicle.

Flanagan was already up and moving around the back of the truck. He keyed his radio as he went. "Angry Ragnar, Woodsrunner. You still alive up there?"

181

"About time you got here, Woodsrunner." Wade sounded simultaneously angry and relieved. More gunfire rattled from uphill, near the house, as the suppressing fire ceased.

"Watch your fires to the west. We're moving up that flank." Flanagan plunged into the trees, mentally cursing the jungle and its constraints on his vision. They'd be right on top of any Green Shirts in the woods before they saw them.

"Roger." The emotion was gone as Wade got a handle on the situation. "Watch yourselves. We haven't had eyes on since the suppressive fire started. They might have moved out onto the flanks."

"Copy." Then he and Javakhishvili went silent and concentrated on moving and hunting the enemy.

Sporadic gunshots rattled through the night, but it was much quieter now that the machineguns had been silenced. The Blackhearts with machineguns had ceased fire as well, since they didn't have targets. Wasting rounds on the jungle would be counterproductive—at worst they'd even simply reveal themselves to the enemy. Muzzle flashes show up easily in the dark, and tracers work both ways.

"On your right." Gomez didn't bother with the radio, but his voice was pitched low enough that it was doubtful that anyone much farther away than a couple of yards could hear him. Especially as a renewed burst of gunfire thundered up ahead and above, answered from the house almost immediately.

The three Blackhearts kept going, moving through the bush as quietly but quickly as they could, weapons up and NVGs scanning for any movement, ears straining for the rustle that might herald an enemy combatant moving through the jungle—or any of the more dangerous Colombian wildlife.

Flanagan slowed as he heard twigs breaking off to his left. He lifted his rifle, and the Green Shirt practically ran into his muzzle, suddenly bursting through the undergrowth, an AK-74 held high in his hands, trying to move up and off to the flank.

He wasn't retreating, so Flanagan shot him. He died with two bullets in his heart before he'd even registered that he wasn't alone.

Then Flanagan had to duck behind a tree as another Green Shirt behind the one he'd just killed opened fire, raking the jungle with a long, rattling burst of automatic fire. Bullets chopped through branches and leaves and *thud*ded into tree trunks, raining splinters and bits of shredded vegetation down before a fast series of shots *snap*ped down from the house and silenced the shooter.

Then a voice was raised out in the terraced cornfield, shouting in Spanish. A moment later, more fire raked the jungle, forcing the Blackhearts into cover. Flanagan moved farther behind the tree he'd sheltered behind, staying low as he eased his NVGs and rifle around the trunk, searching for muzzle flashes. He spotted one, sighted in with his dark-adjusted eye, and squeezed off three quick shots, keeping the rifle braced against the tree trunk. The muzzle flash ceased as the weapon went silent, but the others redoubled their fire, and he had to get even lower as more rounds smacked into the wood above his head.

The fire slackened slightly, but it didn't cease altogether. A moment later, it redoubled again, before slackening.

He knew what was happening. The Green Shirts weren't stupid. They'd learned from the last couple of nights that they had to be more careful. They were maneuvering, some firing while the others moved.

The question was, were they retreating, or assaulting?

He eased out again, only to snatch his head back as another burst of fire spat fragments of bark into his face. One of them must have seen his muzzle blast before, and now they were targeting his position. So, it was time to change positions.

Dropping to his belly, he wormed his way uphill, heading for another stand of trees set close together. The trunks were thinner than his current cover, and they wouldn't provide near as much protection, but they were better than nothing, and staying put was a non-starter.

He passed Javakhishvili, who had dashed a little higher before getting down as they'd taken fire. The long-haired mercenary was down in the prone, and he fired under a fallen log as Flanagan crawled behind him. Flanagan wasn't sure if he could actually see what he was shooting at, but maybe the added return fire would discourage the Green Shirts a little.

Flanagan reached the stand of trees and got up on a low knee, searching for targets. He was a little past the beaten zone of the Green Shirts' suppressive fire. And he suddenly had a better view of the cornfields from that position.

The Green Shirts *were* falling back, angling toward the road and down the hill, but keeping to the far side of the farm, away from the gun trucks and the Blackhearts' machinegunners. Their fire and movement left more than a little to be desired—they were mostly running and shooting behind them, pausing only long enough to pour longer bursts at the trees and the farmhouse above, where Wade, Burgess, and Hank were picking them off. Even as Flanagan brought his own rifle to bear, the man he'd picked out as a target jerked and fell on his face.

It looked an awful lot like they were winning. Until a glimmer of light caught Flanagan's eye, and he looked up to see headlights moving across the ridge on the other side of the valley. If he remembered right, that road linked to the road immediately below, along the edge of the fields. Those trucks—and there were at least six of them—were on their way, right to Galán's door.

This was far from over.

***

Galvez could see the muzzle flashes on the other side of the valley, and he knew that this wasn't going well. The fact that he couldn't see streams of tracers meant that the Green Shirts' machineguns were out of action. Whoever the American had sent, they were far too efficient.

I have to end this tonight. If they don't kill Clemente, then I'll just have to find another way to deal with him. Damn that American pig and his promises! He betrayed me and the revolution as soon as he made the deal! That Galvez had had no

184

intention of keeping his part of the deal didn't bother him in the slightest.

"Hurry up!" He lifted his radio to his lips. "All Revolutionary Force units, move on the Galán farm! We have the counter-revolutionaries cornered! Now is the time to finish them off!"

CHAPTER 20

Brannigan rode in the back of Pacheco's truck, his teeth gritted, holding on for dear life as the former Search Bloc operator sent them tearing along the narrow, rocky mountain road toward Galán's farm and his beleaguered teammates. He could hear the gunfight ebb and flow as the echoes of gunfire rolled across the hills. He prayed like he hadn't prayed in a long time that they weren't too late.

Pacheco slowed as they moved over the ridge and started down the other side toward the farm. They were still on the other side of the ridge from the fight, so he couldn't see the muzzle flashes or tracers. He leaned forward, about to yell at Pacheco not to slow down, but he stopped himself. Just like back in the city, they had to move tactically. They wouldn't do the other Blackhearts any good blundering into the middle of everything and getting shot to pieces.

On that note, he keyed his radio. "Any Blackheart station, this is Kodiak. We are in Sierra Bravo's truck, coming up toward the Galán farm from the west. Watch your fires on the road to the west."

"Kodiak, this is Gambler. Good copy." Curtis sounded calm and collected—once the bullets started flying the man's clownishness flat-out disappeared. "You're going to see our gun truck first. Gamer and I are set in on the road. Woodsrunner,

Shady Slav, and Pancho Villa are in the woods up to the right, so watch your fires in that direction, too."

"Roger. We're coming in." He looked across at Quintana. "Tell your boys that we're coming up on my team. Nobody shoots unless I say so."

The San Tabal cop didn't look happy at being told what to do, but he nodded. There might still have been a touch of resentment in his expression and his body language. He was the closest that the resistance had to a local tactical commander, and this American mercenary was taking command.

Tough shit. Those are my boys out front, and that means I'm calling the shots. Brannigan had been in far too many situations over the years where it was his boys at the sharp end, but someone else was making all the decisions, someone who wasn't taking all the same risks and stood to lose nothing if the decision was wrong. Quintana had plenty to lose, but it was still the Blackhearts in the middle of the fight, right then.

Pacheco came around the bend and halted, the headlights illuminating a shot-up gun truck with a PKM mounted in the back, currently unmanned and pointed at the sky. Movement in the weeds to the right resolved into Vincent Bianco as he stood up, thoroughly camouflaged in his tiger stripes and face paint. He had his Negev slung as he raised a gloved hand to the truck.

Brannigan clambered down and moved to meet him. At the same time, his radio crackled. "Kodiak, Angry Ragnar. Be advised, we just saw a lot of headlights coming from the northwest. We might have a bunch more company soon."

"Copy. What's your status?"

"Everybody's still in one piece, though the civvies are a little shook up." Wade paused. "This house isn't going to provide much cover for very long. The front is shot to hell."

Brannigan looked back as Pacheco shut off the headlights and got out of the truck. "Can we get them out of there? If we're going to have more company soon…"

Pacheco looked back at his truck, then at the captured gun truck with the PKM in the back. "Maybe. I don't know how big Lara's and Galán's families are. And what's the plan after that?"

Brannigan looked up toward the north, where he could see the flickering glow of moving headlights in his NVGs. "If we can, we break contact and move back to town. Securing San Tabal is still the primary objective. If the city is too hard a nut to crack, then we fall back to Fuentes's farm, and we start choking them off by securing the farms and encircling the city with the resistance." He wasn't sure how effective that would be—a rural resistance could be effective, over time, but he doubted they had that kind of time.

No, if we can take out the Green Shirt leadership, and clear out most of the Green Shirts themselves, we might be able to stabilize the situation before bigger forces get involved. Like the Venezuelans.

But first they'd have to break contact with the incoming force.

The gunfire had mostly died down to nothing. The Green Shirts who had been assaulting Galán's farm—and who had survived—had retreated into the jungle on the far side of the cornfields. Either that, or they were playing possum.

"Quintana, can you get your boys up onto the eastern edge of the cornfields to hold security? We need to get the women and children out of harm's way." He kept his tone respectful, and made his op order into a request. There was no reason to antagonize the former deputy police chief, especially after his bristling in the back of the truck.

Quintana nodded. "How are you going to transport them?"

Brannigan frowned. He hadn't thought about that. He'd rather keep the Blackhearts mobile and on the offensive, but somebody was going to have to drive the vehicles. "We'll see if any of the women can drive, or if there are older teenagers who can handle it. I'd rather keep the shooters where they can fight."

Quintana thought about that for a moment, then nodded. It made sense. They were still outnumbered and outgunned. Splitting off shooters to recruit more shooters was one thing. Splitting them off to escort noncombatants—as honorable a task as that was—would only serve to weaken the resistance in the short run.

He barked at his policemen, and started pointing up and to the east. The half-dozen men they'd managed to gather before things had gotten urgent picked up the Galils, M16s, and a couple of Uzis that they'd pulled from Pacheco's arms cache, and headed up through the cornfields.

Brannigan watched them go, noticing that they weren't moving in much of a formation, or very carefully. They clearly thought that the enemy had been routed, so they were just moving to take a post. He almost said something, but a glance at Quintana convinced him to hold his peace until something happened. Colombia had its own version of *machismo*, and he'd already stepped on the pudgy man's toes quite a bit that night.

He keyed his radio. "Angry Ragnar, Kodiak. See if you can push out and set security up there, and start the women and kids moving down to us. We'll get them on the trucks and get them out of here."

"Roger. They'll be moving down shortly."

***

"Stop here."

The driver looked over at Galvez with some surprise. "But *Commandante*, they are still almost a kilometer away. We have not even met up with the rest of our men yet."

"I know. But the road is at the *base* of the hill. I do not want to take our entire force in to try to assault uphill toward the enemy." Galvez didn't have a lot of infantry experience. He was good at murdering people and setting off bombs. Fighting out in the countryside like this was not his preferred way to make a revolution. But he wasn't clueless, either. He knew the value of using the terrain, and that it was easier to attack downhill—or

190

across relatively flat ground—than it was to struggle uphill while taking fire from above.

He'd had a couple of experiences with that when he'd fought alongside the FARC, many years before. Some more recent experience had been had alongside some of the more politically palatable cartels in Mexico.

CJNG might not be proper socialists, but they were good at the combat side of things, and they were hurting the capitalist Americans and their Mexican puppets. That made it worthwhile to work with them from time to time. They hadn't needed to know his real name, or what he stood for.

The column stopped, bunching up on the road, and Galvez got out, waving at the others to follow. He didn't have quite the numbers he would have preferred—there had only ever been a couple hundred Green Shirts to begin with, and the unexpected resistance had killed or maimed at least fifty already—but he still should have enough to sweep the tiny Galán farm.

He had them where he wanted them, now. The farm might be up on a hill, but there were few ways in or out. He held up a hand to stop the driver as he got out. "Not everyone is going. I want about thirty of us up on the ridge. The rest stay with the trucks and move out on the road to cut them off." The mountains to the south of the farm were steep and treacherous, the thick jungle making them even worse. They would have a hard time retreating without the use of the road. He hoped to catch them between the hammer and the anvil—the Green Shirts with the trucks would shut off their escape, while his assault force would drive along the top of the ridge and descend on the farmhouse from above. Then, hopefully, this would all be over, and he could salvage his plans. Ballesteros's death had already done some serious damage, but with Clemente out of the way, Galvez could potentially become the undisputed Leader of the Revolution much more quickly.

"Move out!"

***

Wade stepped outside, hardly sparing a glance for the pockmarked walls, horrifically chewed up by sustained machinegun fire. Galán was going to need to do some serious repairs when this was all over.

Presuming he and his family survived.

He swept the top terrace, just in case any of the Green Shirts had lingered, hunkered down behind the terrace itself where they could pop up and start shooting once the Blackhearts and their allies thought they were safe. But the ground around the house was clear, aside from downed cornstalks that had been splintered and shredded by bullets. A few flames guttered among the drier leaves, where tracers had punched through, or bounced off the terrace itself to burn on the fallen vegetation. Fortunately, everything was still too damp for there to be much of a wildfire risk. Wade stomped on the embers he could see, anyway.

He shifted his position to the corner of the house, watching the jungle to the east, where the retreating Green Shirts had disappeared. One of them sprawled between the edge of the cornfield and the treeline, staring sightlessly at the night sky above. Wade had gotten him with a running snap shot, tearing through his center mass even as he'd dashed toward the jungle.

He was kind of proud of that shot.

Hank was ushering the women and children out, with Fuentes's help. Burgess had quietly moved up the slope behind the house, and was set in behind a forked tree, his rifle laid in the fork, watching the jungle below them.

"Angry Ragnar, Woodsrunner. Probably best to send the civvies down the west edge of the fields. We'll stay in place and provide overwatch."

"Roger." He glanced over his shoulder at Hank. "You hear that, kid?"

If the former captain rankled at the term "kid," he kept it to himself. "Yeah. I heard." He was already motioning Señora Galán toward the treeline. "Makes sense. Keep 'em out of the open."

Wade had already turned back toward the diffuse glow that marked the incoming vehicles. He didn't say anything in reply to Hank's comment. It didn't need a reply.

Movement nearby drew his attention, and he turned to see Lara moving down into the cornfield. "What are you doing?" Given Lara's importance to the resistance movement they were building, Wade might have been somewhat more diplomatic, but he'd never figured he'd been hired for his diplomatic skill. And under the circumstances, he had no qualms about barking at the "important" people if they were doing something stupid.

Lara ignored him, but clambered down toward the third terrace down, crouching in a gap in the cornstalks, where one of the Green Shirts had popped up during those last few minutes of the firefight only to take a bullet through the teeth from Burgess. He rummaged around for a moment, then started climbing back up, an AK-47 and chest rig in his hands. He was huffing a little bit when he knelt beside Wade. "Show me how to use this."

Wade glanced at him skeptically. This was hardly the time or the place for basic marksmanship training. But at the same time, he had to admire the old guy's guts. He let his Galil hang on its sling, the magazine hooked on his knee, the muzzle pointing at the dirt next to him, and reached out to take the old Kalashnikov. He quickly pulled the magazine, then brass-checked the chamber. The mag felt about half full, and there was a round in the chamber. He flipped the selector lever back up to "safe"—also blocking the charging handle in the process—and started to point.

"Lever up is safe, middle is auto, all the way down is semi—that means one shot per trigger pull. Don't use auto, you'll spray rounds all over the place, won't hit much, and might just accidentally shoot one of us in the back. Front sight's here, rear sight's here. Put that post into this slot, and put the post on the target. You can't see that well in the dark, so there's going to be some dumb luck involved. Never point it at anyone you don't want to shoot. So, watch that you don't sweep any of us with the muzzle. You've got a limited amount of ammo, so only shoot when you have to. Make sure you pull the buttstock—that's this part—all the way back into your shoulder pocket, here." He jabbed his fingers into Lara's shoulder. The older man flinched a little, but he nodded his understanding. "That's going to help mitigate the recoil and let you keep control of the rifle. Lean into it." He thought for a second. "The AK doesn't have a bolt hold-open." When he got a blank look, he elaborated. "Some rifles will lock the bolt to the rear when the magazine is empty. The AK doesn't do that—it'll just go 'click.' Then you have to reload." He tapped the lever at the back of the magazine well. "Push this lever, rock the mag out like this." He demonstrated. "Then put the new one in in the opposite direction." He pulled the magazine back until it clicked into place. Then he handed the rifle back. "Remember. Be careful where you point it, keep your finger off the trigger unless you're trying to kill somebody, and let us do most of the fighting. You're too important to get smoked playing hero."

Lara nodded as he struggled to get the chest rig on. "I cannot just sit by. We have all done that too much lately."

"Yeah, well." Wade didn't feel like having that conversation. He couldn't disagree, but what small part of him *did* understand the need for diplomacy was telling him to keep his opinion behind his teeth. If more people stood up to the tyrants, terrorists, and criminals who terrorized them, there might be less need for people like the Blackhearts.

Of course, that meant less work and less money, so it was kind of a tossup to him.

A glance down the hill confirmed that the headlights were getting closer. "Woodsrunner, Angry Ragnar. You might want to get those civvies moving with a quickness. We're going to have company really soon."

"They're in a hurry; the last ones are almost down to the trucks. We're moving up to join you." Flanagan clearly didn't want to be stuck back in the woods on babysitting duty when the balloon went up. Wade grinned fiercely. Flanagan was a quiet one, but he was a killer, and Wade truly appreciated that.

194

He moved up to the edge of the terrace and got down in the prone, aiming his weapon in toward the road. The terrace would provide him some cover when the bad guys showed up. He flipped his selector to "R" and waited as the lights got closer.

***

The phone woke Santelli out of a disturbingly light doze. He squinted at the clock and realized that he was getting to the age where he really probably should get glasses. Then, as the fact that it was just past 0200 registered through the fog in his brain, he snatched at the phone. Melissa turned over, her eyes opening in the dark, and murmured, "What is it?"

"Nothing, baby." He hit the "answer" button as he swung out of bed, hoping and praying that he was right, but without holding out a whole lot of hope. A call at that hour probably wasn't good news, not when the team was in the field. He hadn't even really registered the number on the screen, he'd been so desperate to get a handle on the situation, even though there was nothing he could really do from five thousand miles away.

"What is it?" He stepped out of the bedroom and shut the door, even as Melissa sat up in bed. He caught a glimpse of the worried look on her face in the moonlight filtering through the window.

"Carlo, sorry to wake you up, but we might have to move on this quick." It was Mark Van Zandt.

Santelli's blood ran cold. "What happened? Is anybody hit?"

It took Van Zandt a second to answer, and when he did, it was with a tone of some chagrin. "Oh, no. Nothing like that. As far as I know, everybody's still in one piece." He blew out a breath, the sound rasping in Santelli's phone speaker. "Sorry. Didn't even think about that."

Santelli bit back a curse. The fact that Van Zandt *hadn't* thought of that possibility spoke volumes about the man and how separated he'd long been from real operations, even as the Blackhearts' main facilitator.

"Anyway, the client himself just called me, screaming about the team going off the reservation and off-mission. Said that they've violated the ROE—not that *I* ever got any formal ROE, even if there could be any such thing for a deniable op like this—and that they've disrupted the whole plan.

"Carlo, I think we've got him. He gave a couple things away in that conversation. I've already got a plane heading up to Boston. It should get there in an hour. I need you on it. Abernathy's going to meet us in Arlington."

Santelli rubbed his gritty eyes. "Sir, you're going to have to spell it out for me. I just woke up, and my brain's been worn out worrying about the team." *Which suggests that I really shouldn't let John retire me. Dammit.*

"I'll explain in person, Carlo. But this guy's threatened to blackmail your team and my office over this. Except we just caught him with his hand in the cookie jar. Get down here. I think we can have him off the team's backs by lunchtime."

CHAPTER 21

Bianco had taken up a new position, this time closer to the east side of the Galán farm, down in the prone behind his Negev. He was on the side of the road, most of his body cocked off into the lower ground below, with the machinegun's bipods up on the road itself. He was still wrestling with the PVS-14s. The ProTec helmet didn't fit his big head all that well, and so he was having a devil of a time getting the NVGs to line up right. He had to tilt his head well back to be able to see, and it was putting a crick in his neck.

The headlights were still around the bend. He'd more than half expected them to have come around already, but maybe they were being cautious. Or maybe his own perception of time was getting skewed by the adrenaline and the stress of waiting for the first rounds to crack off.

His hands were sweating inside his gloves. He could feel it. His heart rate was up, and his mouth was dry. *Every damned time.* He knew that it would pass once the bullets started flying. It usually did. But he was always scared just before a fight.

Sometimes it spilled over into the fight itself. He still remembered that ditch in Chad, when he'd been caught dead to rights by the bad guys. He'd frozen, just for a few seconds. It still haunted him. He didn't know if the rest of the Blackhearts had noticed—it had been the middle of a firefight, and he'd gotten back up and into the fight. But he owed his life not to his own action, but to Wade, who had shot the man who was about to shoot him.

Never again. He clenched his gloved fist, as if he could force it to stop sweating, and readjusted his position behind the gun. The headlights were coming, and he forced his breathing into a low, steady rhythm. Sure, he was scared. But he'd never let that make him freeze again. Even if it meant he'd have to hold the line and die.

He didn't even think about the old aphorism, "Courage is being scared and saddling up anyway." He just knew that he was going to be a better man, a better warrior, and he was never going to let his brother Blackhearts down again.

The glow ahead brightened as the lead vehicle started to come around the curve. He squinted through his NVGs, trying to make out details and positively identify the enemy. He pulled the buttstock back into his shoulder and his finger slipped inside the trigger guard.

He really wished that they had some explosives. Pacheco had said that he had some, but all Bianco had seen had been weapons, gear, and ammo. But even if they'd had the kind of explosives they could have turned into IEDs, there had hardly been time to set them in.

The headlights were right in his face, whiting out his NVGs. He couldn't be one hundred percent sure they were the bad guys. If there were up-gunners on the trucks, they were hidden behind the glare.

Hesitation kills. He fought the urge to readjust—he was right in the cone of light from the headlights, and if he moved at the wrong time, and those were gun trucks with the gunners on alert, movement would only get him killed. But at the same time, he didn't want to jump the gun and murder a bunch of farmers.

Then the lead truck bounced over a rock, momentarily moving the headlights away, and he caught a glimpse of the man up on the PKM in the back. His finger tightened on the trigger.

The Negev's rate of fire was about the same as the M-249 SAW that Bianco had learned inside and out during his years in the Marine Corps. It all felt perfectly familiar, as he walked the tracers up the hood and toward the up-gunner.

One of the headlights shattered, and suddenly he could see better, but the driver had reacted faster than he'd expected, wrenching the wheel over and flooring the accelerator, diving off the road and into the jungle. The gunner was almost thrown clear, but still survived, as the truck lurched to a stop behind the trees.

The next vehicle back had already stopped, and the gunner opened fire, spraying the trees and the side of the road with bullets. Green tracers spat through the foliage and kicked dirt and rocks off the road itself, coming uncomfortably close to Bianco's position. He ducked, burying his face in the dirt, as the incoming rounds flew overhead with painful *snap*s and smashed and shredded the vegetation around him.

***

Brannigan helped the last of the women into the back seat of the truck, trying not to shove her too hard, even while his NVGs brightened with the approaching glow of the incoming headlights. The Green Shirts were almost on top of them, and they had minutes at best—seconds at worst—to get the noncombatants out.

The woman drew her feet inside and he slammed the door, smacking his hand down on the hood. "GO!" Lara's wife, a stocky but handsome woman in her mid-fifties, threw the truck into reverse and twisted around in her seat, watching out the back window as she sent the vehicle careening backward down the bumpy mountain road and around the curve below. The gun truck followed, with one of Galán's teenage sons driving. There had been some arguing in Spanish before the kid had taken the wheel. His mother had prevailed, apparently. It seemed as if the young man had wanted to stay with his father, the resistance fighters, and the Blackhearts.

Both vehicles made it around the curve—though the teenager almost wrecked along the way—just before machinegun fire split the night on the other side of the fields.

Brannigan, Jenkins, Pacheco, and Quintana were already moving up into the trees when Bianco opened fire. The Negev's ripping roar was readily identifiable, compared to the heavier and slower *thudthudthud* of the PKMs or M60s that the Green Shirts mostly seemed to be using.

A moment later, Bianco's fire was answered. First one, then two PKMs opened up, and Brannigan looked through the trees just in time to see green tracers pouring into the woods on the side of the road where Bianco had set in, just before Bianco's fire went silent.

Oh, hell. Not Vinnie.

Curtis opened fire from about halfway up the hill, pouring his own stream of tracers toward the glow of the headlights, but it was almost futile. The Green Shirts' gun trucks were still behind the arm of jungle that stretched down on the east side of the cornfields from Curtis' position. Curtis was pouring fire into the jungle, hoping that he hit something on the other side.

Brannigan paused, even as Jenkins and Quintana kept going. Pacheco noticed and slowed, looking back at the big mercenary commander.

Brannigan looked back toward the road where Bianco had been set in. Every fiber of his being screamed at him to go down there and pull Bianco out, dead or alive. But a moment later, the first of the gun trucks came roaring out into the cleared section of the road, the M60 mounted in the back spitting flame, raking the cornfields with red tracers.

The policemen threw themselves flat, all except for an overweight man named Muñoz. His back arched as bullets punched through his spine and his lung, and he fell on his face against the next terrace, sliding down to roll on his back, his eyes staring sightlessly at the thin clouds moving in over the night sky.

Curtis shifted fire, raking the truck as it skidded to a halt in a cloud of dust, and the incoming machinegun fire momentarily slackened. But then the next truck back hove into view and added its own fire, beating down the cornstalks and sweeping the terraces with a deadly rain of bullets.

For a moment, the Blackhearts' fire died down to nothing, as those not already in cover crawled toward the treeline and some semblance of cover and concealment. Cornstalks waved as they thrashed through the fields, but the gunners down below weren't so much aiming as they were spraying fire all across the open ground, either trying to suppress or just hoping that enough volume of fire might hit someone. That was the only reason no more of the Blackhearts or their allies got hit.

With Curtis silenced, the first gun truck opened up again, adding its fire to the second's, even as two more trucks rumbled up behind them, stopping on the road and letting more Green Shirts with rifles and submachineguns pile out.

Then a shot from up above, near the house, suddenly silenced one of the gunners. *That had to be Wade.* It was quite a shot, given the lack of lasers or optics and the near-impossibility of using iron sights with NVGs.

"Move! Get up the hill and get cover!" The loss of one gunner had only made the Green Shirts intensify their fire, pouring bullets up the hill toward the house. Sheer numbers gave them fire superiority, and soon every one of the Blackhearts was pinned down, flat in the dirt and cursing their chest rigs for keeping them a little bit higher off the ground.

This was not going well.

Then Burgess yelled something from up behind the house and opened fire. Brannigan couldn't see where, at first, but then the flickering muzzle flashes in the jungle to the east, up on the ridgeline, told him all he needed to know.

***

Bianco returned fire for a moment, half-blindly, spraying another long burst down the road. Tracers sparked off the one vehicle he could see clearly, forcing the gunner back behind a tree, and giving him a momentary breather. But the second vehicle's gunner responded almost instantly, raking his position with more accurate fire, and Bianco snatched the Negev to his chest as he rolled down the slope and off the road altogether. More machinegun fire chased him, but he was below the lip of the road and in cover.

Rolling to his back, he got his feet under him and skidded a couple of yards down the narrow draw where he'd set in. This wasn't a great position—they'd needed to stop the convoy cold, but it hadn't quite happened. Of course, the Green Shirts had to have expected contact, given what had already happened, so this wasn't a huge surprise.

Unfortunately, the terrain and the timing had limited the Blackhearts' contingency planning. Now Bianco found himself in the low ground, packing a belt-fed light machinegun, with only a limited number of options.

He was on the wrong side of the road, and now there was a linear danger area, covered by enemy fire, between him and the rest of the team. The sides of the narrow draw he'd ducked down were relatively steep—the only easy ways out were up to the road or down into the valley below—and covered in more thick vegetation. He had to either fight his way out or run for it and try to circle around again.

The gunfire up above him had redoubled as more trucks moved in, and the Blackhearts' return fire had died down to almost nothing. This was bad.

He craned his neck, still partly on his back, to look up toward the road. He caught a glimpse of a figure jumping out of one of the trucks, but even as he shrank down into the weeds, he saw that they were all moving toward the fields above, ignoring his little hidey hole.

Gritting his teeth, he rolled to his side and started to scramble up the low slope to the west. If he could get clear, get around that curve, he might be able to get up on some higher ground—or just onto the Green Shirts' flank—and hit them hard enough to at least gain some maneuvering room for the rest. He had to move fast.

***

Flanagan was deep enough in the trees, with Gomez and Javakhishvili, that he was outside the beaten zone and therefore could maneuver more easily. He'd started moving uphill even faster as soon as the shooting started, his legs burning, all too aware that he'd already been in one intense firefight that night, and he wasn't getting any younger. But survival is a competitive sport, and he didn't intend to lose.

In a matter of a couple more minutes, he was level with the house, just as Burgess opened fire on the Green Shirts' assault element. Ignoring the bullets that *snap*ped and zipped overhead, chopping through some of the higher leaves in the canopy, he turned and dashed for the house, keeping his head down as best he could while still moving fast. For a moment, he was fully exposed to the storm of death roaring up from the road, but a lot of those rounds were going high, and he got to the corner of the Galán house in seconds, dropping to a knee and bringing his rifle up.

The iron sights were all but invisible, though he still tried. He found he could just barely pick up the front sight through the NVGs' aperture, though everything beyond it was sort of black, at least until one of the Green Shirts returned Burgess's fire.

Muzzle flash makes for a pretty good target in the dark. Flanagan shifted his aim and fired. The Green Shirt was either hit, or the bullet passed close enough that he was shocked into ceasing fire and dropping prone to get out of the line of fire.

Flanagan gave him two more rounds just to keep him honest. Precise aim wasn't all that doable under those circumstances, but aggression was more important.

Then he was moving again, dashing to the next corner, even though there wasn't as much cover there. Burgess was holding his position behind a massive tree, about ten yards uphill, mag-dumping into the figures that had begun to dash forward toward the house.

It was a bit surreal. Their targets were little more than dark green silhouettes, barely visible in the shadows under the jungle, and the most they could do was point shoot and hope they got close enough. Gomez dashed up between Flanagan and Burgess, dropping prone and hammering a pair into another charging Green

Shirt. That was definitely a kill—the man staggered and fell on his face.

But there were a lot more behind him, and soon the Blackhearts were simply raking the trees with fire. But the Galils didn't have the ammo capacity that the belt-fed Negevs did.

"Reloading!" Burgess went dry and ripped his mag out, letting it fall to the dirt as he snatched a replacement out of his chest rig.

Flanagan knew he was getting close to empty, himself. "Mario! Get inside and get set!" This was about to become a siege. *If* they could get the team inside, without getting mowed down in the open as the fire from below continued.

And the Green Shirts had far more firepower and ammunition than the Blackhearts.

CHAPTER 22

Bianco was panting hard, sweat pouring into his eyes and drenching his fatigues under his chest rig. He'd slipped twice already in the last ten yards, but he was almost over the little finger that ran down from the side of the road. That didn't mean that the worst part was over, but at least he'd have a little more cover, and he'd be closer to a better position.

The crackling roar of gunfire above him seemed to be intensifying, but that might have just been because he knew that his buddies were on the receiving end, and until he got a little bit farther, he couldn't do a damned thing about it.

Maybe I should just get up there and open up. Sure, they'll probably kill me, but at least the others will get a fighting chance. If they're still alive.

That twisted his guts a little. He didn't want to die. His earlier determination, now that he was genuinely staring such a sacrifice in the face, seemed like so much empty bravado, now.

Don't puss out. He got over the top of the little finger and crouched in the undergrowth. He felt himself start to slide and caught himself by wedging one boot against the nearest tree. The angle started to squeeze his foot, but he ignored the pain. *They'd do it for you.*

That tore it. He turned back toward the road and started struggling through the vines and weeds, every gunshot hitting his nerves like a cattle prod. He tripped and fell on his face, almost losing his grip on the Negev. The noise almost made him freeze where he was, but the shooting up ahead was far too loud for any of the Green Shirts to have heard it. He scrambled back to his feet, hauling the machinegun back up, hoping and praying he hadn't just speared the barrel full of dirt, and scrambled toward the top of the slope.

He came out farther down the road than he'd thought he would, almost at the curve. He gulped as he saw how close the nearest truck was, its headlights spilling white light down the road, right in his face.

It almost made him turn and engage right there, but none of the Green Shirts he could see were looking in his direction. All their attention was directed uphill, where even more gunfire thundered and crackled, the cacophony echoing across the darkened hills.

With a lunge, Bianco dashed out across the road, keeping his head down and crossing in three lurching strides, his chest rig bouncing against his torso, the Negev's weight tearing at his arms. He probably hadn't run that fast in a long time.

One of the Green Shirts must have spotted him, because a half dozen shots followed him, a few kicking up dirt at his heels while others sailed out into the night with hissing *crack*s.

Then he was in the trees and he pivoted, dropping prone behind one of the largest ones and dragging the Negev to bear. He had half a belt left.

It would have to be enough. He leaned into the bipods and went to work.

By luck, he'd dropped into a near-perfect position. The Green Shirts on the road—only a handful of the men on foot had started to venture up into the cornfield—were spread out along the shallow curve of the roadway that faced Galán's farm, but they were all within an arc that he could easily cover with the belt-fed simply by shifting his aim a few inches to the left and right.

Starting on the left, he held down the trigger, leaning into the gun to control the recoil, stitching tracers across the line of vehicles and men. The first man, the one who had shot at him and was still moving forward with his rifle up, caught the first burst at the knees and crumpled, screaming, to the roadway. Bianco had already traversed past him, though, raking the road and the up gunners on the trucks.

Several more Green Shirts collapsed, dead or wounded, and the fire slackened considerably as they scrambled for cover or died. Bianco reached the end of his arc and started back, but the Negev ran dry halfway across, before he could reach the first man he'd shot, who lay in the dirt, writhing and still screaming.

Scrambling to his feet, he flipped the ammo tray cover open and ripped the drum off as he started to run into the jungle, heading up the hill toward the house.

***

Brannigan couldn't tell exactly what had happened down below, but they suddenly had a lull in the incoming fire. "Get up and move! Get to the house!" He rose to a knee and added his own fire to whoever had just jumped the Green Shirts down on the road. He ripped half the mag down the hillside at the trucks, and at least one round shot out one of the headlights. Brannigan didn't consider that an achievement. Better if he'd hit one of the men.

Curtis had recovered and let rip with a long, ravening burst from the next terrace up. Brannigan turned and ran, struggling up the hillside to the right, finding the shallower slope beside the terraces, rather than trying to climb the three-foot-high earthen walls. He got to the next one up and dropped prone again, resuming his fire and giving Curtis some cover.

Curtis turned, hefting the gun and running the other way, toward the trees on the east side of the farm. Unfortunately, that was where the other Green Shirts were coming from.

Brannigan didn't hear the curse, but he sure heard the panic fire as Curtis skidded to a halt, snatched up the Negev like it was a carbine, and laid a twenty-round burst into the trees directly in front of him, even as more rifle fire from the house chopped into the shadows nearby.

"Everyone get to the house! *Now!*" Flanagan was ordinarily a quiet man, but he could make himself heard when he needed to. His bellow sounded even over the thunder of gunfire. "Move your ass, Kevin!" A moment later, more fire plunged into the trees, answered by a pained scream.

Curtis put his head down and sprinted up the hillside, his short legs pumping, the machinegun in his hands swinging from side to side.

Brannigan had already started moving, grabbing Jenkins as he went and propelling him toward Quintana, who'd retreated farther up the hillside, but was moving more slowly. "Get him moving!"

Jenkins ran forward and grabbed hold of Quintana, dragging him upward as Brannigan turned back and dumped the last of his magazine down through the cornstalks. The former policeman stumbled and almost fell, but Jenkins hauled him to his feet and kept moving. Then, as the fire from the house redoubled, Brannigan followed, stripping the empty mag out and rocking in another.

Another burst of machinegun fire roared out of the night nearby, entirely too close for comfort. Brannigan pivoted as he chambered a round, bringing his rifle up, searching for the muzzle flash, knowing he was too late.

But just before he fired, he realized that the automatic fire had been directed *downhill*. He shifted, added his own fire, and a moment later, Bianco burst out of the trees, panting for breath, clutching his Negev to his chest as he staggered toward the house.

Brannigan was right behind him, as Curtis opened fire from the house itself, raking the terraces and the road below. The two Blackhearts raced the last handful of yards to the door and plunged inside.

"Headcount!" Brannigan looked around the darkened interior of the bullet-riddled structure, praying that he had everyone. Bianco was on the floor next to him, gasping for breath but already shifting his position to point the Negev out the partially open, thoroughly holed door. Curtis was at the window with the other and Flanagan was at the west window, while Burgess, Javakhishvili, and Gomez held the east side against the increasingly ragged fire coming from the Green Shirts' assault element. Hank and Wade were also at the south-facing windows, while Fuentes, Pacheco, Quintana, Lara, Galán, and the handful of police who'd made it to the dubious shelter of the house covered the north and west sides.

It was awfully crowded in that tiny house, and it was going to get worse as gunfire continued to erode the cinderblock walls. But they had some cover for the time being, as inadequate as it might have been.

Flanagan had come away from the window to make the same assessment. "We're up, Colonel." He blew out a breath. The fire outside had slackened some, especially since the Green Shirts no longer could be sure where their opponents were. Burgess fired twice, and a yell of alarm sounded outside. A sporadic burst of fire smacked bullets into the cinderblocks, mostly high, and then it went quiet again.

"Well, this is the Alamo." Brannigan's voice was grim as he peered out the doorway. "At least until we come up with a better plan."

He was met with silence. A better plan was going to be tough. They were pinned down, outnumbered, and outgunned. And unless Van Zandt had a relief force on the way that he hadn't mentioned, the entire resistance was right there in one place. All the Green Shirts had to do was kill everyone in that rapidly crumbling house, and the mission was over.

Brannigan wracked his brain. He wasn't ready to lie down and die. And he'd be damned if he let a bunch of druggie Communist thugs be the end of him.

There had to be a way out, a way to turn this to their advantage. He just had to think of it.

In the meantime, the Green Shirts started to move, the gun trucks beginning to edge their way up the sides of the cornfields. A burst of machinegun fire from Curtis shattered a windshield and discouraged that approach.

They could hold their own for a while. But as soon as their ammo ran out, they were dead.

***

Abernathy had indeed been waiting when Van Zandt and Santelli arrived at a small business park in Arlington, Virginia. While Santelli suspected that Abernathy was deeply involved in the dark side of special operations, there was nothing about the plain blue Ford Explorer that screamed "government" or "operator." Abernathy himself, sitting in the passenger seat, was wearing a flannel shirt and jeans, far more casual than Santelli had ever seen him.

"Get in." It was early in the morning still, but the old man was as keen-eyed as ever. "He won't leave the house for another hour, so we've got time, but let's not push it." He jerked a thumb at the big blond man in the driver's seat. "This is Hauser. He's one of mine. He'll provide security if we need it."

"What about the client's security?" Santelli was still a little hazy as to who their client was—Van Zandt hadn't wanted to say over the phone, and it had been a very short drive from the airport. They'd covered more logistical matters than who their target was.

Abernathy snorted. "Senator Briggs treats his security like dirt. And I've already spoken to his detail lead. They won't interfere." He smiled coldly. "After all, we're just there for an early meeting." He nodded to Hauser, who'd already put the Explorer into gear, and they pulled away, heading toward the far more upscale part of Arlington.

***

Senator Alford Briggs lived in a massive, two-story, sprawling stone mansion that filled most of its one-acre lot. Built in a roughly Victorian style, it could only be described as "ostentatious."

Two black, up-armored Yukons sat in the driveway, just inside the small, landscaped island in the center. Neither appeared to be occupied at the moment, as the considerably older and more beat-up Ford Explorer pulled up and stopped between them, right in front of the front door.

"You need me to come in, Clay?" Hauser scanned the entire front of the building.

"I don't think we'll need you inside, Cole, but on the other hand, we might want to leave in a hurry." There was a hard gleam in Abernathy's eye. "I'm pretty sure we've got Briggs's balls in a vice, but he might not take kindly to that fact, and he's not known for being particularly circumspect when he gets agitated. And we're about to agitate the hell out of him."

Abernathy led the way, swinging out of the passenger seat and striding up the steps. He shoved through the carved double doors, and pinned the young security staffer who was hurrying across the massive, two-story foyer with a glare. "Where's the Senator, son?"

The kid knew authority when he saw it, even though Abernathy was wearing civilian clothes. Neither Santelli nor Van Zandt looked like a hit team, but they didn't look like aides or staffers, either. Van Zandt still carried himself like a Marine officer, his back straight and shoulders back. Santelli looked slightly dumpy next to the other two, but at the same time, he had the build of a gorilla and almost the strength.

"He's... uh... he's upstairs. You were the ones who called? General..."

"General Abernathy, yes." The hard-eyed old man kept moving toward the huge, grand staircase at the far end of the foyer. "Which room?"

The kid hustled to catch up. "I'll show you, sir." Santelli watched the young man with some sympathy. The kid looked like he was in his mid- to late-twenties. He was probably either former law enforcement or former military—that was a tossup, given Briggs's documented prejudices toward both professions—and he took his responsibilities seriously. He had a wedding ring on his finger, so he was probably more worried about keeping his job and maintaining his family's lifestyle than any loyalty to the senator.

From what Santelli knew about Briggs, any such loyalty would have been strictly one-way, and the men and women who worked directly for the man would know that even better.

They reached the top of the stairs and the kid led the way to the right. The hallway that encircled the foyer was high-ceilinged, with white walls and molding along the ceiling, deep, gray carpet on the floor, and dark wood doors leading to the rooms off the central foyer. A wrought-iron handrail kept anyone from falling back down the stairs, and a massive crystal chandelier hung over the base of the steps.

The kid stopped at one of the gleaming, walnut doors, and knocked. He leaned in to listen to the muffled voice from inside. "It's General Abernathy, sir. He called ahead last night."

Another muffled word came from inside, and the young man opened the door and ushered the three of them inside.

The room was apparently Briggs's home office, or something of the sort. A massive oak desk stood in the center of the room, and the walls were lined with bookshelves. The shelves didn't hold many books, but a lot of photos of himself with various celebrities, other politicians, and world leaders, along with various extremely expensive souvenirs. The few books that Santelli could see were all brand new, untouched, and whatever was currently considered "important" in the media and political circles.

It was the most carefully arranged façade that Santelli thought he'd ever seen.

Briggs himself was in his mid-sixties, but his slicked-back hair was still entirely brown. His chiseled face was starting to show some wrinkles around the eyes and mouth, but every bit of his appearance seemed carefully manicured, down to his polo shirt and khakis.

"Well, this is certainly somewhat unexpected, General." Briggs came around the desk with his hand extended, until he glanced at Van Zandt. He stutter-stepped, ever so slightly. Santelli saw the flash of uncertainty, even fear, in his eyes.

"Oh, I don't think it really is, Senator." Abernathy ignored the proffered hand and sat down in one of the leather armchairs

212

across from the desk, pulling a cigar out of his pocket. "I believe you know General Van Zandt."

Briggs tried to play it off. "I… I think we might have met. Some Pentagon function, or maybe a Senate hearing." He stepped back toward the desk as if seeking cover, ignoring Santelli altogether.

"Look, Senator, I'm a busy man and I don't like bullshit, so I'm going to cut to the chase. I know that you hired a team of operators through General Van Zandt here to intervene in a nasty little situation down in Colombia. Not a bad thing, on the surface, especially considering that there's some fishy stuff happening in the background that's keeping the Colombian National Army out of it. Except that some of the strictures you put on the mission raised some eyebrows."

Van Zandt settled in the second chair, while Santelli leaned against the wall by the door with his arms folded. "When you called me last night, Senator, you made some references to events happening on the ground that even Sergeant Major Santelli here—" he jerked a thumb back toward where Santelli was leaning against the door jamb "—hadn't been apprised of. They *were* confirmed later, but that raised the question of just how you'd gotten those details. How did you know that the team had gotten involved with the local resistance, instead of simply following the canned operational plan you handed me?"

Briggs had gone a little pale, but he leaned against the desk and folded his arms. "So, you admit that your little team of contractors has already gone off the reservation?"

Abernathy snorted. "Only a moron would use a canned op plan put out by a politician without question. Only the crown prince of the kingdom of morons would go in to set up an ambush on an insurgent leader without prior reconnaissance. And from what I've been able to glean, that reconnaissance confirmed that there was no follow-up plan at all."

"I don't recall reading you in on the operation, General." Briggs's voice was cold.

Abernathy lit the cigar, daring Briggs to object with his eyes. The senator couldn't meet that stare for very long. "I read myself in. If you're on the Senate Intelligence Committee—which I know you are—you know that there is very little that happens in the special operations world that I *don't* know about. Which also means that I know that there are no other teams in the area, none of our units assigned to look into this little revolutionary problem right on the Colombian border with Venezuela." He kept Briggs pinned with an unblinking stare through a cloud of tobacco smoke. "So, the question once again arises, how did you know the details about events on the ground that are otherwise not being publicized or reported on by American assets?"

Briggs wasn't giving up yet. "You seem to have a theory, General." He leaned back, his arms still folded, looking defiant.

"Oh, I've got more than a theory. I've got call records."

Briggs blanched, but held his peace.

"See, there's an individual down there that my operation's had an eye on for a long time. Hell, we've been trying to kill him for more than a decade. Does the name Diego Galvez ring a bell? No? How about Adolfo Aguirre? Or maybe El Verdugo?" Abernathy inspected his cigar as he blew a cloud of smoke toward the ceiling. "Don't play coy, Senator. I know you know who I'm talking about." He glanced over at Van Zandt. "Nobody's entirely sure what his real name is—he switches aliases fairly often. But we're pretty sure they're all the same guy. He's been active for the last fifteen years, and we've been actively hunting him for the last ten. He's a slippery bastard, though. One of the most cunning terrorists I've ever gone after. He's like a nightmare mashup of Carlos the Jackal and Che Guevara. And he's bound and determined to surpass both of them."

He turned his gaze back on Briggs. "Well, he did get a little sloppy, recently. He's used the same phone for a bit too long. And we've been tracking some of his calls. Still can't quite listen in—there are some legal issues there, for one thing—but we can tell who he calls, and when." He took another long puff, still staring Briggs down. The senator looked suddenly ill, and couldn't meet Abernathy's eyes.

"Care to explain why you've been talking with a terrorist on the Most Wanted list, Senator? We know which numbers are your 'secret' phones, too, by the way." Abernathy watched the senator as he took another deep puff on the cigar. "And we know that you've been using the same phone to talk to your worthless, coke-dealer cousin, too."

Santelli watched the play of emotions cross Briggs's face. Shock turned to fear, to anger, to cunning, and back to fear as he watched Abernathy's face.

"Don't even think about it, Briggs," Abernathy snapped. "I've got copies and copies of copies. And while some of those are in the hands of otherwise disinterested parties who *will* dig into something that smacks that heavily of serious compromise, others are ready to be delivered to political opponents of yours, who don't really give a damn about the ethics of the situation, but would *love* to see you go down."

Briggs's face had gone still and gray. "What do you want? You wouldn't be in here talking to me if you didn't have something in mind."

"I want to know what the game is. I want to know how thoroughly compromised you are. I want to know how deep this goes. What was the deal? Cocaine for a dead rival? What?" Abernathy sat up, leaning forward through the cloud of cigar smoke.

Briggs looked around the room, meeting Van Zandt's and Santelli's eyes, if only for a moment each. He turned back to Abernathy, as if he was trying to judge whether the old man was serious.

He was. And Briggs knew it. He seemed to shrink a little. "It was nothing like that. After I found out about the coup, I started to speak out about it. Some of my constituents were getting a little heated—after all, there's supposed to be a peace deal with the FARC. And that was part of the problem. The situation there is very delicate, and I recognized that. I warned against destroying the peace with the FARC, and antagonizing the Venezuelans.

"Then he reached out to me. I never learned his name. He said he was one of the revolutionaries, and that he was concerned about the way things were going. He said that Clemente was losing his mind, that he didn't really stand for the revolution anymore." Briggs seemed to wilt a little bit more. "He promised that if I managed to quietly take Clemente out of the picture, he could bring things under control. I could hint at some black operation that of course I couldn't talk about openly, score some political points, and he'd at least tone things down for stability's sake."

"And you believed him." Contempt dripped from Abernathy's voice. Contempt, and something more. He didn't believe Briggs for a second.

Santelli suddenly remembered Abernathy's reference to Briggs's "worthless, coke-dealer cousin."

"There's a fine line that statesmen have to walk to make things happen!" Briggs was getting some of his bluster back.

"Oh, right. I forgot about how you never met a dictator you didn't like to bargain with." The old general took another long puff. "It's a nice act, Senator, but don't forget that I know that you've been covering for your cousin's drug-running for a while. I'm sure that has *nothing* to do with this." Abernathy sneered. "Well, here's a slightly less morally compromised bargain for you. Since you *did* hire General Van Zandt's associates to take down a Communist/narco dictator, some good is going to come out of it. So, on the condition that you don't even *think* about or mention said associates *ever* again, and certainly don't initiate any action to retaliate in any way for messing up your little sweetheart deal, then the information about your association with Galvez need never become public." He took another puff. "Believe me, Senator, you're getting off light this way. I can bury you, and I will if you cross me."

Santelli wasn't entirely sure what to think about this little byplay. Abernathy had certainly always struck him as a hard old cuss, but this was a level of ruthlessness that he hadn't quite imagined. And he wasn't sure if he liked it.

On a fundamental level, Carlo Santelli was a simple man, with simple and clear ideas of what constituted justice. And that this corrupt bastard, who had made a deal with a terrorist—and while he certainly hadn't said as much, Santelli suspected that the Blackhearts were supposed to get sold out somewhere along the line as part of this deal—was going to walk, scot free, bugged him. Deeply.

But if there was one thing that he'd learned in almost three decades in the military, most of them as a Staff or Senior NCO, it was that sometimes you had to take the little victories and ignore the little defeat that was the tradeoff.

Briggs stared at Abernathy for a moment, almost as if he were in shock that he—Senator and Important Person that he was—found himself at the mercy of an old soldier who was even more ruthless than he was. But he hadn't gotten where he was by being a complete idiot when it came to this sort of thing. He knew when he'd been outmaneuvered. And he knew what he had to lose if Abernathy wasn't bluffing.

He nodded, but behind the fear and the defeat, there was a little flicker of hate in his eyes as he acquiesced.

There would be a reckoning for this. And from the look in Abernathy's eye as he stood up, he knew it, and he was ready for it.

"Let's go." Without another word to Briggs, Abernathy led the way out of the room. As he headed for the stairs, he pulled a phone out of his pocket and brought it to his ear. "Cole? Get the boys moving. I think John could probably use some help."

CHAPTER 23

Galvez stared at the carnage and cursed viciously, directing every bit of hatred and venom up toward the mercenaries and their bourgeoise allies huddled in the battered farmhouse. It looked almost like half his force was dead, dying, or gravely wounded and moaning in pain.

The American mercenaries had mauled the Green Shirts, badly. It would be a challenge to maintain control in San Tabal now. But perhaps if he had the mutilated bodies of the Americans and their local allies to parade through the streets, the psychological effect would be enough to keep the people in line until they could recoup their numbers.

And he would do just that. Already he was picturing the bloody spectacle, and it raised his spirits as he savored the images. He didn't even know what most of the mercenaries looked like, but that hardly mattered. They wouldn't be all that recognizable, anyway, not when he was through with them.

"Spread out, salvage the machineguns, and lock that building down. No one gets out." He thought a moment, then grabbed Lorenzo by the arm. "Go round up some of the local farmers. Preferably those who have grumbled or caused trouble. We'll give them empty weapons and drive them up through the fields, force the gringos to waste their ammunition." A lot of bullets had been expended that night. Once the resistance was out

219

of ammunition, taking the farmhouse and dragging them out would be easy.

He stared up at the farmhouse again. The eastern sky was getting lighter. The sun would be up in the next half hour. Soon, this would be over.

Then he'd have to deal with Clemente himself. He cursed again, glaring his hate toward the farmhouse.

***

"Hey, Colonel? You see that guy down there, just behind the least-shot-up gun truck?" Wade was squinting over his sights, having taken his turn at one of the southern windows. Since the Green Shirts had fallen back and the fight had died down to the occasional sporadic burst of fire from a distance, the weary and beleaguered mercenaries and their local allies had dropped to fifty percent security.

In reality, that had meant that the Blackhearts were up on guard, while the locals mostly collapsed. Pacheco seemed to be the only one who was alert and ready to fight. The rest—even though they were farmers and used to long hours of hard work, they weren't used to the stress of combat—had just sort of slumped to the floor, staying low and away from the windows and doors, especially since the enemy fire had never *completely* stopped.

Brannigan moved carefully to peer out the window over Wade's shoulder. "I see him."

"Looks important, don't he?" Wade was clearly sighting in on the figure. "Just saw him giving somebody orders."

"Think you can hit him from here?"

Wade snorted. "Easy shot." His finger tightened on the trigger. Unfortunately, right then the man pivoted on his heel and stalked out of sight behind the gun truck. "Fuck."

"Don't sweat it." Brannigan turned away as another shot *snap*ped through the east window to smack more plaster off the west wall. "That's getting a little annoying."

"They're trying to draw us out." Flanagan was set in on that window, standing well back in the shadows. "Some of them might just be idiots shooting for the sake of shooting, but I think they're trying to draw fire."

"What good does that do them?" Curtis patted his Negev, though he only had one drum left for it.

"Gets us to waste ammo. Gets us engaged in one direction so that they can rush us from another. Keeps us pinned down and occupied while they go get mortars or RPGs to flatten the house." Flanagan shrugged without taking his eyes off the jungle outside the window. "Take your pick."

"Fuck that." Wade fired. Even without looking, Brannigan knew that another Green Shirt had just taken a bullet. The big Ranger was pissed, and he was on the hunt. He'd killed at least two more in the last half hour, until they'd learned that standing in the open wasn't a good idea. Even the man that Wade had just spotted, clearly a commander, had still been *behind* the truck, only his head and shoulders visible.

That Wade had still been more than willing to chance the shot wasn't a sign of desperation. It was rage. None of the Blackhearts liked being pinned down, but Wade took it as a personal affront. He was out for blood.

"If we just sit here trying to whittle them down one by one, we'll be here until next week." Burgess shifted his position, squinting as he eyed the trees below, on the west side of the ragged, battered, bloodstained cornfield. "In the meantime, they bottle us up so they can bring in those mortars or RPGs." He spared a glance at Brannigan. "We've got to try something else."

Brannigan mused on it, rubbing his chin. At times like this, he really missed Roger Hancock. Flanagan was a good tactician, as was Wade. But Roger had had a flair for it. And Flanagan was taciturn enough that he was less likely to have a burst of brilliance and just drive ahead with it, the way Hancock might have.

Again, that was nothing against Joe Flanagan. The man was solid—Brannigan wouldn't have chosen him as Hancock's successor otherwise. But his style was just different, and right then, Brannigan wanted to have Hancock with them.

But Roger Hancock was in a shallow grave in the Altiplano, and would never proffer an unorthodox solution again.

"All right." He couldn't say it was genius, but it might work. "They think they've got us cornered."

"Uh, they *do* have us cornered, Colonel."

"Shut up, Kevin. So far as they know, we're just mercs. They've got to know that we're not locals at this point." Brannigan scratched the stubble on his chin as he thought. "We need to make them think that we've bolted, that either the locals abandoned us, or we abandoned the locals." He looked up at the ceiling. It had been a long day, with a lot of fighting, and he was tired. His brain wasn't quite firing on all cylinders. He glanced over at Pacheco. "Who are they going to be more likely to want dead first?"

Pacheco snorted. "Probably you. They'll figure that with you out of the picture, they can deal with the people of San Tabal at their leisure."

Brannigan frowned. That complicated things a little. "Okay. Here's what we're going to do…"

***

Galvez paced restlessly. Sporadic gunfire continued to echo across the valley, but his Green Shirts were slow getting into position. And Lorenzo still wasn't back with his cannon fodder. He chewed the inside of his cheek as his impatient rage mounted.

"*Commandante!*" He didn't know the young Green Shirt's name, but Galvez swung on the man abruptly, making the skinny former ELN recruit stagger back a half step.

"What?"

The boy—he couldn't be much older than sixteen or seventeen—gulped. "Some of them are trying to run, *Commandante*." He pointed up toward the farmhouse, where some commotion had broken out.

Galvez hurried around the back of the gun truck, careful to stay in some cover, just in case. Sure enough, there was some shooting going on up there, and a voice was raised, bellowing in English.

222

"You pussy sons of bitches! Get your asses back here!" Another burst of fire rattled out, aimed up toward the top of the ridge, away from most of the Green Shirts.

Are the Americans and the locals fighting each other? He hardly dared think it, but a wolfish grin split his features as he watched what was happening. *The farmers are leaving the Americans to their fate. Perfect. I might not even need Lorenzo's hostages.*

"Fuck!" The rage in the American's voice was palpable.

You shouldn't have crossed me. Now I'm going to kill you and drag your corpses by their heels through the streets of San Tabal.

All thought of his plan to draw the Americans out and make them waste their ammunition supplies vanished in a wave of eagerness and bloodlust. "Suppressing fire! Get in there and finish them off!"

***

Brannigan paused as he topped the ridge, panting and soaked in sweat. It wasn't just the lack of sleep—they hadn't eaten or had much water in a while, either.

He turned back, peering through the trees, then scanned the slope below them. The sun was up, but the vegetation was still thick enough that it was hard to see more than a couple of yards. Flanagan and Wade joined him.

"Curtis missed his calling. He should be an actor." Wade sank to a knee, bracing his other foot against a tree. The slope was fairly steep there. "Think we're far enough outside the cordon?"

"We'll see." Brannigan kept it short. "Keep low. Move fast."

Flanagan nodded and turned east, paralleling the ridgeline above and slipping through the vegetation as quickly and quietly as the terrain allowed.

***

Curtis turned back down the slope, leaning into his Negev and sighting through the open door. Down in the prone, he found himself in a similar situation to the one Wade had faced earlier.

The angle of the terraces and the slope meant that he didn't have a great shot.

"That was convincing." Pacheco was on the other side of the door, barricaded on the jamb and watching the Green Shirts moving down below.

"Well, I can't say I'm all that happy about being the sacrificial lamb." Curtis grimaced and got up on a knee, jamming one of the Negev's bipods against the doorjamb to brace the gun. *Now* he could see the enemy. Which meant he could hit the enemy. "Just 'cause I'm short. Fuckers."

"It does mean that we have a machinegun here in the house, so I am not going to complain." Pacheco craned his neck to see a little better, and then ducked as a renewed storm of machinegun fire hammered the house from below. "Especially since they haven't hesitated to take advantage of the situation we just played out for them." He looked over his shoulder, and Curtis followed his gaze. They had about half a dozen men with rifles, with about three magazines left for each.

Hurry up, Colonel.

***

Flanagan had gotten about fifty yards before he had to stop, freezing in place and slowly easing himself down to the ground. He couldn't see the enemy yet, but he could hear low voices speaking Spanish and the crunch of footsteps in the undergrowth.

There hadn't been time to warn the others, but Brannigan had still been within line of sight, so Flanagan had to trust that they'd taken cover as well. He peered over his rifle's sights as he listened to the Green Shirts get closer.

He had no doubt that these were, in fact, Green Shirts. After what had already happened on the other side of the ridge, there was no way that any of the locals would be stupid enough to get this close to Galán's farm before things quieted down.

Flanagan had seen some pretty insane things in warzones over the years, but it still seemed unlikely.

Ideally, they would have kept pushing, getting more distance from the farmhouse before circling around to hit the Green Shirts from the flank. But their allies—not to mention Curtis—didn't have that kind of time. And the deception had required the enemy to see them running, so there was no hiding the fact that they'd escaped.

The footsteps were getting closer. Flanagan gritted his teeth. Over years of combat tours and dozens of firefights, he'd never set a rifle to "auto." Aimed fire was his preferred method of engagement. But as the Green Shirts closed the distance and he still couldn't see them, he knew he was going to have to break his own rule.

Flipping the selector to "A," he leveled the rifle at about knee height. The Green Shirts were only a handful of yards away.

Pulling the stock firmly back into his shoulder to control the recoil, he opened fire. The Galil shredded the vegetation in front of him with a chattering, rattling roar, slightly higher-pitched and faster than an AK.

Bullets chopped into flesh and bone, barely three yards away. Screams erupted, nearly drowned out by the rifle's reports, and at least one body went tumbling down the hill. Flanagan caught a glimpse of the falling man as he ceased fire, the body fetching up against a tree trunk with a sickening *crunch.*

At least one was still moaning and screaming in pain just ahead. Flanagan rose to a knee as Brannigan moved past him, a little higher up the hillside. The terrain was pretty restrictive, which meant that this fight was going to get really interesting, really fast.

Brannigan fired a burst of his own at something or someone ahead in the trees Flanagan couldn't see. He tried to dash forward, but almost lost his footing as the rock underfoot rolled away down the slope as he put his boot on it with the next step.

I hate the jungle. He caught himself, keeping his rifle up and ready, and scrambled a little higher, his muzzle tracking in on the groans.

Three bodies were crumpled on the hillside just ahead, two obviously dead and the third not long for the world. The screams and moans were fading, and the dying man's breathing was getting faster and shallower as he bled out. Flanagan moved close enough to kick the M16 away from the man's limp hands, but the dying man didn't even seem to notice. He let out a last, gurgling rattle of breath, and died.

But then something else moved up ahead, thrashing through the brush.

Flanagan hesitated just long enough to confirm that it wasn't Brannigan. The big man was still up above him, braced against a tree, searching for targets over his sights. Whoever was out there was not a friendly, and was coming closer.

As much as he hated engaging what he couldn't see, the rules of jungle warfare were unforgiving. He leveled his Galil and ripped off the last of the magazine, holding the barrel down as he pinned the trigger to the rear. The muzzle flash flickered and stuttered as he raked the hillside with 5.56 fire, shredding more vegetation, spitting splinters and bits of bark off tree boles, and tearing holes through the next couple of Green Shirts who were rushing toward the screams.

The rifle *click*ed. Like the Kalashnikov it was partially based on, the Galil didn't have a bolt hold-open. He ripped the mag out, let it fall, and rocked in another, racking the bolt as Brannigan opened fire up above him, and Burgess pushed up downhill to his right.

Flanagan kept moving. The hillside was almost too steep to move from tree to tree, but he did the best he could.

He found the bodies in another few steps. They must have been moving close to each other. He'd taken both with one burst. One lay with puckered, red-soaked holes in his shirt tracking from his armpit up to his clavicle. The other had taken the last of the rounds through the throat and face.

Both were still twitching, but they weren't breathing anymore.

Gunfire roared and thundered on the other side of the ridge, but the Blackhearts didn't encounter any more Green Shirts as they swept along the military crest. It seemed like Curtis and their local allies were keeping the enemy's attention.

Now they just had to move fast enough to keep their friends from being slaughtered. The weight of numbers was still on the Green Shirts' side.

They pushed another hundred yards before turning back up toward the top of the ridgeline. It took longer than it felt like it should—the terrain and the jungle were implacable enemies. But by the time they came over the ridge, they were clear of the beaten zone centered on the beleaguered house.

The jungle was a hell of an obstacle, but in this case, it also worked in their favor. Brannigan signaled to spread out, and a ragged skirmish line with Bianco at the far left—closest to the house—descended toward the enemy that was pouring fire at their friends, still concealed and undetected.

The Blackhearts held their fire at first, as they got closer and closer. It wasn't hard to find the Green Shirts—they were advancing toward the house, standing up and pouring fire into the rapidly-disintegrating cinderblock. The noise alone was enough to guide the mercenaries in.

Finally, Brannigan passed the nod. Bianco opened up first. The others joined in a split second later.

It wasn't a Mad Minute. They didn't have the ammo for that. It was more like a Mad Ten Seconds. But that ten seconds of hell did the trick.

The entire skirmish line opened up on the Green Shirts' flank from about ten yards away, pouring a total of a couple hundred rounds into the remaining fifteen or so Green Shirts that had just reached the edge of the cleared yard around the house. Muzzle blasts spat thin smoke and flame and bullets turned leaves into flying green confetti before smashing through guts, ribs, lungs, hearts, throats, and skulls. Galvez's assault force was torn to bloody, rapidly cooling meat in a matter of seconds, the bodies collapsing and falling on top of each other as bullets passed through one man and into another.

Then they drove past the bodies and through the jungle, staying clear of the open ground, Javakhishvili, Brannigan, and Jenkins reloading as they went.

They continued to sweep down the east side, staying in the jungle. Ahead, Flanagan thought he heard someone thrashing through the brush, but the sounds were receding, not advancing.

The fire from the base of the hill, on the road, had slackened somewhat, possibly due to shock as the Green Shirts on the gun trucks realized that their maneuver element had just been wiped out in a handful of seconds. Either that, or at least two of their up-guns had gone dry at the same time, and they were reloading.

The downhill slope helped the rapidity of the Blackhearts' advance, to the point that Hank and Jenkins both started to outrun the rest of the skirmish line and had to dial it back.

Brannigan signaled again, pointing to the southeast. They needed to move to the right a little farther. They wouldn't do anything for their besieged comrades if they got flanked. So, they pushed out farther, making damned good and sure they were outside of any cordon the Green Shirts had gotten in place before sunrise.

The jungle, of course, fought them every step of the way. And the terrain wasn't great, either. Soon Flanagan noticed that they were getting crowded back toward the west and the cornfields, by a combination of thicker and thicker vegetation and the increasingly broken terrain. Galán's farm was apparently bordered on the east by a sharp finger with an even deeper draw on the other side. And that finger was a tangled mess of vines, undergrowth, and tight stands of trees.

Of course, that probably meant that the Green Shirts hadn't penetrated far to the east, either.

He heard voices ahead, but it took a second to realize that one of them was someone down on the road yelling at the half-dozen men in the jungle, much closer and driving uphill. That realization hit almost at the same time he came out of some denser undergrowth and almost ran into the Green Shirt out on their left flank.

Fortunately, Flanagan was already on the hunt, his rifle held ready and off safe. The Green Shirt was puffing, his G3 held in slack hands, his head down as he struggled through the vegetation and up the hill.

He never had a chance.

Flanagan had left his Galil's selector on "A," just because of the short sightlines and the need for a glorified brush-cutter in close-in jungle combat. But with his muzzle barely three feet from his opponent, all it took was a single stroke of the trigger. The shot was deafeningly loud—not because it was any louder than the rest of the firefight that had gone down already, but simply because nobody had been expecting it right then and there.

And it cored out the Green Shirt's heart. He crumpled where he was as Flanagan shifted toward the dim figure just beyond him, letting rip with another long, roaring burst into the weeds.

He'd moved out to the flank, probing the bush along the steep finger to their right, so he was on the outer flank. And when he opened fire, the rest of the Blackhearts did, too. More bullets swept through the jungle in a scythe of death that tore through flesh as easily as vegetation.

Bianco held his fire. He was waiting for more important targets. And this little skirmish was over quickly.

"Up!" Brannigan had just reloaded, but that wasn't the only reason he called out. They had to push. Speed and ferocious violence were their only hope at this point. Flanagan drove forward, still careful to watch his flank and any bit of cover he could see ahead of him, while maintaining the line with Gomez on his left.

They swept down through the last bit of jungle and burst out onto the road with a stuttering storm of gunfire. Three more Green Shirts went down, sprawled in their own blood on the road.

Two more had ducked behind the rear gun truck and tried to return fire, but they were shooting blind around the taillight and over the bed, while the gunner tried to swivel around to bring his M60 to bear. Bianco was ahead of him though, and blasted him onto his ass in the bed, his torso ripped open and blood splashed against the shattered glass of the truck's rear window.

More return fire came their way as the Green Shirts realized they were under attack from behind. In the meantime, Curtis, Pacheco, and the rest of their allies up at the battered farmhouse redoubled their own fire, now that the suppressive fire from below had all but ceased.

Bianco hadn't quite come out on the road itself, Flanagan saw. He had popped out on the first terrace, about five yards back from the road and at least four feet above it. And he had a hell of a sector of fire from there.

Dropping prone behind the machinegun, Bianco went to work. In long, ten-to-twelve-round bursts, he raked the column of gun trucks from back to front and back again. Glass shattered, metal sparked, and blood flew as he dumped the last of his ammo into what remained of the Green Shirts' base of fire.

Flanagan raced across the road and into the low ground on the other side, snapping his rifle up and hammering a burst at one of the Green Shirts crouched behind one of two technicals in the center of the fields. He'd forgotten that the weapon was on auto for a second, and the recoil kind of got away from him, the rounds climbing into the body of the truck after the first two. Those had hit, but not fatally, and he ducked as the wounded man sprayed a desperate burst of 5.56 at him in reply.

Then Gomez shot the Green Shirt through the throat, and that was over.

The technicals at the front of the column were starting to pull away, bodies piled into the beds. One still had a gunner up, and he tried to spray bullets down the road at the Blackhearts, but a half dozen rounds knocked him off his feet and on top of another Green Shirt, who shoved him off to fall out of the bed and flop onto the road.

230

Then there was no one left to shoot. The echoes of gunfire died away, replaced with the moans of the wounded as a thin, misty rain began to fall.

CHAPTER 24

Galán's farm was in ruins. His crop was smashed, burned, and shredded by gunfire, stalks flattened under corpses leaking blood and other bodily fluids into the soil. His house was shattered, the walls holed in several hundred places by bullets, every window smashed. The interior looked like a hurricane had hit it, the floor and the furniture strewn with plaster dust, broken glass, and bits of pulverized concrete.

Of the six policemen that Quintana and Brannigan had gathered, four were still alive. By some miracle—and most likely because of the sheer speed and ferocity of their counterattack—none of the Blackhearts had been killed. A few minor shrapnel wounds were overshadowed by the pain of exhaustion, dehydration, and numerous cuts, scrapes, gouges, and battered joints from negotiating the terrain and the jungle itself.

Brannigan, Lara, and Pacheco stood on the top terrace, just outside the house, surveying the bodies strewn across the cornfield and the road.

"How many men did the Green Shirts ever have in total?" Brannigan turned to Lara and Quintana. The former policeman was covered in blood, having been clipped by a bullet through his right trapezius as well as having his scalp torn by flying glass as a burst of rifle fire had shattered the window he'd been peering out of. "Did you ever get a rough count?"

Quintana winced as he squinted against the misting rain. "I don't think anyone ever got a complete count. And they weren't exactly posting how many men they had. But our best estimates were less than two hundred."

Brannigan squinted as he scanned the carnage below, adding in his head. "Joe, how many do you think you guys killed at Ballesteros's house?"

Flanagan thought about it for a second. "Maybe a dozen? Twenty at the outside?"

Brannigan nodded as he kept adding up the last several engagements they'd had with the Green Shirts. "Were they actively recruiting at all?"

"Yes. Successfully, too. Mostly among the street gangs in the city."

"So, even on an optimistic assessment, with as many as we killed here, we might have cut their numbers by... what? A third?"

"Maybe half." Quintana sounded a little hopeful, but there was still a note of doubt in his voice.

"Don't underestimate the effect that word of this will have on the rest." Pacheco sounded a little more sure of himself than Quintana. "Even if the thugs flocked to them—and there is never any shortage of such people—and if Galvez goes to great lengths to frighten his surviving men out of talking about it—and he will—word will get around, and many of even the most vicious will start to look for an escape plan. You rarely have to kill all of them. Kill just enough, and the rest will scatter."

"The question is, how many is enough?" Brannigan had fought insurgents all around the world over the past thirty years. He'd seen many hard lessons driven home in blood and fire. And seen just as many of them ignored.

One of the hardest was the fact that no two insurgencies are ever exactly the same, and by definition, they're hard as hell to eradicate.

"How dependent are they on the leadership?" He was still thinking through contingencies and courses of action. They'd dealt the Green Shirts a severe blow here, but as long as Clemente, Galvez, and possibly others were still at large—and still in control of San Tabal, even if only through terror—then this wasn't over.

"More than FARC or ELN." Pacheco had clearly done some study, even as a relative outsider. "Clemente isn't the type to plan for a legacy. He's a creature of appetite and pride. He'd probably sooner see San Tabal burned to the ground at his death than plan for a successor. Galvez is more cunning. He'll have contingency plans, though once again, they probably don't allow for his own capture or death. He's the outlaw hero, the great revolutionary. He wants to see himself on top of the revolution, not a martyr for it."

"So, if we take them out, then at least we can throw the Green Shirts into enough chaos that we might be able to secure the city and the surrounding farms, drive them back into the jungle, and maybe even get the situation shifted to a state where we can get Bogota to intervene."

Pacheco nodded. "It seems like the most workable plan at the moment. We should continue to recruit police and concerned citizens as we go, of course." He gestured to the bloody mess below and around them. "We have more weapons and ammunition to go around, now."

Brannigan cracked his knuckles. "Let's get them divvied up and get moving. They're off balance for now. We need to move quickly, before they can regroup."

***

Galvez hadn't told Clemente about his fallback camp. He'd found the cavern back during his days working with the FARC. An operation had gone bad, and he had fled into the jungle, pursued by the Colombian National Army. He'd almost fallen into the tiny hole that had led into the cavern, and as the helicopters had come closer, he'd wormed his way into the dark. He'd marked where it was, and over time, as he'd come in and out of Colombia in the service of The Revolution, he'd turned it into a fallback position, one that he could even get to if he had to run from any of the other northern countries of South America. Now, while it had always been his personal hiding place, it was the best place to take his surviving Green Shirts.

He'd considered trying to weed out a few of them, the ones he wasn't sure of, on the way, but his assault force had been whittled down to a handful of fighters. He'd need them all in the days ahead, as much as he hated it.

Rage and hatred burned in him as he paced the cavern floor. This entire plan had gone terribly wrong. That damned American had turned on him. *I'll make sure he dies, too. Someday. He'll beg me for mercy before the end.*

Despite the fury that made him want to strike out, to kill, to crush, to burn, a plan was slowly forming in his head. The American mercenaries were still few in number. He'd underestimated their aggressiveness. He wouldn't make that mistake again. He had stocks of explosives secreted in the hills around San Tabal. He'd draw them into an ambush, then blow them all to bloody pieces.

But first he had to eliminate Clemente. He didn't have a great reason, but he was beyond reason at that point. He'd set all of this in motion to kill Clemente and take over. He had to finish that.

He continued to pace, his fevered mind racing to find a way to snatch victory out of this bloody defeat.

***

San Tabal was eerily silent as the morning eased toward noon, the rain slowing before it stopped, though the clouds remained, settling atop the peaks of the hills.

Brannigan, Wade, Flanagan, and Pacheco watched from the hillside above. "Looks like everybody's waiting for the other shoe to drop."

"I'm sure they are." Brannigan peered through a pair of binoculars that Pacheco had brought along, scanning the empty streets. A face showed in a window for a split second, then disappeared. "Did the Green Shirts have any central positions within the city that they might have fallen back to?"

Lara pointed. "The police station, there on that hill, has been their primary headquarters. Clemente himself has generally stayed in the mayor's house, there." His voice turned even grimmer. "They hanged Jurado outside it, in the plaza, after forcing him to watch as they executed his friends and family."

The police station, in its elevated position about halfway up the hill from the plaza, was easy to pick out, especially since it had the Green Shirts' flag, red and yellow separated by a slash of black with a red star in the yellow, flying above it.

Clemente's stolen mansion wasn't that hard to pick out, either. The fact that Clemente had more of the red, yellow, and black flags dangling from the balcony above the plaza helped, but it was also the largest structure in view, as well.

He scanned the deserted streets and quiet houses. There was a tension on the air, a tension that he could feel even from up there on the hillside. Like he'd said, it was the sense that everyone was waiting for the other shoe to drop. The Green Shirts were hunkered down, waiting for the Blackhearts and their allies to come after them following the slaughter in the mountains, and the locals were hunkered down waiting for either the collateral damage that would come from an assault on the city, or for the Green Shirts to take out their rage on the local populace.

He'd seen it happen before. Mostly in Africa. Those who fancied themselves warriors, but who lacked the moral ethos of protection of the innocent, or the training to stand against those with greater skill and firepower, usually came away from getting their asses kicked with a great deal of wounded pride. And without that moral ethos, wounded pride was often salved by proving they were still "stronger." And it's easy to prove greater strength when beating on people who can't defend themselves.

Brannigan had seen it all too many times, and he hoped to keep it from happening again here in San Tabal. But that meant they'd have to move fast. And that could present its own problems. Moving fast in urban combat was not always a recipe for success.

Or survival.

"Joe, you get the mayor's house. Wade, take the police station." He turned to Quintana. "Pick one of your most trustworthy cops to go with each element. They'll pick out others—cops or civilians who know how to use guns—and recruit them along the way." He glanced at the weary, dirty band of mercenaries. "We're going to need numbers to carry this through. The ten of us aren't going to be enough."

Quintana nodded. "What about me?"

"You'll come with me to grab more, in areas that aren't along Wade's and Flanagan's route. Again, we're going to need as many as we can get, and we'll act as a mobile reserve. If one of those two teams gets in trouble, we'll be their backup."

"And Lara?" Quintana glanced over his shoulder at where Pacheco was keeping an eye on the farmers, all of whom were armed, but were still holding back.

Brannigan followed Quintana's gaze. Lara looked tired and grim, as if he were already feeling the burden that he was going to have to take on as a part of this plan. He would be even more of a target if this worked—the Green Shirts probably had allies elsewhere in the country, and they would remember the man who returned to the office of mayor after overthrowing the "revolution."

He'd be looking over his shoulder for the rest of his life.

Welcome to the club, buddy.

"I'd be inclined to say that if he wants to be a leader, he's going to need to take some of the risks, but on the other hand, unless you've got a replacement handy when the new mayor gets killed before even entering office, we're probably going to have to keep him back here, out of harm's way." He glanced blandly at Quintana, waiting for the other man to suggest another option. Like perhaps making *him* mayor, should Lara not survive…

But that suggestion didn't come. Quintana watched Lara for another moment. "No, best to keep him here. If he gets killed in the attack, we will never be able to get the city stabilized in time."

238

"He's that respected?" Brannigan was feeling Quintana out a little with that question, and he suddenly thought that the other man was quite well aware. Perhaps the dullard dishrag of a yes-man cop was more than he appeared.

"He *was* the mayor for many years." Quintana nodded. "Yes, the people will rally to him, if he stands in the plaza and announces that the days of the Green Shirts are over." He looked Brannigan in the eye. "I will follow him." He smiled crookedly, and Brannigan thought it was the most genuine expression he'd seen on the man's face. "After all, if he is mayor, he will be more of a target than the deputy police chief."

Brannigan decided to let that go. It wasn't his decision, and it wasn't his city or country. If they kept Lara alive, it would be his worry, his decision, going forward.

"All right." He looked around at the other Blackhearts. "One more push, gentlemen. I'll see you on the other side."

CHAPTER 25

Wade was by nature a grounded, down-to-earth guy. He didn't get creeped out. He preferred to creep other people out, mainly with matter-of-fact expressions of his complete comfort with violence, delivered with an icy, unblinking gaze that could have given Roger Hancock a run for his money in the "basilisk stare" department.

But the empty silence on the streets of San Tabal was giving him the willies.

He was on point—Flanagan and Gomez had teamed up again, so he figured he was one of the best fieldcraft men in his element, between him and Burgess. Plus, he just preferred to be on point himself. Behind him, Burgess, Bianco, and Jenkins led about a dozen local cops and volunteers who had joined them along the way, mostly recruited by Contreras, one of Quintana's cops who had survived the fight on Galán's farm. They were spread out in a rough tactical column, split along both sides of the street as they worked their way around toward the police station.

He and Flanagan had finally resorted to Rock, Paper, Scissors to decide who got which target. The police station was probably the more vital target, but the mayor's house was where they'd probably find Clemente. Flanagan was a quiet, unassuming dude most of the time, but he still had that killer instinct and didn't want to just let another Blackheart take the big prize.

It's the little things.

Movement drew Wade's eye, and he flicked his Galil's muzzle toward it, only to see the curtain behind the barred window slip back into place. He didn't relax, but kept the rifle up, covering that window as he continued to move up the street, maintaining as much awareness of every other angle he couldn't close off as he did. Urban combat is a complex dance of multiple angles and threats that could appear at close range without warning.

And with how quiet San Tabal was, he fully expected one of those threats to appear at any moment. It was as if the city was holding its breath, waiting for the ambush to kick off.

He had to expand his scan ahead as he continued down the street, but he kept coming back to that curtain. For the most part, he was keeping his weapon and eyes trained on the other side of the street, while Burgess covered his side ahead of him. He still had to be careful of openings on his side, but it was easier to react and engage with a little distance.

The curtain moved again. His Galil rose until he was peering just over the sights, his finger resting on the trigger guard. The selector was already on "R."

But he lowered it as he registered the small face of a kid who couldn't be more than about five, peering out from behind the curtain. No target. It didn't mean no threat—he'd certainly been places where the bad guys had had no qualms about using little kids as human shields—but he wasn't going to smoke a little boy just because.

If the threat did materialize, he'd go so far as to kill everyone in the house if that was what it took to neutralize it, and sleep like a baby afterward. But he wasn't going to deliberately just murder a kid.

They kept moving. The cops and volunteers were a little too bunched up, but the Blackhearts in the lead maintained as careful movement and constant, three-hundred-sixty-degree security as they went.

He paused, holding up a fist, as he reached the alley that would form their last covered and concealed position before the police station. He could see the compound up ahead, just around the next bend in the street.

The police station was a walled compound with a white plastered, blocky building with the almost ubiquitous red tile roof standing above the outer wall, which was also whitewashed plaster over cinderblock, topped with barbed wire. The closed gate faced the street, about two-thirds of the way down the wall.

Wade got most of his assault force into the alley, except for Jenkins and Bianco, who set in behind another house across the street, just in case.

Wade leaned out just far enough to get a decent look at the compound and the gate. Not only did the certainly locked gate appear to be steel, painted black and rusting a little where the paint had chipped over time, he was sure that any Green Shirts who were holed up in the police station would have every weapon they possessed aimed in at it. It was the only real way in, and that made it a death trap.

He wasn't inclined to go in that way. If he'd had his way, and a platoon of Rangers with him, he'd hit the wall with a Carl Gustaf and go in through the hole. But he didn't have a Carl G, or a breaching charge, or even a satchel of C4 or Semtex. He didn't even have any grenades. For whatever reason, the Green Shirts they'd looted after the killing out on the farm hadn't had any explosives on them. It had seemed weird to him, but they had to make do with what they had, which wasn't much.

Wade's icy blue eyes scanned the street and the intersecting alleyways, looking for a solution. Going over was a possibility, but that barbed wire was going to present a problem, and without a serious base of fire to keep the bad guys inside pinned down, they'd get slaughtered as they climbed over.

Then his eyes lit on a big panel truck parked just down the street, before moving to the T-intersection almost directly across from the gate. He had an idea…

***

Flanagan was taking a somewhat different tack to Wade's. He was still moving through the streets as quietly and stealthily as he could, but he only had Gomez, Curtis, and Hank with him. Pacheco and his handful of San Tabal police had split off early, rounding up more volunteers. They would stage around the plaza, waiting for the signal to move in.

Flanagan and his element would provide that signal. Mainly when the shooting started.

The mayor's mansion and the central plaza were in the middle of the old part of town, most of which was surprisingly open, though not as affluent as some of the old colonial plantation towns. The buildings were mostly solid and well-built, but they were showing their age. The plaster was cracking or chipped off entirely, a few of the roofing tiles had fallen to the street. A few trees grew in pots on the sidewalk, but the place wasn't exactly landscaped.

Somewhat to his surprise, given what Quintana and Lara had said about the Green Shirts' terror campaign, Flanagan didn't see bodies hanging from lampposts or lying in the streets. That must have happened elsewhere in the city.

It could be surprising, sometimes, how little it takes to terrorize a population that isn't prepared to fight back.

The four Blackhearts had a straight shot at the low wall that surrounded the loading area at the back of the house, leading into the service entrance. Flanagan looked around at the others, who were all on security, watching the roofs and windows above as well as the alleyway behind them. "Ready?"

He got three nods. "Let's go."

Almost as one, the four of them got to their feet and dashed for the wall. Speed was now their security.

The wall itself only stood about four feet high, almost more of a fence than a wall. Rifles snapped to either side as they crossed the street on the way toward the rear of the mansion, but there was no opposition out on the streets.

Inside, however…

Glass shattered as gunfire roared out from the second floor. A voice was raised in alarm as bullets *snap*ped over the Blackhearts' heads, the shooter not quite leading them enough.

244

The rounds kicked dirt and fragments of the pavement into the air behind them.

The four of them flattened themselves against the wall, weapons out and up, Curtis leaning out just far enough to return fire, smacking plaster, glass, and bits of window frame back in the shooter's face. The incoming fire died away.

Flanagan had paused at the base of the wall for only a second. He popped up, cleared the loading area with his muzzle, and then vaulted the wall, almost kicking Hank in the head—the younger man had taken cover a little too close. Gomez was right behind him.

The two of them held on the service entrance and the single window next to it just long enough for Hank and Bianco to get over and join them. Then they were moving on the door.

The window was dark on the other side, but that didn't mean much, so they were all careful not to silhouette themselves as they passed. That meant some creative movement, but they were at the door in a second. Curtis stepped out, kicked in the door, then turned out of the way as Gomez, Flanagan, and Hank rolled in.

They entered into a darkened kitchen, with a large storage room immediately off to the left. Both were currently deserted, but Flanagan could hear shouts and footsteps from upstairs. Between the fire from the window and the crash of the door getting kicked in, the Green Shirts in the house knew they had to counterattack quickly.

Flanagan and Hank had gone left, while Gomez had gone right, Curtis flowing in behind them to take up security on the door itself. His Negev would be of only limited use inside—they had no intention of just mowing down everyone in the house—but he couldn't just stay outside, either.

Boots clattered on the stairs nearby, and Flanagan turned to train his weapon on the door as a silhouette with a rifle in his hands appeared in it.

The Green Shirt clearly hadn't been trained. He came through the door alone, and with his rifle still pointed off to one side.

Better than if he just came in spraying, but too bad for him.

Flanagan and Gomez both shot the Green Shirt at almost the same moment. He stopped dead in his tracks as the 5.56 rounds tore through his torso, then Gomez's follow up shot snapped his head back and he collapsed in the doorway.

If any more of his compatriots had been following him in, they changed their minds really quick. The door stayed open and empty, and the thunder of the reports had deadened the Blackhearts' hearing enough that Flanagan couldn't be sure if he heard movement on the other side or not.

He didn't want to risk going through that doorway, though. If there were Green Shirts on the other side, they were probably crouched down as close to the near wall as possible, their weapons pointed right at the door.

Keeping his Galil trained on the open door for as long as he could, Flanagan turned and stepped through the door into the storage room, pivoting to clear the corner as he did so, then sweeping back as Hank followed him through. The shelves were stacked, and there were all too many hiding places where a Green Shirt could be crouched weapon pointed and waiting, but no targets immediately presented themselves.

With a nod to Hank, he started to move up, Galil held ready, careful to check each angle as he moved through the standing shelves, stacked with boxes of every foodstuff that had probably come into San Tabal since just before the coup. As per, the Communist revolutionaries would eat like kings, while the people they were supposedly "liberating" struggled and starved.

History might not quite repeat itself, but it sure comes close.

The two of them reached the end of the rows of shelves, and found another door leading deeper into the house. It was still closed, but they moved quickly toward it, Hank covering the door while Flanagan reached for the doorknob.

He wondered a little that no more Green Shirts had tried to make entry through that door to flank them. They had to know the layout of the mansion by then. While there hadn't been much evidence that these thugs ever really trained or drilled, by the time they knew that the resistance was coming for them, they had to have figured out that some kind of preparation was needed.

But the answer reached his ears a moment later, as he grasped the doorknob and threw the door open. The sound was a bit muffled, but just then a storm of gunfire erupted out by the front, near the plaza.

The local volunteers had arrived and were attacking the mansion. Clemente was probably throwing every remaining Green Shirt he had at the front door.

Hank went through the door, going right. Flanagan went left.

The Green Shirts had fallen back to the corner of the hallway, all the way to the left, and barricaded on the corner itself. Muzzle flashes flickered in Flanagan's face, but he was moving fast, dashing toward the corner and pivoting as he went, already answering the Green Shirts with a devastating storm of rapid fire, bullets chewing into the plaster and forcing them back, as he hoped that he was fast enough to keep Hank from getting shot in the back of the head.

***

Wade was starting to feel the urgency. He could hear the shooting down by the plaza and the mansion. Flanagan had already opened the ball. The Green Shirts in the police station were going to be even more alert now. But it had taken some time to get that big truck around the block and pointed at the gate. They'd taken some sporadic fire from the upper windows, but nothing accurate enough to worry about.

The Green Shirts knew what was coming. Or at least they thought they did.

Wade made sure the truck was aimed about as well as it could be, put it in gear and sent it surging toward the gate as he made himself as small as possible behind the engine block. If he'd had any other option, he'd have tried to wedge the accelerator and bail, but there wasn't time, and there was no guarantee that it wouldn't have swerved off course or simply stalled out. So, he was riding this train all the way to the end of the line.

Bullets smacked into the hood and the windshield. Glass rained down on him, and then the truck hit the gate.

The impact was brutal. Even braced as he was, he was thrown against the steering wheel as the shock slammed his teeth together painfully. For a moment, he couldn't be sure if it had worked, or if he'd just put himself in the middle of a catastrophic vehicular accident for nothing.

But while he stomped on the gas and the engine roared, something creaked, groaned, then shrieked horribly and the truck suddenly surged forward, bouncing up and over as the gate was torn off its hinges and the bar holding it closed broke. The gate folded inward and the truck slanted upward as it went over the broken barrier, then one of the front tires dropped over the edge and stuck. More bullets poured into the front of the truck, but the engine block was absorbing most of the punishment. For the moment.

He kicked the driver's side door open and bailed, dragging his Galil with him, hoping that Bianco hadn't picked that side to lay down covering fire.

He hadn't. The Negev opened up on the other side of the cab, hammering the front of the police station with bullets, as Wade dove for the dubious cover of one of the handful of green and white Toyota Hiluxes parked against the wall. He waited for more fire to reach out to punch through the flimsy body of the pickup, but Bianco was playing his Negev like a concert pianist, moving from window to window, putting a burst through each seemingly at random. He wasn't wasting ammo on the wall. Every round was calculated to keep the Green Shirts' heads down.

Taking a split second to catch his breath, Wade got his feet under him and checked that the rest of his assault force had come through the gate. Burgess and Jenkins had led their recruits along the wall, protected from the police station itself, while Wade and Bianco had gotten the truck ready. Now they were moving through the wrecked gateway, picking their way over the smashed, twisted ruin of the gate itself and squeezing between the wall— and the jagged remnants of the hinges—and the side of the truck. The truck itself had come to rest at a bit of an angle to the police station, so it provided some cover.

Wade got Jenkins' attention. He'd have preferred Burgess, Flanagan, or Gomez, but Jenkins was there, and he'd have to do. "On me." Getting to his feet, he sprinted across the dirt parking lot toward the front door.

Bianco saw him move and shifted fire to the windows on the right. Unfortunately, that meant that one of the Green Shirts on the left stuck his head up, saw the figures in tiger stripe cammies running toward the front door, and sprayed fire out through the shattered window.

Fortunately, he wasn't exactly aiming, and his position wasn't great, either. The muzzle climbed fast, the bullets quickly drilling holes in the sky. He stopped shooting altogether as Wade put a burst through the window on the move. It wasn't accurate by any means, but it did what it was meant to do.

Then he was at the door. He didn't bother trying to stack up, even though Jenkins was still a pace or two behind him. He just lowered his shoulder and hit it like a battering ram.

The realization that this could be a really bad idea if the door was barred or otherwise barricaded hit just before he did. But the Green Shirts had apparently been banking on terror, firepower, and the barred front gate to protect them. The door splintered and slammed inward.

Wade had overbalanced a little, and he went down on one shoulder as he went through the door. *FuckfuckfuckfuckFUCK!* He rolled to one side as he tried to kick his way out of the doorway, searching for targets and hoping he could kill them faster than they could turn to engage him.

A Green Shirt was crouched beneath the window right in front of him as he rolled to his right, trying to stay out of Bianco's line of fire, and they locked eyes for a second. The Green Shirt looked older than Wade would have expected. He was a grizzled *indio* who might have been anywhere from his mid-forties to his early sixties. At a glance, Wade realized that the Green Shirt might have been doing this almost as long as he had.

But the Green Shirt was no Ranger. He had crouched down as far as he could get as Bianco's machinegun fire scattered broken glass and smashed plaster over him, and his M16 was pointed at the ceiling.

Wade's Galil was already pointed almost directly at his heart.

He hadn't taken the selector off "A" when he'd gone through the door. The five-round burst tore the Green Shirt open from his belly button to his face, the last round punching through his eye and tearing out the back of his skull in a spray of red.

More gunfire thundered behind and above him, and brass rained down on his back where he lay on the floor.

Then he was rolling out of the way, onto his stomach, as more of the San Tabal irregulars flooded through the doorway, shooting at anything that moved.

***

Flanagan was committed, rounding the corner with his weapon up, dumping the last of his magazine into the three or four Green Shirts huddled behind the corner itself. Bullets thudded into flesh as his momentum carried him past the corner and up against the opposite wall. The Green Shirts tried to pivot to follow him, but the closest was already dying, and the other two couldn't move fast enough, especially as the dying man slumped back against them.

With that short window of hesitation, Flanagan quickly hammered controlled pairs into each before finishing them off with headshots as they staggered back against the wall. The three of them slid down toward the floor in eerie synchronization, leaving a broad smear of red against the white plaster.

He shifted his eyes to check on Hank, only able to spare a glance. He was exposed as hell to the whole corridor, but it was otherwise empty for the moment.

The younger Brannigan was fine. He was still up, his rifle held ready, as Gomez moved to join Flanagan. "Junior, Gambler, bring it in." They couldn't afford to get separated at the moment.

Pacheco entered next at the head of a handful of San Tabal police. They took the other side of the corridor as the Blackhearts headed up the one Flanagan had covered.

***

By the time Wade had regained his feet, gunfire was thundering through the entire police station. It wasn't a large building—the irregulars had moved fast. He could only imagine the pent-up bloodlust after being forced to cower at the feet of these Communist thugs for weeks. With Jenkins and Burgess in tow, Bianco holding on the door with a couple of the irregulars and Fuentes, he pushed toward the police commander's office.

He remembered a time when he would have been worried about the locals just killing *everyone* inside. Not that he'd ever particularly cared on a *personal* level. But his position would have demanded that he keep the regulars and irregulars under his command under control. Now? Now the only reason he didn't want the irregulars to slaughter every Green Shirt in the building was just because he wanted a few more to add to his tally.

The commander's office was on the second floor. The ground floor had gone quiet—Green Shirt bodies were strewn on the floors of the offices and the jail post, along with several of the locals. The Green Shirts had gone down fighting, but they'd been killed, nevertheless. After what they'd done in San Tabal, there would be no quarter.

While the ground floor was quiet, gunfire thundered and roared upstairs. Somebody up there was putting up a hell of a fight. Pulverized concrete and plaster rained down from the impacts on the wall over the middle of the stairs.

Wade ducked under the shower of debris and slowed as he neared the top of the stairs. He didn't want to go charging out into the open before he knew what he was facing. That was a good way to get shot. He was aggressive, not stupid.

The landing opened onto a T-shaped hallway that led to the commandant's office. Given how small the station was, and the fact that the stairs only went up one flight, instead of turning and going up for two, with a landing halfway up, he found himself at the top of the stairs, and covered from the raging automatic gunfire pouring down the hallway and hammering into the rapidly eroding wall.

Burgess was with him as he moved to the corner, but both Blackhearts stayed back, out of the hallway. They didn't have long to wait.

Wade hadn't been entirely sure that there was only one shooter. But when the gunfire fell silent without being immediately picked up by a second shooter, he moved.

Barreling around the corner, Wade charged the commandant's office. He heard Burgess curse behind him, but the former SEAL was right on his heels a moment later, as he went through the door like a freight train.

The Green Shirt was crouched behind the desk, cursing in Spanish as he tried to reload his AK. Wade had cleared his corner in an eyeblink—just in case—before pivoting back toward the desk and quickly stepping around. He locked eyes with the Green Shirt for a split second as his Galil came level. The man was still trying to get the mag locked in.

Wade shot him three times through the heart. The Galil's reports were painfully loud in the small office, and the bullets smashed the man back against the commandant's leather-upholstered chair. He stayed upright for a second before he crumpled, his head bouncing off the edge of the desk with a *clunk*.

The police station was clear.

***

Flanagan and the rest cleared the mansion room by room, careful to communicate with Pacheco as they moved. There was

252

definitely some risk that they'd give their progress away to the enemy, but with the locals going the opposite direction through the house, they couldn't afford to lose track of each other. That was a good way to get a friendly killed. Or a lot of friendlies.

So far, though, the rooms had been empty. It was as if the defenders they'd killed near the entrance had been all that was left.

Flanagan didn't trust that they had been, but that was why they were continuing to clear. He hadn't heard anyone call out that they'd seen Clemente's body yet.

The locals and the Blackhearts reached the master staircase at about the same time. Flanagan and Pacheco exchanged nods, and they headed up, weapons pivoting to cover the doors to either side of the balcony above.

Most of them were closed. They'd have to clear each of those rooms, as well. But for the moment, the primary target was the big double door at the top of the stairs.

There was no stack up. Flanagan didn't have time to even suggest it. Pacheco went in and kicked the doors open, riding the right-hand door to the wall as Flanagan rushed to catch up, taking the left. He came up against a wardrobe set behind the door, but he cleared the corner before pivoting toward the center of the room.

It appeared to have been an entertainment room, but it had been retrofitted into something of a command center. A field desk stood in the center, while the entertainment center had been shoved against another wall. Crates and cases had been stacked up haphazardly around the room, several open to reveal piles of expensive things like silver platters and fancy vases.

He took all that in at a glance, even as one of the San Tabal volunteers came through the door behind him and took a shotgun blast to the face.

The man's feet flew out from under him and he crashed onto his back in the threshold, his skull a bloody ruin. At almost the same time, Pacheco and Flanagan pivoted toward the field desk, which had been overturned.

The man behind the desk had fired over the top. But the field desk was hardly what anyone would consider cover. Both Flanagan and Pacheco opened fire right through the desktop.

Green-painted plywood splintered and cracked under the onslaught, as close to a dozen 5.56 rounds tore through the flimsy barrier and punched into the body beyond. The man grunted and collapsed, the shotgun clattering to the floor.

Flanagan moved forward, his weapon leveled, careful not to over penetrate to expose himself to some of the dead spaces behind the crates. He advanced just far enough to see who they'd shot.

There was no mistaking the identity of the blood-soaked, bullet-riddled body. He'd studied the target photos enough.

Ramon Clemente was dead. The contract, such as it was, had been fulfilled.

Now they just had to finish securing the city and get Lara installed as mayor.

Except that even as the gunfire fell silent, he could hear the distant growl of helicopters. And he didn't think that they were friendlies, either. Not that close to Venezuela.

CHAPTER 26

Brannigan heard the helos, too, in the sudden hush that had fallen over San Tabal. Bursts of sporadic gunfire still echoed over the city, but that would probably continue for a while. There would be holdouts, people celebrating with gunfire, and some people would take advantage of the chaos to carry out vendettas or seize what they could.

The gunfire didn't concern him nearly as much as the helicopters.

Brannigan, Javakhishvili, Quintana, and Lara had been joined by nearly two hundred volunteers. They'd run through Pacheco's remaining stores of weapons quickly, but one of the policemen—a weaselly-looking man of questionable loyalty, who had taken a job with the Green Shirts but quickly changed sides once one of Quintana's men had knocked on his door—had fingered another cache that the Green Shirts had placed for "the defense of the city against the Colombian governmental regressives." It still hadn't been enough, so those farmers, shopkeepers, and other local citizens who'd joined up who hadn't gotten an AK, FNC, or M16 were now carrying machetes, pitchforks, and rocks.

If those helicopters were hostile, these people wouldn't have a chance.

He stepped out into the street, scanning the hills above the city. There. He squinted for a moment, then turned to Quintana. "Get one of your most trustworthy lieutenants and get half these guys up to the police station. Herc will go with them. Have them report to Wade and get ready to defend it. The rest of us will move to the plaza and the mayor's house." He hoped that the sudden

255

silence meant that his Blackhearts had taken the two centers of gravity in the city. Since neither Wade nor Flanagan had called for help over the radio, that was probably a good guess. Sometimes no news really is good news. Neither man would have let themselves get pinned down or outflanked without calling for support.

"What if those are Colombian helicopters?" Quintana asked, even as he started dividing the mob of volunteers up.

"They might be. The Colombians *do* have Mi-17s, if I remember correctly." The helos were still a good distance away, but the profile was unmistakable. "But so do the Venezuelans, and those birds are coming in from the north."

Quintana's face turned grave as he looked up and noticed that, as well. Brannigan gripped his shoulder. "It's not over yet. We don't know who they are. Get your people moving; we'll set in defenses and if they're friendlies, we can stand down. If they're not, then we keep fighting."

He didn't say that the odds were stacked against them if the Venezuelan Army had decided to enter the fray. Ten mercenaries, a couple dozen cops, and a bunch of eager but untrained and inexperienced irregular volunteers wouldn't last long against even the less-than-impressive National Army of the Bolivarian Republic of Venezuela.

Maybe they wouldn't need to hold for long. Maybe with the Venezuelans making the first move by invading Colombian territory, they'd only have to defend themselves until the Colombian National Army responded.

But a lot of them would still be dead by that point.

They were committed, though. If they gave up the city to the Venezuelans, they may as well pack it in. And then their allies would probably all be slaughtered.

His face set with grim determination, he headed uphill, toward the plaza.

***

Wade had reacted quickly when he'd heard the helos, before even setting eyes on them. He knew enough about their situation that he didn't immediately trust *anything*, and knew that without comms, they had to assume that the incoming forces were hostile until proven friendly. He'd seen too many green-on-blue or blue-on-blue incidents brought about through simple lack of communication to think that it was in any way time to relax.

"Get everyone under cover. Vinnie! Get up here and get on a window! I want that belt-fed in place to cover any approaches to the building!" He glanced around, but nobody had any smokes. *Flares. The cops have to have flares or something.* He started downstairs, looking for the police gear room.

He was just starting to dig into the lockers when he heard his radio crackle. "Angry Ragnar, Shady Slav. Coming up from the southeast with a large group of friendlies. Watch your fires toward the street."

"Roger. Police station's secure. Bring it in." He glanced up as he thought of something. "Be careful of the wreck in the gateway—it got shot up pretty good, and it might be leaking fuel."

"Copy. We're moving in pretty quick—looks like those helos are about two minutes out." There was a pause, and then Javakhishvili's voice turned grim. "Be advised, they've got Venezuelan roundels on their tails. They are not friendlies."

Wade just grinned wolfishly. "Then we get to kill some Venezuelan regulars. Dead Communists are dead Communists. I'm not choosy."

***

Galvez had waited until he saw the helicopters moving in over the mountains above the city to make his move.

He was certain that Clemente had called the Venezuelans as soon as he'd realized just how badly the entire war was going. In fact, Galvez was sure that he'd called them as soon as the assault on the Galán farm had failed.

It only went further to prove that Clemente wasn't the man to lead the revolution. If he was even still alive.

Galvez was still determined to snatch victory out of this disaster. His plan was still nebulous, but if he could at least retake the mayor's house, he might be able to work things out with the

Venezuelans. They didn't want to control this part of Colombia, after all, but simply to spread the Revolution, just like he did.

It had taken entirely too long to round up a decent attack force, and even now, he was getting sidelong glances from some of the hardened FARC fighters who had responded to the call. They'd been on the way for the last several days, filtering down out of the camps in the Norte de Santander Depot, drawn by Clemente's call for reinforcements. But their leader, a mustached man known only as Fabian, had been decidedly unimpressed by what he'd seen so far, and hadn't hesitated to express his opinion.

Galvez was already considering how he might kill Fabian without triggering an instant mutiny from the other FARC fighters.

He and his small, fifty-man assault force had watched from a hill on the south side of the valley as the growing crowd of local volunteers had moved up toward the center of the city. Now, as he saw them split up and run as the Venezuelans closed in, he saw his opening.

"We have to attack now. We can hit them from behind as they are disorganized and looking at the Venezuelans. We'll take the mayor's mansion, fortify it, and then once the Venezuelans have cleared the rest of them out, we can negotiate the rest." He was sure he could work that out—he'd fought alongside the Venezuelans before. The solidarity of the Revolution was important to them, too.

He got up and ran down the hill toward the handful of trucks they'd gathered to make the assault. Time was short.

***

Flanagan met Quintana and Brannigan at the plaza. Some of the locals, seeing many of their neighbors gathering around the fountain with weapons, had started to come out of their houses and apartments. Quintana's cops were trying to convince them that it still wasn't safe, pointing to the circling helicopters overhead. Some had seen the birds and immediately sought cover again. Others were still getting it through their heads.

But when automatic fire erupted from the street to the south, a lot of them figured out that the danger wasn't past.

Unfortunately, it was too late for some, as several of them were smashed lifelessly to the cobblestones in a welter of blood. The screams were almost drowned out by the gunfire.

Brannigan turned, dashing to the corner of the mansion and dropping to a knee, bringing his Galil to bear and searching for targets. Two ancient Land Cruisers were hurtling up the street, with Green Shirt fighters leaning out the side windows, spraying bullets at anything that moved.

Then Curtis opened fire from the roof.

He didn't have a lot of ammo left for the Negev, but bullets chopped into the hood of the lead vehicle, walking up into the windshield and smashing into the driver. A faint adjustment drove the last of the burst across the windshield and into the passenger.

Brannigan took a shot at the man leaning out of one of the rear windows, but the man had ducked inside just as the Land Cruiser swerved and bounced over the curb to smash into a storefront on the side of the street.

The lead vehicle was screwed, but the Land Cruiser behind it braked hard and skidded to a stop. The Green Shirts bailed out and scrambled to cover in and around the surrounding buildings, still spraying fire up the street toward the plaza. Brannigan had to duck back as bullets smacked plaster off the mansion's wall above his head.

More fire erupted off to the west. The Green Shirts were trying to flank them.

***

Flanagan and Gomez had already faded around the corner of the mansion, working their way around to flank the Green Shirt assault, so they had just slipped away from the plaza when the flanking attack opened fire.

When Flanagan took a knee for a second to assess the situation and glanced back, he saw that Hank had joined them, racing along the street and skidding to a halt behind Gomez, pivoting to cover the north. He pointed his Galil toward the Mi-17s that were still circling above. "How the hell are we supposed to fight *more* Green Shirts *and* the Venezuelans?"

"The Venezuelans aren't on the ground yet. Worry about the Green Shirts for now." Flanagan got up and moved toward the next corner. "Mario. High-low?"

Gomez nodded. "I'll go high."

Flanagan took a knee and leaned out around the corner, while Gomez stood above and behind him, leaning out at a slightly different angle. Both men came around and brought their weapons to bear at almost the same moment.

The men clustered around the ancient Ford at the next corner a block away, dumping fire toward the mansion and the plaza, didn't look like Green Shirts. They were dressed in woodland camouflage, with black tac vests and black and green berets or woodland boonie covers. They blazed away down the street with an M60 and half a dozen AKMs.

They weren't wearing the red, yellow, and blue armbands, but Flanagan had seen enough photos of the FARC's pseudo-uniform to be pretty sure he knew what he was looking at.

Neither he nor Gomez hesitated. As soon as they identified their targets and found their sights, they opened fire.

Flanagan shot the M60 gunner three times, smashing two rounds into his side before the third punched through his temple. The thickset, mustached man fell over sideways, his joints gone loose, blood pouring from his shattered skull onto the machinegun.

Even as the FARC fighters realized that the flankers had just been flanked, Flanagan and Gomez raked fire across the vehicle, bullets punching into flesh and metal and shattering glass. Three more FARC gunmen collapsed, dead or bleeding out.

Two more, however, scrambled behind the dubious cover of the old pickup and returned fire. Long, stuttering bursts stitched the side of the building where Flanagan and Gomez had taken cover, smacking debris into their faces and forcing both men back around the corner.

260

Then one of the Mi-17s roared overhead, flying low enough that the rotor wash rattled the windows in the building. Hank tracked it with his Galil, though the rifle wouldn't do much against the massive transport helicopter. Fortunately, it didn't appear to have a door gunner.

But as it came to a hover over the intersection, the side doors slid open, and rappelling ropes spooled out. A figure appeared in the doorway, leveling an AK-103. More dark figures were moving behind him, preparing to rappel to the street.

Before the first man could descend, though, a delta-winged shape flashed overhead with a deafening thunderclap. The Mi-17 rocked as the Colombian IAI Kfir fighter's sonic boom swept over it.

The two-plane flight banked hard over the eastern ridge and circled back around. The Mi-17 dumped the ropes and dipped its nose, pulling hard away from the intersection and heading for the north as fast as its rotors could move it.

Hank audibly let out a sigh of relief. "The Colombians finally decided they didn't want the Venezuelans getting involved."

Flanagan didn't answer. He'd dropped to his side and shoved out into the street as the surviving FARC gunmen kept shooting.

Flanagan fired twice. The first bullet missed, spitting dirt and gravel off the street. The second tore through the FARC shooter's ankle and the man collapsed, screaming. Two more shots silenced him.

The remaining FARC fighter turned tail and ran.

***

When the Colombian Kfir's drove the Venezuelans running hard for the border, the last of the starch seemed to go right out of the remaining Green Shirts.

Most of those near the second vehicle began to look up at the receding helicopters before throwing their weapons down and come out of cover with their hands up.

But four of them, led by a gaunt, wolfish man wearing a black beret, dashed toward the south, covering their retreat with a storm of automatic rifle fire.

"Galvez!" Fuentes was back by the fountain with Lara, his FNC leveled over the lip of the fountain. He dumped the last of his magazine toward the retreating Green Shirts, though his marksmanship left a bit to be desired. He sprayed bullets down the street, but he hit little besides the wrecked Land Cruiser and the walls on either side of the street.

Fuentes's rifle ran dry with a *click*. He stared down at it for a moment, as Brannigan came out of cover. "Blackhearts, on me!" If that really was one of the Green Shirts' leaders, he couldn't be allowed to escape.

He barely avoided getting his head blown off from behind as one of the San Tabal irregulars ripped off another mag down the street. The man didn't hit anything, and in the meantime, Galvez and his handful of killers disappeared around a corner.

"Galvez is on the move, heading south." Brannigan panted into his radio as he ran back into the street and pursued. "Woodsrunner, head due south and see if you can cut him off. Angry Ragnar, have you got any police vehicles you can use up there?"

"Already moving." Wade wouldn't want to be left out.

Brannigan sprinted down the street, his boots hammering the pavement, his joints feeling all of the thirty years or more that he'd been fighting in foreign lands. He only slowed as he neared the corner that Galvez had disappeared behind.

Easing around the corner behind his weapon, he didn't run into the ambush he'd feared, but he caught a glimpse of Galvez and the Green Shirts hustling between the vehicles parked on the street toward the next intersection.

They suddenly stopped, the lead man falling to the ground with limp finality, as bullets chewed into him and the side of the van parked right at the corner. The three survivors shot back as they retreated into a two-story storefront behind the van.

Brannigan, Javakhishvili, and Pacheco closed in on the store as Flanagan, Gomez, and Hank came around the corner, guns up. More gunfire from inside the shop forced them back, but Flanagan and Gomez quickly adjusted, crossing the side street and getting out of the line of fire as they continued to circle toward their quarry.

Engines roared on the far side of the block. "Angry Ragnar, lock down the streets for two blocks south of the plaza. Galvez has gone to ground."

"Roger." With another growl of engines, a green-and-white police Hilux surged into the intersection.

Brannigan, Javakhishvili, and Pacheco had quickly crossed the street to the same side as the shop that Galvez and his companions had retreated into. They hurried along, keeping close to the buildings. So far, it appeared that the Green Shirts were only aware of Flanagan, Gomez, and Hank. Flanagan and Gomez were closing in from behind the Hilux. Hank was on the corner, barricaded on the building, exchanging sporadic fire with the gunmen inside.

The front of the store had been covered by large picture windows. Bullets had shattered the windows and the glass door. Most of the shop—which appeared to be a grocery store—was now deep in shadow on the other side of the broken glass, shards of which reflected the scene on the overcast street.

Brannigan held just before the first window, briefly wishing he had some grenades. He didn't know much about this Galvez, but he'd seen enough that he knew that those were no longer really men in there. They were cornered animals, and therefore they were more dangerous than they'd ever been before.

He momentarily locked gazes with Hank, across the intersection. He didn't have to say anything. His son just nodded, lifted his rifle, and mag-dumped into the storefront.

The Green Shirts' fire ceased as they sought cover. Brannigan made his move as soon as Hank's mag went dry.

He didn't bother trying to get to the door. Instead, he kicked out the last of the broken picture window and stepped over the low wall and into the store, his rifle up and ready.

One of the Green Shirts was crouched behind a standing rack of baskets holding corn and beans that had been half shot to bits. Shattered corncobs and scattered beans littered the floor. The Green Shirt saw the shadow moving in the window and pivoted toward it, but Brannigan and Pacheco shot him before he could get all the way around. Bullets punched through his chest and neck, and he collapsed next to the rack.

The second stood up to try to engage the two of them with his M16, but Hank shot him through the side, and he crumpled.

The store fell silent.

Brannigan advanced carefully, Pacheco and Javakhishvili in tow, broken glass and dried beans crunching under his boots. Flanagan and Gomez entered from the other side, keeping pace as they swept the store.

There was no sign of Galvez. But there was a stairwell going up to the apartment on the second floor, and as he neared it, Gomez suddenly froze, threw up a fist, and then pointed up.

Brannigan and Javakhishvili finished a cursory sweep of the very back, but it was empty, a police Hilux beyond the back door with half a dozen of Quintana's volunteers in the back. And they could hear some scuffling upstairs, along with what sounded like a faint, frightened moan, quickly cut off.

The Blackhearts fell into a practiced stack as they mounted the steps, rifle muzzles shifting to cover the opening angle on the top of the stairs as they padded up to the second floor. The landing ended in a single door leading into the apartment. The plaster on the walls was cracked and dingy, the door scuffed and ill-fitting.

Gomez had reached it first. He put his back to the narrow wall, got the nod from Flanagan, and kicked the door in.

Flanagan raced through the doorway, his weapon leveled. A bullet smacked splinters off the door just above his head, and he kept going, even as Galvez, a young woman clasped to his chest in front of him, his arm around her throat, tried to track him with a Jericho 9mm.

Brannigan went in behind him, took two steps to the wall, and leveled his own rifle, his finger already on the trigger.

Galvez saw the movement and hesitated, just for a split second. It was enough.

He might have cursed, but the word was drowned out by the deafening thunder of the Galil in the enclosed space. Galvez's head snapped back under the impact and his pistol fell from a suddenly nerveless hand. The girl screamed as Galvez fell to the floor behind her, and Gomez moved to pull her away from the corpse.

The rest of the Blackhearts spread out to quickly clear the rest of the apartment, but as Brannigan looked down at what had once been Diego Galvez, alias El Verdugo, he knew that, at least for the moment, it was over.

EPILOGUE

Cole Hauser stood by the plane with his massive arms folded across an equally massive chest. "Well, this is fucking embarrassing." He eyed the filthy, tired mercenaries as they got out of Pacheco's truck and headed for the white, unmarked Casa. Half a dozen tough-looking men in plainclothes, but carrying themselves in that way that unmistakably identified them to anyone who was looking that they were soldiers, were loading equipment cases from the plane into a pair of SUVs nearby. "We finally get the spare manpower and the authorization to come down here and play, and you boys have already cleaned house."

Brannigan shrugged. "What can I say? We were hired to do a job." He looked up as Van Zandt himself stepped out of the plane's door. "Mark."

"John." Van Zandt waved them up into the plane. They'd already handed off their weapons upon reaching the airfield. Pacheco had taken them, accompanied by a Colombian officer who treated the old Search Bloc operator with noted deference. Brannigan wasn't too concerned about him. "Job well done."

Brannigan waited until the rest of the Blackhearts had gotten aboard before he trudged up the steps into the plane. He sank down onto one of the jump seats, running a hand over his face. He was desperately tired. As uncomfortable as the utilitarian interior of the Casa was, he was probably going to be asleep within minutes of takeoff.

The handover with the Colombians had gone surprisingly smoothly. Lara had stepped into the leadership role immediately, addressing the crowd of San Tabal citizens who'd come out of their homes as the gunfire died away. Lara had immediately tapped Quintana to lead the new police force, and with Pacheco's help, Quintana had set about securing the important parts of the city right away.

When the Army had showed up, Pacheco, Lara, and Quintana had gone to meet them while the Blackhearts had kind of faded into the background. Pacheco had spoken with the officer who was now standing next to him, and a few minutes later had come to pick the Blackhearts up, quietly, on a presently abandoned street near the edge of town. Things had been a little tense at first, until Pacheco had assured them that there were Americans at the nearest airstrip, with the approval of the Colombian government, and they were not heading for prison or a firing squad.

They'd still wondered, up until they'd stopped, gotten out, and seen the Casa with Abernathy's mysterious operators unloading it.

Van Zandt sat beside him as the door shut. Brannigan, leaning back against the padded wall of the plane's interior fuselage, turned to look at him. "So, are we going back to a quiet paycheck, or an investigation?"

"A quiet paycheck." Van Zandt nodded toward the exterior, where Abernathy's operators were mounting up and joining the Colombians. "We had a bit of a chat with the client." He looked a little chagrined. "Turned out that Abernathy had a lot more information about this little situation than my office even thought existed. The client won't be messing with you for the foreseeable future."

"Who was the client?" Brannigan had closed his eyes, but his voice was a low, hard growl.

When Van Zandt didn't answer, he opened his eyes and fixed his old superior officer with an icy, pitiless stare. "Who was the client, Mark?"

"Senator Briggs."

Brannigan snorted. "Figures."

"It wasn't as much the corruption that we expected as it was political naivete." Van Zandt grimaced a little. "Dumbass thought he could score some points by getting behind a 'reformer.'"

Brannigan eyed him narrowly. It was pretty clear that while Van Zandt mostly believed what he'd just said, he was leaving part of it out. And he thought he knew which part. "Given the fact that Ballesteros apparently screamed that Galvez was trying to kill him just before he died, I don't think there were any real 'reformers' in that bunch. That leaves two possibilities. Either he got played by a thug trying to off another thug, or he lied to save his own skin." He dug into his pocket and produced a small envelope. "And it ain't the first one."

Van Zandt's eyebrow lifted as he took the envelope. "What's this?"

"It's a ledger found in Clemente's office." Brannigan turned to watch Flanagan come up the ramp and give him a thumbs up that everyone was aboard. "Well, a copy of it. It has their whole cocaine distribution plan in it." He met Van Zandt's eyes coolly. "I think you'll recognize one of the names on it."

"Briggs's cousin Hatteras?"

Brannigan nodded as he sat down and buckled in. The Casa's engines were spooling up. Van Zandt joined him. "Thought that name seemed familiar. Probably not enough to put the Senator away, though, knowing how things work in DC."

"Either way." Van Zandt shrugged. "He's had the fear put in him. Abernathy's a scary son of a bitch when he wants to be. I don't think he'll be causing us any problems in the near future."

"Maybe not the near future." Brannigan shut his eyes again. Damn, he was tired. "But people like him rarely forget and never forgive." He snorted again. "But who am I kidding? We've been looking over our shoulders since those Humanity Front bastards went after Sam. Nothing's really changed. We've just got a couple new enemies to add to the list.

"Let 'em come. They'll regret it if they do."

BRANNIGAN'S BLACKHEARTS

BLOOD DEBT

Mercenaries strike a hidden base…

…But it's a trap.

Now they have only one hope – Brannigan's Blackhearts

When Mitchell Price's black bag team hit a mysterious former Soviet military base in Kyrgyzstan, they thought they knew what they were in for. They're professionals, and they've been on this hunt for a long time.

But things can go bad in a heartbeat.

Now with the team dead or captured, one man knows where they are, and he's going to have to convince Brannigan's Blackhearts to help. He's not just going to hire them, though. He's coming with them.

Dan Tackett is coming out of retirement.

And he and the Blackhearts are about to venture into the heart of darkness in Central Asia.

AUTHOR'S NOTE

Thank you for reading *War to the Knife*. I've had something like this one in mind since I started the series. A bit of old-school *Jagged Alliance*-style mercenary liberation of a captured population. I hope you enjoyed reading it as much as I enjoyed writing it.

To keep up-to-date, I hope that you'll sign up for my newsletter—you get a free American Praetorians novella, *Drawing the Line*, when you do.

If you've enjoyed this novel, I hope that you'll go leave a review on Amazon or Goodreads. Reviews matter a lot to independent authors, so I appreciate the effort.

If you'd like to connect, I have a Facebook page at https://www.facebook.com/PeteNealenAuthor. You can also contact me, or just read my musings and occasional samples on the blog, at https://www.americanpraetorians.com. I look forward to hearing from you.

Also By Peter Nealen

The Maelstrom Rising Series
Escalation
Holding Action
Crimson Star
Strategic Assets
Fortress Doctrine
Thunder Run
Area Denial
SPOTREPS – A Maelstrom Rising Anthology

The Brannigan's Blackhearts Universe
Kill Yuan
The Colonel Has A Plan (Online Short)
Fury in the Gulf
Burmese Crossfire
Enemy Unidentified
Frozen Conflict
High Desert Vengeance
Doctors of Death
Kill or Capture
Enemy of My Enemy

The American Praetorians Series
Drawing the Line: An American Praetorians Story (Novella)
Task Force Desperate
Hunting in the Shadows
Alone and Unafraid
The Devil You Don't Know
Lex Talionis

The Jed Horn Supernatural Thriller Series
Nightmares
A Silver Cross and a Winchester
The Walker on the Hills
The Canyon of the Lost (Novelette)
Older and Fouler Things

Made in the USA
Middletown, DE
18 May 2024